"I've missed you

said Grady.

Anna tried to move away, but he wouldn't let her. She felt a thrill of fear, because she doubted she would be able to resist him, and she would hate herself if she didn't.

"Don't pull away yet," he murmured.

She met his eyes. He was smiling at her, and it was seeping through all her defenses. "Don't come in here and start messing with my life, Grady Clayton."

"I've already messed with your life, Anna Fitzgerald. And I plan to keep right on messing with it, too." His fingers brushed her cheek. "Maybe I'll mess with it slowly, and maybe I won't. Whatever I do, though, it's for the long haul. I don't take this lightly. I don't take *you* lightly."

Dear Reader:

We at Silhouette are very excited to bring you a NEW reading **Sensation.** *Look out for the four books which will appear in our new Silhouette* **Sensation** *series every month. These stories will have the high quality you have come to expect from Silhouette, and their varied and provocative plots will encourage you to explore the wonder of falling in love – again and again!*

Emotions run high in these drama-filled novels. Greater sensual detail and an extra edge of realism intensify the hero and heroine's relationship so that you cannot help but be caught up in their every change of mood.

We hope you enjoy this new **Sensation** *– and will go on to enjoy many more.*

We would love to hear your comments about our new line and encourage you to write to us:

Jane Nicholls
Silhouette Books
PO Box 236
Thornton Road
Croydon
Surrey
CR9 3RU

EMILIE RICHARDS
The Way Back Home

Silhouette Sensation

First published in Great Britain in 1991 by Silhouette Books, Eton House, 18-24 Paradise Road, Richmond, Surrey TW9 1SR

© Emilie Richards McGee 1990

Silhouette, Silhouette Sensation and Colophon are Trade Marks of Harlequin Enterprises B.V.

ISBN 0 373 58202 1

18 – 9107

Made and printed in Great Britain

Chapter 1

If there hadn't been a momentary lull in the fighting, no one would have heard the doorbell. As it was, the bell—which had once been tampered with by a boy whose single ambition was to shut out the world—sounded more like an outraged gasp than a summons. The fighting began again.

"Man, I know you took my shirt out of my pack. Someone saw you! Give it back or you're gonna pay!" A slight, still-forming young man doubled up his fist and waved it under the nose of a boy almost twice his size.

The larger boy, whose left arm was in a cast, spat on the floor. "Pay? Pay who? You? Who'd pay for one of your dirty little rags?" Contemptuously, he turned his head, as if taking in the whole room, but his eyes never left his opponent.

"Give it back!"

"I don't have your shirt. Who'd want it? It's probably crawling with bugs!"

The smaller boy moved in for the kill, although it was clear to all the fascinated kids watching the confrontation that he was going to be ground right into the frayed carpet.

The same thing was clear to Anna Fitzgerald. She had heard the screaming all the way from the director's office, where she'd just been dragged to hear a week's worth of bad news.

The fight was almost a relief.

Anna leaped down the stairs, three at a time, springing off the bottom step like a championship diver. Cleanly and with infinite skill, she parted the troubled waters.

"Stop it, both of you!"

The small circle of kids split neatly in half. Revealed in the middle were Wesley and Fang. Anna had known who was fighting before she raced out of Tom Schneider's office.

"Hit him with that cast and you'll end up having surgery on your arm," she warned Wesley as she darted between the boys, pushing Fang backward a foot or two. Fang, so-called because of one horizontally tilted front tooth, tried to stand his ground, but Anna had caught him off balance. He melted into the circle of kids. Nobody caught him when he fell.

Anna put her hands on her hips and faced Wesley. His cast-covered arm was still raised. "Put a torch in your hand and you'd look like the Statue of Liberty," she observed.

There were snickers behind her, but she didn't take her eyes off Wesley.

Wesley smiled. The smile was angelic, but there was something unholy in his eyes. "Move out of the way, Annie babe."

"Why? So you can say we threw you back on the streets? That's what you want, isn't it? Hey, you might make something of yourself if you stay around here."

"In this two-bit flophouse?" Wesley moved closer, arm still raised.

Anna didn't even blink, although Wesley outweighed her by fifty pounds at least. Somewhere inside her she registered the click of the front door. She couldn't take her eyes off Wesley long enough to see who had come or gone. She hoped it was an arriving counselor. "You're not scaring me."

"You don't have much sense, then."

"I tell myself that every day."

"Get out of the way. Fang wants trouble."

"Since when is it your style to give anybody what they want?"

Welsey stood over her, his arm still raised. He moved as if to hit her. "I'm warning you."

Anna didn't move an inch. "Back off, Wesley. I know—"

Before she could finish, a man in a dark brown suit materialized out of the group of kids behind Wesley, grabbed the arm not sporting a cast and spun Wesley around. Anna, who had never counted on seeing any real emotion on Wesley's face, saw a momentary flash of surprise.

Wesley landed in a faded chintz armchair. In a moment the man was standing over him, making it perfectly clear that he wasn't to move. "Touch that girl," the stranger said in a menacing voice, "and you'll be listening to a cop read you your rights."

Wesley sat back casually, as if he were enjoying himself. "Oh, I'm scared. Real scared."

"Out," Anna said quietly to the kids staring open-mouthed at the tall stranger. "Go in the kitchen and start on supper." She didn't wait to see if they had done as she'd asked. She started toward Wesley.

The man barred her way. "Stay away from him."

"Look, I don't know who you are—"

"If you want to help, go find somebody who works here. If anybody does," he muttered under his breath.

"*I* work here."

The man gave her one quick glance. "I mean staff," he said, dismissing her.

Anna caught Wesley's eye. He was laughing at her, although you had to know him well to tell. One of Wesley's few admirable traits was his sense of humor. She had used it more than once to help him find his way back to civilization. She tried it now. "See what you've done?" she asked, ignoring the stranger for the moment. "You've *completely* subverted my authority. Tonight you wash dishes. All of them."

"You have to *work* here to tell me what to do," Wesley sing-songed.

Anna managed a smile and turned her attention to the stranger. He had been a blur to her during the excitement. Now she took in a lanky broad-shouldered body and shining mahogany hair. His eyes were a matching brown. He had wide cheekbones and a narrow-lipped mouth that hadn't once relaxed its grim line. She tried to change that. "I'm Anna Fitzgerald, the assistant director of this zoo. Step away from Wesley, please. He's been known to bite."

The man turned to face her, although he didn't turn his back to Wesley—which lifted him a notch in Anna's estimation. "Assistant director?" This time his eyes took a leisurely tour from the toes of her ragged Reeboks to the short golden spiked locks framing her impossibly young face. "First Day's being run by a rock band?"

Anna held out her hand. "And you are?"

He hesitated, then took her hand. "Grady Clayton."

She'd heard the name before, but so had everyone else in the city of Ponte Reynaldo. Grady Clayton. She should have known.

"Mr. Prosecutor." Anna dropped his hand immediately. "We weren't expecting you for another hour."

"I have no trouble believing that."

Her polite smile died. In Tom Schneider's office, only minutes before, she had discovered that First Day was going to be visited by Sun County's popular acting State Attorney. A week wouldn't have been long enough for Anna to steel herself to be nice to a politician. Now she had already tapped her entire reservoir of good manners. "Move out of that chair before I get back and you're a dead man," she said to Wesley, who was watching the conversation with interest. She turned back to Grady Clayton. "I'll take you to Tom's office. I believe you came to see him."

"I think I've seen what I came to."

She spoke before she thought. "You'd need to have your eyes open for that, Mr. Clayton."

Grady's expression didn't change. He was under fire from a disheveled teenager with a self-righteous frown as expressive as her astonishing turquoise eyes. He didn't allow his grudging respect to show. "My eyes are always open, Miss Fitzgerald. What I've seen here is chaos. It's easy to recognize."

"Then you're going to have to decide if you're willing to look any deeper. If you aren't, you're wasting your time." She lifted her chin and stared straight at him. "And our time is precious. Just like our kids."

They stared at each other, taking each other's measure, until Wesley interrupted. "Hey, the cop-fink gets to make decisions, just like we do. Maybe you should put him through the program, Annie babe. Teach him how."

"Stay in that chair." Without another word to either male, Anna turned and started up the stairs. She was almost surprised when she reached Tom's door to find that Grady had followed her.

"I always come a little earlier than I'm expected." Grady sat back in the chair beside Tom Schneider's desk. Coffee steamed enticingly in front of him, but he ignored it. "I get a better idea of what's going on."

"Some might say that's wise," Tom said, nodding pleasantly. "And some might say it was downright sneaky."

"The second group doesn't interest me much."

"Since you're a man who goes straight to the point, I'll do the same. I'm not going to apologize for what you saw when you got here. Fights occur every day. First Day isn't a Sunday school, and the kids who live here aren't angels."

"And the girl trying to get control of the situation wasn't old enough to *teach* Sunday school."

Tom made a tent of his stubby fingers and regarded Grady over them. He was a quiet, good-humored man who could size anybody up in ten seconds or less. He already knew he liked Grady Clayton. "That bothers you?"

"You know my reservations about your program. Now I find you've got teenagers running the place. How can kids adequately supervise kids?"

"Anna's twenty-two."

Grady reached for his coffee to hide his surprise. "She looks fifteen."

"She can look her age when she has to, but what does that have to do with her ability to handle runaways? She's effective precisely because they can relate to her. Anna's young enough to know what they're feeling and old enough to help them deal with it."

Grady impatiently waved aside the other man's words. "We both know I'm not here because your assistant looks like a runaway herself."

"No, you're here because you're afraid that First Day is involved in drug dealing."

"One of your charges was caught with a roll of cash in one pocket and an illegal pharmacy in the other."

"And that's unfortunate."

Grady lifted a brow. "Why? Because he was caught?"

Tom smiled. "You and I are on the same side, Mr. Clayton. I hate drugs as much as you do, and so does all my staff. We have strict rules against them. The kids who live here know they're out of the program if they use or deal."

"The kid we caught was still in the program."

"The kid you caught drifted in and out of it. He was never a long-term resident. He came in occasionally for rest and shelter and a hot meal. We don't turn kids away if they come in clean and stay clean while they're here. What they do on the outside is out of our control."

"Isn't *everything* they do out of your control?"

"This is a runaway shelter, not a prison."

There was a perfunctory rap on the office door, and Anna entered, taking the empty chair beside Grady before either man could stand.

Grady watched as she sprawled beside him. She hadn't changed out of her faded denim shorts, rolled up to the tops of her thighs, and her sunshine-yellow blouse was still knotted loosely around her midriff. But she had made a stab at combing her hair. The punky spikes had become soft golden fluff with delicate wisps decorating her neck and cheeks. He noted pale freckles on the bridge of her nose.

"I was just trying to tell Mr. Clayton a little about our program," Tom told Anna. "Is everyone settled downstairs?"

"Craig just got in. Car trouble again. He's keeping his eye on things in the kitchen, but Fang had to go to work anyway, so he and Wesley will be separated for a while."

"Fang?" Grady couldn't help himself.

"He won't tell us his real name." Anna fidgeted in her chair until she was facing Grady. She'd had a few minutes to get her temper under control. She was hoping it was enough to do the trick. "When Fang first came three months ago, he was so black and blue we couldn't even write an accurate description of him for our records."

"Have you done anything to find out who he is?"

"We've tried to make him feel safe enough to tell us. But we don't do detective work, if that's what you mean. We'd have a lot of empty beds here if we did."

"Maybe they'd be empty because the kids would be back home."

Tom interrupted. "We do know that Fang's father as good as put him here when he beat him in a drunken rage. We're less interested in Fang's real name than in helping him grow up without bruises." Tom leaned across his desk. "You're going to have lots of questions, all of which I'll answer later. Let Anna show you around first. Ask her anything you want." He turned his attention to Anna. "Be polite," he warned her.

A faint blush colored Anna's cheeks, and she made a face. Tom knew her better than anyone in the world. It was Tom who had held her hand through the worst days of her own life, Tom who had given her the courage to become the woman she was. Now, behind thick spectacles, his blue eyes shone with confidence. "I am always polite," she said primly. She pushed herself out of her chair. "Unless I'm rude."

Grady laughed. He hadn't known he had a laugh left inside him. The day had been grueling, beginning with meetings at six a.m. and continuing straight through without a break, or even without two things to do at once. It was din-

nertime already, and he couldn't remember one meal he'd
eaten, with the exception of stale doughnuts at a campaign
coffee with a local ladies' guild. He didn't really want to be
here. And he didn't want to laugh—couldn't even manage
one. Except that he just had.

The laugh somehow freed the knot of fatigue and tension inside him. He stood. "I'm afraid I'm the one who's
been rude."

"Arrogant." Anna looked up at him. She was surprised
to see him smiling. It was a down-home smile, Davy Crock-
ett-gone-to-Congress with the polish of urban sophistica-
tion instead of a coonskin cap. She understood for the first
time how this man had so charmed conservative Sun County
that despite his relative youth, the voters might make him
their offical State's Attorney in the upcoming election.

"I think it's more exhaustion than arrogance," Grady
said candidly. "But at least part of it's genuine concern.
This county is my responsibility now. Your program is under scrutiny."

Tom answered. "You'll find nothing here to worry you.
We exist to help kids, not to feed their bad habits. But we
don't work miracles, we give chances. Some kids are too far
gone to take what we offer. Maybe Paco Hernandez was one
of them."

"Maybe?"

"We know Paco pretty well," Anna broke in, before Tom
could explain. "He's been on the streets since he was fourteen. Like a lot of kids, he figured out right away that he
could sell drugs or his body to survive. He chose the first.
Who's to say he made a bad decision?"

Grady grunted noncommittally.

Anna went on. "By the time First Day was there to give
Paco a third choice, we didn't add up to much next to the
limousines and beachfront villas of the guys he was working for. But he kept coming back for a day or two, anyway.
There always seemed to be a chance with Paco." She met
Grady's eyes. "Maybe there still will be, if he's put in a rehab program instead of jail."

"We're pushing for the maximum sentence."

"A shortsighted mistake."

Grady wondered how he could have believed Anna was a teenager. Looks had never so completely deceived him before. Now, as he stared into her turquoise eyes, he saw what he had missed at first. Anna looked fifteen, but she was at least a hundred. His mother, who studied reincarnation, spoke often of old souls. If there was such a thing, its name was Anna Fitzgerald.

"You have very strong opinions," he said carefully, "yet you're obviously just out of college. Have you really had enough experience to be so sure of yourself?"

"I didn't learn what I know from books."

"No?"

"I learned it on the streets. The hard way." She turned and started toward the door. Once there she paused, then looked back over her shoulder to see if he had followed her. "Come on, Mr. Prosecutor, let me show you a little of what I know. These kids are your constituents, too. Give them a chance."

Half an hour later Grady had decided that if these kids were his constituents, a political career was out of the question. If he had been tired when he started, he was dead on his feet by the time they made it to the first floor staff room.

There had been kids everywhere. Long-haired kids with pale, unhealthy faces. Short-haired kids who looked as if they belonged on high school football teams. Madonna-like teens lugging babies on their hips. Mary Magdalene-like teens wearing provocative clothing and size-'em-up looks on their faces.

There had been mass confusion and a surprising regimentation beneath it.

He had watched the kids with Anna and reluctantly agreed with Tom Schneider's assessment of her. She was one of them, but not quite. They respected her, although they didn't show it in the traditional ways, and when she told them to do something, they listened.

He had also watched the looks on their faces when he had been introduced. He was a cop to them, or, in Wesley's

words, a cop-fink. These were kids who had lived beyond
the law and probably still considered themselves above it.

Which was why he had come.

Anna closed the staff room door behind them, and the
noise, a blend of loud rock music, shouting teenagers and
dinner preparations, ebbed to a comfortable roar. Anna
flung herself on the sofa, but Grady noticed she still tapped
her foot in rhythm, as if she was anxious to move on.

"We used to call this the staff lounge, until we realized
that nobody ever got to lounge here. We use it for just about
everything else, though. Talking with kids, writing up re-
ports, phone calls, whatever has to be done."

The room was like every room in the old house, cool and
dim. First Day was located in a huge stucco mausoleum with
pretensions to Spanish architectural design. The walls were
thick and laced with crushed coquina shell, and there were
minimal windows decorated with black iron grillwork to let
in the blistering Florida sunshine. Entryways were grace-
fully arched, and the white walls were set off with dark
woodwork. Outside, a red tile roof rose above the two-story
house and looked out over three acres of trees and gardens.

The house had once been a showplace. Now it had the
marks of an institution. Clean but shabby. Smoke alarms
and overhead sprinklers. Department store furniture and
cheap poster art. There was nothing wrong with the house
that half a million dollars and a team of interior designers
couldn't cure, but what would be the point? The house had
been donated, forever hallelujah, to First Day. It would
never again be the site of pre-opera cocktail parties or oh-so-
posh charity fund-raisers. It would remain a shelter for
runaways until it fell down around its new tenants' ears.

Anna waited for Grady to respond. He looked like a man
who had just survived the London blitz. "I gather we're a
bit overwhelming," she said dryly.

"I knew Mrs. Garson. I was just wondering what she
would think about what you've done with her house."

"Mrs. Garson willed us the house because she believed in
what we were trying to do. The First Day program has

served over a thousand kids since we moved here. I think she'd be proud."

Grady frowned. "A thousand kids?"

"Give or take a few dozen." Anna tried to smile and hoped it would be contagious. "Surprised?"

"The house is big, but not that big."

"A lot of those thousand kids only stayed a night or two at our intake shelter on West 15th. First Day Inn. Remember, this is our long-term facility. The kids here are committed to staying off the streets and making their way back into society. The kids who come through our intake shelter are fed and housed and counseled on a short-term basis. A lot of them head home, others go to different programs more suited to their needs, others just disappear back onto the streets."

"Like Paco?"

"That's right."

"So Paco wasn't here?"

Anna weighed her answer carefully. "He showed up from time to time. A lot of the kids know each other, and they visit back and forth. Sometimes the intake kids come here to see what we're about. And sometimes, if we have a spare bed, they come here because First Day Inn is filled to overflowing."

"Then Paco had contact with kids who are still in your program?"

"I won't deny it."

Grady slouched comfortably in a chair and watched her fidget. Sitting still seemed to be impossible for her. "What would you do if you caught a kid who was staying here using drugs? Turn him back out on the streets? Call the cops? Have a heart-to-heart talk?"

Anna wondered how he had managed to keep cynicism out of a question made for it. "We've done all three of those things. It depends on the kid."

"Then you don't necessarily turn in kids who are breaking the law?"

"If you were a parent, Mr. Clayton, and you caught your kid smoking marijuana, would you take him right to the local precinct house or would you try to get help for him?"

"I don't know."

"Then you're kidding yourself. What kind of parent puts his own kid in jail for a first offense? And what kind of program would this be if we didn't look at each case individually and give our kids the benefit of the doubt whenever we possibly can?"

Grady didn't smile. "A program that wasn't out of compliance with the law."

"We don't break the law. And we don't give our kids permission to break it, either. But we're not dealing with your garden-variety suburban sweet peas here. These kids have problems you probably don't even know the names for. They come here sick and hungry and battered. And even after they get here, they make mistakes."

"Did you know that Paco Hernandez was selling drugs? Did you overlook it in hopes you could make a good little boy out of him again?"

"You have an evil mind, Mr. Clayton."

"Which is why I'm the State's Attorney."

Anna was on her feet, pacing the room, before she spoke again. Even though he was engulfed in weariness, Grady admired the way she moved. She was neither graceful nor clumsy but so filled with vitality that the air around her seemed to shiver. Watching her almost energized him.

She pointed to the door. "Did you see anything out there except possible tenants for your filthy, overcrowded prison system?"

"You'd prefer your criminals on the streets?"

She ignored his logic. She was moving past the point of logic herself. He was treading on sacred ground. "These kids are not criminals! They're kids, scared kids, sad kids, angry kids. Some of them have done horrible things to survive. Some of them have had horrible things done *to* them. They need a chance now. They don't need a pogrom."

"Pogrom?"

She waved her hands. "A purge, a hysterical law-and-order demonstration!"

Grady stood, too, his exhaustion fading away. "I wasn't having Auschwitz readied, if that's what's worrying you."

Anna stopped pacing. The last cautious voice inside her was now silent. "It's not so different, though, is it? You come here with preconceived notions of who's good and who isn't, who deserves a chance and who doesn't. You look at the faces of these kids and you see trouble! They'll never elect *you* to office. They'll never be part of the elite power structure that makes the decisions that affect us all. So why bother with them? Why give them a second chance? Why not just shove them somewhere so they'll never see the light of day again?"

Exhaustion had disappeared. Grady moved forward so that he and Anna were only a step apart. His face was a thundercloud. "You know nothing about me and what I believe!"

"Look, I know your type! You think what you are is a secret, but I understand all about you."

"What in hell are you talking about?"

"You go after power and damn the foolish who get in your way! You say whatever your voters want to hear and do whatever brings you the greatest glory. I know your type, all right. And I know that eventually you get to the point where you think everyone in the world was put there to serve your whims, no matter how twisted or evil they are, no matter who you destroy—" She stopped, and, slowly, her eyes widened.

As Grady watched she seemed to grow paler. He took the last step toward her, anger forgotten. "Anna?"

But she was in the grip of something else. She moved away from him, growing paler still.

He lowered his voice. "Anna? Are you all right?"

She shut her eyes, as if to block out the sight of him.

He reached out to put his hand on her arm. "Maybe you'd better sit down."

She jumped as if he had burned her, and her eyelids flew open. "Don't touch me. Don't ever touch me!"

Grady's patience evaporated. "Who in hell are you looking at? I'm sure it isn't me!"

"Anna!" Tom's summons came from the doorway. Neither Anna nor Grady had heard him open the door.

Anna turned to look at Tom, her eyes bewildered, defeated.

Tom stuck his thumb over his shoulder. "They're about to serve dinner. You're needed to figure out the cleanup schedule."

Anna's eyes flashed back to Grady. She stared at him for a long moment, almost as if she were trying to figure out exactly who he was. Then she turned and left the room without another word.

Tom closed the door behind her and waited for Grady to speak.

"How much of that did you see?" Grady asked at last.

"Enough."

"What's going on here? The staff's as confused as the residents!"

"The staff and the residents are people with pasts. I would guess that Anna was just living a little of hers."

"How much of her past do you know?"

"Not a bit."

Grady ran his hand through his hair in exasperation. "You hire staff without knowing their credentials and checking their references?"

"I hired Anna *because* I knew her."

"You just said you don't know her past!"

"Not her past before she came here. Anna was a First Day resident before she started working for us. In the four years I've know her, she's never even told me her real name. I suspect she just told you more about who she used to be than she's ever told anyone here."

"Am I supposed to be flattered?"

Tom's smile was sad. "Flattered? No. Compassionate? Yes, Mr. Clayton. And maybe just a little sorry that you provoked her."

Chapter 2

Compassion. Grady drove to his parents' home with Tom Schneider's words ringing in his ears. Compassion. Wasn't that one of those words like "maturity" that was linked more to age than to a Princeton summa cum laude or the Stanford Law Review?

Exhaustion had blotted out what compassion he had accumulated in his twenty-nine years. He had baited Anna Fitzgerald, striking at the things she obviously held dear. And why? To make a point? What did it matter what she believed? Exhaustion and tension had pushed him over the edge of good sense.

Except that exhaustion wasn't the whole truth. He didn't like to admit the rest. Perhaps if he wasn't driving alone, forced to endure his own silent company, he wouldn't even *think* it. But the truth was painfully clear to him as he swung his car onto the beachfront avenue that led to the Clayton estate.

He had baited Anna Fitzgerald because she was so alive, so vibrant in her defense of the kids she worked with, that just watching her had energized him. Stimulated him, if the truth was acknowledged. He had been so caught up in

Anna's vitality and passion that he had baited her like a schoolboy waving a bullfrog under a little girl's snub nose. He had been thinking with his hormones, not his brains.

Good old sexual attraction. His reaction to Anna had been no more serious than that hypothetical schoolboy's, but with the same predictable results. He had sent her running. Which was just as well, but it had hardly been a mature way to do it.

Grady slapped his palm against the steering wheel of his Audi and wondered why good manners and good sense had simultaneously deserted him. He couldn't afford to let that happen again. He was in a race for State's Attorney that was going to take every bit of concentration and maturity he possessed. If he won the right to represent his party in November, the election would probably be a shoo-in. But he had a tough primary to get through first. Nobody his age had ever won such an important honor in Sun County.

Still, nobody else had exposed corruption in the State's Attorney's office, either. Not that he'd collared Harry Traltor hoping to get his job when the former prosecutor was indicted. Grady had never considered that he would be given Traltor's position, but there had been such a public outcry when Traltor was linked to a drug running mob and such a flood of praise for Grady's efforts to expose him, that the governor had been given no choice but to appoint him to finish Traltor's term.

Now *he* had no choice but to run for the job in the upcoming primary.

The palms lining Reynaldo Avenue swayed in the salt-tinged breeze as he drove. With twilight's approach the sky was a deepening blue merging seamlessly with the ocean. Sea gulls squawked under blooming clumps of oleander, and from the public beach, laughing children called goodbye to a perfect summer day.

Grady made good time. He had long since left rush hour traffic behind. The Clayton estate was far enough out of the city, and in an area so sparsely populated, that Grady could unleash a little of the sports car's power.

The area was sparsely populated because there were no housing tracts here, no miles of one-story, cement block, gravel roofed houses with sand-splattered yards and cluttered carports. The residents of Reynaldo Beach were surrounded by space, manicured lawns and all the surf and sand the eye could behold. They paid for the privilege, although for the most part they were too well-bred to even notice. Reynaldo Beach was old money and older codes of conduct. A person was born to Reynaldo Beach. Those few who had dared to enter without the proper credentials found their existence mocked and lonely.

Grady blazed past the house that Susan Powell, his fiancée, wanted him to buy. It was small by Reynaldo Beach standards, a snowbird's former winter cottage. The architectural style was eclectic, the ambience more cozy than correct. He had been surprised when Susan asked him to tour the house with her. He still wasn't sure if she wanted to live there because it was the only house available in "The Beach," or because the house itself touched some poignant chord inside her. He hadn't asked, and she hadn't said. And that was a description of their relationship.

Susan Powell, of the Palm Beach Powells, was twenty-five, and twenty-five-times charming. They had been engaged for a year. Their wedding was set for the fall, and by all accounts would be the biggest social event of the season. She had stood beside him when his own job was jeopardized during the Harry Traltor scandal, and she stood beside him now as he campaigned. She had a knack for making things easier for everybody around her, and he loved her for the way she took his life in her capable hands and soothed away its hurts.

He thought of Anna Fitzgerald as he made the turn onto the Clayton estate grounds. Anna would never make life easier for anyone. She would challenge, provoke, stimulate. Life with Anna would be a roller coaster ride. Life with Susan was going to be a glider flight.

As he parked his car in the circular driveway in front of his parents' home, he shoved away thoughts of Anna and the way he had treated her. The house was brick and cypress, all verandas and French doors and massive square pillars. Despite the sandy soil and salt-laden air, there were gardenias and azaleas, wisteria and camellias. Gardeners kept the estate blooming and verdant, never taking no for an answer. Money might not be able to buy everything, but in Reynaldo Beach, it could fool Mother Nature.

Susan came out on the porch as he turned off the ignition. Her streaked brown hair shone in the light of the setting sun. She walked to the edge, but he knew she would come no closer. She would consider that an intrusion on his privacy, a demand for attention. Instead, she would wait to determine his mood and his needs, then adjust her own accordingly.

He found that thought surprisingly irritating.

"One of those days?" Susan stood on tiptoe to kiss him when he joined her. She was tall and willowy, but no match for his six two.

He held her close, trying to be grateful that she cared enough to be considerate. "I'm beat. If I have to shake another hand I'll run screaming into the night."

"I'm sorry, sweetheart, but there are half a dozen hands to shake inside."

A rough groan of disappointment caught in his throat.

Susan went on. "Your parents invited the Matsons and the Briggs for dinner. And old Mr. Steinburg and his sister, too. They've all made sizeable contributions to your campaign fund."

He buried his face in her hair. She smelled of Shalimar and sunshine. The combination was intriguing. "Run away with me. Let's drive to the other side of town and eat smoked mackerel at some beachfront bar. Let's play miniature golf until the sun comes up tomorrow."

"I had a fresh shirt and your dinner jacket laid out. If you sneak through the front hall you can shower and change before you have to see anyone. I can have Sarah stall dinner."

"Let's shack up at some shabby motel and make wild, passionate love until the primary results are in."

She stiffened a little. "Grady?"

He sighed and stepped away from her. There were questions in her pansy-blue eyes, and he couldn't answer them. "Go ahead and stall dinner. I won't be long."

She seemed relieved. "All this is going to be over with soon. After our wedding we'll go away. We'll play all the miniature golf you can stand."

He waited for her to say she'd fulfill his last fantasy, but he knew he would have to wait forever. Their relationship was founded on mutual interests and respect. They were lovers, but only just. She was giving in bed and made no demands, just as she made no demands in any other area of her life. Passion was something she didn't understand.

He kissed her forehead. "I'll be down in a few minutes."

"Grady?"

"Yes."

"I'm sorry about tonight."

He was sorry, too, but for exactly what, he wasn't sure.

"So, bunny-nose, did Isabelle teach you any more Spanish today?"

"Si, señorita." Ryan Fitzgerald burst into laughter, as if he had just made a wonderful joke. Anna was learning that to a four-year-old, almost anything was funny.

"This little one of yours, he keeps me on my feet."

"Toes." Anna swooped Ryan into the air and hugged him close. He immediately began to wiggle. "And Teresa, she keeps you on your toes, too?"

"They have decided to marry. A fine couple, you think?"

Anna pretended to examine her wiggling son. His hair was white-blond and so tightly curled that it looked as if he had just escaped from a demented beautician. His skin was milk-white and his eyes a Florida-sky blue. Like his father's.

Teresa, Isabella's three-year-old daughter, had black hair, like her mother's. Her skin was creamy and her eyes the light brown of coconut husks—again, like her mother's. She already knew how to use her eyes to tear a man's heart in two. It was no wonder that Ryan had fallen under her spell.

"I think Teresa will be a woman for a rich man. I'm going to go out and enroll Ryan at Harvard tomorrow."

"I tell her not to marry a man with fast talk. Now I should tell her to marry a Harvard?"

Anna laughed, and, still holding Ryan, gave Isabella a quick hug, too. "Tell her to marry for love."

Isabella poured out a flood of Spanish which Anna couldn't decipher, but she guessed the sentiment. Isabelle had married for love, and Enrique, her *amore*, had left her with Teresa and another child on the way. By all accounts he was now back in Central America living with another woman.

Isabella's misfortune had been Anna's blessing, because after Enrique's desertion, Isabella had needed a job, and caring for Ryan and two other neighborhood children paid her bills. She and Anna were next-door neighbors, living in a crowded, shabby neighborhood where the Cuban refugees were the old guard and the Haitians and Central Americans the new. Latin music filled the air from morning till night, and the shrill wake-up calls of roosters were as commonplace as hubcap thievery.

Anna's house had three rooms, built in a single row from front to back. Isabella's had four. There were four feet of weeds between the houses, and walls so thin that secrets couldn't exist. After Enrique's departure, Anna had heard Isabella's weeping. The two women had made short work of the language barrier. Feelings were the same no matter what their country of origin.

Anna loved her neighborhood, and she loved Isabella. She felt protected here, although in reality petty theft was a typical annoyance. But the theft was from outsiders. She knew every family on the block and trusted them implicitly. She cuddled their babies, lectured their teenagers and traded recipes with their matriarchs. Her neighbors were teaching her Spanish and French, and she was honing their English. Ryan, a blond throwback to his Swedish ancestors, was growing up without prejudice or false values. And that was a source of pride for Anna.

"I'd better get bunny-nose here home." She wrestled her son into submission and started toward the front door. "I get paid tomorrow. Want to go out for pizza? My treat?"

"You save your money for an air...air..."

"Conditioner."

"Cone-deesh-ner. I will cook food for us here, yes?"

"I'll bring a surprise."

"Save your money. You spend it, it's gone. You save it—"

"Then it's gone later." Anna blew Isabella and Teresa kisses and loyally nodded at a well-executed statue of the Virgin that was Isabella's pride. Ryan called the statue Mother and regularly decorated it with flower wreaths and Isabella's jewelry, like a Hindu goddess. Anna often thought that her Lutheran relatives would have been surprised at her son's eclectic religious instincts. If they had known about Ryan in the first place.

In her own house she turned on lights and set Ryan down to roam. He had a regular route he followed, and tonight was no exception. She watched as he checked his toy chest, then his bed. His beloved blanket, which wasn't allowed out of the house, was just where he had left it. Satisfied, he turned on the light in his tiny aquarium and counted fish, then counted the leaves on a wilting philodendron that he was killing with kindness.

"Everything okay?" Anna asked as she started water for his bath.

"Can I water my plant, Mommy?"

Her heart always beat a little faster when he called her Mommy. She could never quite believe that he was there, warm and sweet and real. He was a perfect child from an imperfect woman. Sometimes she was afraid she would wake up one morning and find that he was nothing more than a dream in a world filled with nightmares.

"I don't think you'd better, bunny-nose. Not tonight. We've got to let it dry out a little, or it might die."

"*I* have to have a drink every night," he said with four-year-old logic.

"How would you feel if I made you wear wet shoes all the time? That's how your plant feels when you give it too much water."

Ryan seemed to consider. "Could I wear them inside, too?"

She gave up on the analogy. "Hop in the bathtub. I'll get your toys."

Later, she heard him splashing and humming contentedly as she tidied up the morning's dishes. It was the time of night when she always thought of Matt. Matt Fitzgerald who had never seen the son playing with a flotilla of rubber animals in the next room.

It was the time of night when she always thought of Matt, but it was not Matt's face that came to mind tonight. The man she saw had hair of mahogany brown and eyes the same, rich color. And he was reaching out to her while all she could do was turn inward to the black void that was her past.

"Bunny-nose?" She stopped clanking dishes and listened for the familiar splashing. "Bunny-nose?"

"Maybe my plant would like milk to drink. I like milk."

Anna released a long breath. Dreams and nightmares and a hard man with concern in his dark brown eyes. A child with the face of her dead lover. A perfect child from an imperfect woman.

"Finish up now," she called to Ryan. "We'll just have time for a story before bed if you hurry."

On her precious days off Anna usually stayed as far away from First Day as she could. Today, though, she had two reasons for making a stop there. She had to pick up her paycheck, and she had to see Wesley. The morning had been a momentous one for him, although he would never admit that. He had taken the exam to see if he had passed the basic skills course First Day had enrolled him in. It was the first step toward a high school equivalency diploma, an admittance ticket into the society he ridiculed. Anna had doubts whether he would pass. Wesley's potential was extraordinary, but cynicism and an eternal search for the easy way out stopped him from working to develop it.

Still, even though he hadn't studied as hard as he'd needed to, he had taken the exam. Anna wanted him to know she was proud of him.

Days off were sacred time with Ryan, so today Ryan went with her to First Day. He called it First Home, because he and Anna had lived there when he was born and for many months afterward. Sometimes there were babies or toddlers to play with, and almost always there was a teenager who could be persuaded to give him endless horsey-back rides.

Anna always kept Ryan's visits short. First Day was not the place for a child his age. The atmosphere was unpredictable, the language and information he might pick up unfortunately *too* predictable. Still, she liked him to see where she worked so that he was able to envision her here if he missed her during the day. And she thought that Ryan, in small doses, was good for the residents. Kids with the manners of hyenas and the empathy of jackals somehow softened under Ryan's steady, innocent gaze. Even Wesley, who was one of Ryan's favorite people, seemed a different person around the little boy.

They arrived during a lull. The counselors had just changed shifts, and the new staff, with their reservoirs of energy still untapped, had gotten the residents organized. Some of the kids were out at jobs, some in classes. Those at home were quietly occupied.

Anna left Ryan downstairs with seventeen-year-old Jill, who would be a mother herself soon. Jill was undecided what to do about her baby, and privately Anna thought that spending time with Ryan might help her make her decision. Ryan was life itself, pure, unadulterated energy and love, but like any child, he drained energy and love from everyone he came in contact with, too. She wanted Jill to understand the huge commitment she was taking on if she kept her baby. She also wanted her to understand what she might be giving up if she didn't. Anna, of all people, knew that no one could make the decision for her. They could only help her see the choices without blinders.

Upstairs, Tom's door was open, as it always was unless he was in conference. He had the telephone receiver tucked neatly under his chin, and he was shuffling papers on his desk, but he motioned Anna inside when he saw her standing in the doorway.

He spoke into the receiver. "Yes, I know you're sorry. I'm sorry, too, sorry you're backing out of your commitment." Tom paused. "No," he continued. "Frankly, I don't care about your other guests, don't give a hang about them, in fact. We'll use another hotel and we'll be sure the other social service agencies in town know how you've treated us in case they're looking for a place to hold a conference." He hung up without listening to a response.

"Trouble?"

"When was there ever anything but?" He smiled to take the sting out of his words. "The hotel where I wanted to house most of our guests just decided that they don't want to cater to the staffs of the country's runaway shelters if some of the residents are coming along, too."

Anna sat down. Because of the fight with Wesley and the confrontation with Grady Clayton yesterday, she had almost forgotten the rest of the bad news Tom had given her.

"Have you thought any more about what I asked you yesterday?" he asked now.

Anna shook her head. "I guess I blocked it out."

"I'm counting on you to help me run this conference next month, Anna."

"I don't know anything about running a conference! I'll take on any of your other jobs, but please don't ask me to do something I won't be any good at."

"Who says?"

She stared at him.

"Well?" he prompted.

"How many times have you said that to me?"

"One hundred? Two?"

"You expect too much. You always have."

"And I've never been disappointed."

"How about yesterday?"

He smiled. With his bald head and thick glasses he looked like a placid, nearsighted Buddha. "Yesterday was tough, huh? Grady Clayton stirred something up, didn't he?"

"That's what he's paid to do, I guess."

"Something inside you."

"I can't talk about it, Tom."

"Okay. Let's talk about the conference, then."

Anna pitched herself out of her chair and began to roam the room. "Do you really trust me to oversee all those details? How come *we* have to sponsor the damn thing anyway?"

"Because it's our turn. And come on, Anna, you know it'll be a chance for our staff to hear some of the top people in the country talk about programs and possibilities. We can't afford to do much in-service training. This will be a tremendous opportunity."

"Tremendous responsibility."

"I'll be here if you have any problems or questions. You're not going to be alone."

She knew she could say no, but she also knew Tom expected her to say yes. He had always expected her to do more than try her wings. He expected her to fly. "You're pretty pushy, you know that?"

"Of course."

"I'll do it, but I'll probably be here every hour on the hour checking with you."

"Fine." He rummaged on his desk for her paycheck and handed the envelope to her. "I'll have a list of things to do on your desk by Monday."

"My desk?"

"I'm having Earl clear out the small storage room on the third floor. It's not much of an office, but it will be something."

"I don't want an office, Tom."

"Tough. You'll need privacy and a telephone to make all the arrangements, and a place to store all the paperwork. Boiled down that means an office. And it's long overdue."

"I'm becoming a bureaucrat."

"An administrator."

"You never give up. You just keep pushing and pushing." She stopped pacing and bent down to kiss his cheek. "Have a good weekend."

"Did you bring my boy?"

"He's downstairs."

"Send him up to see me before you leave."

Before Anna went downstairs to retrieve Ryan, she searched for Wesley, but found that he hadn't returned from his test yet. She left him a note, then went to find her son.

He was on the front porch. With Grady Clayton.

Ryan was chirping away. "I can hop all the way to the other side on one foot. Wanna see?"

Grady was squatting comfortably beside him so their eyes were level. "Bet you can't."

"I can hop *all* the way over and all the way back."

"No. Really?"

"My mommy calls me bunny-nose 'cause I hop so good and 'cause I can do this." He wiggled his nose expertly.

Grady nodded seriously. "Excellent. Now let's see you hop."

"Okay." Ryan began his demonstration. Grady's gaze didn't flicker. He watched the little boy with the concentration of an official timing an Olympic event.

Ryan was on his way back, hopping for all he was worth, when Anna spoke. "He doesn't vote, you know."

Grady didn't turn. He waited until Ryan had successfully completed his goal, then reached in his pocket and pulled out a deflated balloon. "Your prize."

"It's got writing on it."

"Grady Clayton. That's my name."

"Tom wants you to run up and see him," Anna said, walking over to stand beside Ryan. "Why don't you take the balloon and show him."

"Thanks, Grady!"

"Mr. Clayton," Anna corrected.

"Grady will be just fine." Grady stood. It was only when Ryan was gone that he spoke to Anna. "You have a fine little boy there."

"How do you know he's mine?"

"He has your energy and exuberance." He turned to look at her. "And your chin."

"I'm surprised to see you here again."

Grady folded his arms and leaned against the low stucco wall enclosing the wide porch. "I'm surprised to see you. I was just told you didn't work today."

"Checking so you wouldn't run into me?"

"You and I got off on the wrong foot yesterday. I'd like to change that."

There was none of yesterday's challenge in his voice, only quiet good manners. She leaned against the wall, too. They weren't going to play yesterday's games, and she was glad. "I overreacted."

"And I bullied."

"Why did you?"

Grady certainly wasn't going to tell her the truth. He had slept on it and woken up convinced that he had imagined his attraction to Anna. He had been exhausted and irritable. Nothing made him more irritable than people who stood between him and a drug-free county, and in his exhaustion he had seen Anna's defense of Paco that way.

Now, with Anna beside him, he knew he had spent the morning lying to himself. He had only briefly glanced at her. Even now, he was staring at the wall instead. But he could describe in absolute detail everything about her from the colors and botanical names of the flowers on her Hawaiian print shorts to the number of freckles on her ridiculously aristocratic nose.

"I guess it was because you reacted so violently," he said at last.

"So it was my fault?"

"Not at all. I guess you were just a terrific audience for my self-righteousness."

"Are you trying to charm me, Mr. Prosecutor? I have no faith in the political system, or politicans, either."

He turned so he could see her. "Would I waste my time that way?"

Anna was uncomfortably aware of how attractive Grady was. He was wearing cream-colored trousers and a cream-colored shirt with thin blue stripes. He carried a matching jacket over his arm, and his blue tie was loosened as a sop to the summer heat. In addition to excellent taste in clothing, he had a personal magnetism that would carry him farther than the State's Attorney's office. Someday she could say she knew him when.

"Why *are* you wasting your time?" she asked flippantly, pushing herself away from the wall to rearrange three potted ferns sitting on an iron table.

"I don't consider an apology a waste of time."

She succumbed. Just a little. "Then thank you. And I apologize, too."

"I've got something else to ask you."

For one dizzying moment she almost believed he was going to ask her to go out with him. There was something peculiar in the air between them, and though she didn't dare give it a name, it confused her and made her feel ready for almost any turn of events.

"I'd like you to go on a stakeout."

Almost any turn of events. "Stakeout?" She looked up from her plants. "Me?"

"We need to know who was supplying Paco with drugs. We're missing one link in a chain that could help clear this county of drug running. At least by this particular cartel," he added wryly.

"What does this have to do with me?"

"Your staff knows Paco well. Correct me if I'm wrong."

She shook her head.

"Then when he was here, you also saw the people who were with him. Friends that hung around, people who showed up at odd times."

She tried to think if that were true. "It's been so long since he stayed here. And he was only here for three or four days, just until a bed cleared at the Inn."

"Can you remember anyone who came to see him? Anyone at all?"

Reluctantly she shook her head again. "I'm sorry."

"But you might recognize faces."

"It's possible. But what does that have to do with a stakeout?"

"There's a grocery store on the other side of town. A place called Guerrando's."

"That's close to my house."

Grady looked surprised. "You live on the West Side?"

"I'm not allowed to?"

He recovered immediately. "I'm sorry. I'm not really a snob."

"No?"

"No. I was thinking about little bunny-nose. Can he play in his own yard?"

"I live in a good neighborhood. We watch out for each other."

He thought how easily he could get off the track with Anna. He wanted to know about her, even though it made no sense to take the time to do it. She was obviously a woman with a husband. She had a son to prove it. And he was engaged to be married.

"Guerrando's is an interesting place." He didn't add that it was a known distribution point for drug shipments coming into the county. "We've got reason to believe that the people supplying drugs to Paco spend a lot of money on groceries there."

She heard all the things he didn't say. "How could I help?"

"By watching the people who come and go and telling us if any of them are familiar."

"Watching from where?"

"A safe place, I promise."

Anna considered. "For how long?"

"One day. Maybe two."

"Of course I'll do it."

Grady was taken by surprise. After their encounter yesterday he had expected to fail at convincing her. "May I ask why?"

"Do you really think you're the only one in Ponte Reynaldo who hates drugs?" She stopped rearranging the plants and faced him. "I *see* what drugs do to people. I work with

kids so controlled by them they'd willingly sell their souls for
their next hit. Do you think I don't know the damage they
do? But we weren't talking about drugs yesterday, Mr.
Clayton. We were talking about kids and chances and starting over. I'll help you, but I want you to do something for
me.''

"I can't—"

"You can look at Paco's case again. Look at it hard.
Then ask yourself if you're doing the best thing for Sun
County by sending its hope for the future to prison instead
of a rehab program." She held up her hand to stop him
when he tried to interrupt. "I'm just asking you to look at
his case again. Just one case. That's all.''

She was Joan of Arc in surfer shorts. Grady looked at her
and felt impending doom. Something deep and primal
twisted inside him; he tried desperately to ignore it. His
expression didn't change. "My college roommate died from
a drug overdose. I look at everyone who sells drugs and see
the face of the man who supplied Travis. I have no sympathy.''

She stretched her arm toward him and touched his arm,
giving him sympathy. "Ryan's father was killed in a gun
battle between two drugs gangs in Miami,'' she said softly.
"He never saw his son. But if he had lived, Matt would have
fought for Paco. Can't you do it, too?''

He wanted to tell her no, but he had the indisputable
feeling that telling Anna Fitzgerald no about anything was
going to be the most difficult task of his life. "I'll pick you
up myself, tomorrow morning,'' he said instead. "About
six. I want to be there.'' As he said the words he realized
what a bad idea being there would be. But it was too late.

"I'll be ready.'' Anna gave him her address, then realized her fingers were still grazing the sleeve of his shirt. She
dropped her hand.

He nodded a curt goodbye. Only when he was in his car
and miles away did he let himself wonder if he was losing his
mind. The possibility that it might be his heart was buried
too deeply to consider.

Chapter 3

Isabella was honing her English at an extraordinary speed, but idioms were still a problem. Anna had just finished explaining to her that a stakeout was not a fancy barbecue. They were sitting on Anna's front porch, trying to catch a faint breeze, but for every puff of fresh air that came their way there was another of automobile exhaust.

"So I have to be gone all day tomorrow. Almost from dawn. What do you think I should wear?" Anna leaned back in her chair and fanned herself with her hand. "Black from head to toe? A trench coat?"

"What is this trench coat?"

Anna explained. Then added, "Or maybe something to make me look like a schoolgirl again, so no one will suspect me."

"You look like a schoolgirl now."

Anna looked down at her red halter and skimpy green shorts. Her feet were bare, the tops of them sunburned, as was her nose. She and Ryan had spent the late afternoon at the beach. "Grady Clayton's a very formal man. He'll expect me to be appropriately covered."

"I've seen this Grady in the papers. He is a very hand-some man. How you say...?" Isabella floundered for the right word. "A hulk?"

"Hunk."

Isabella frowned. "This hunk, does it not mean a piece of something? Like a hunk of meat?"

"Same thing."

Isabella giggled. "This hunk, this Grady, does he smile at you like the man at the grocery store smiles?"

"He frowns. Like this." Anna made a horrible face. "And he growls. Like this." She gave a ferocious grown that brought Ryan and Teresa running out of the house to see what had happened.

"You scare the children."

"Grady scares me." Anna thought about her statement and knew it was true. Some of the reasons were obvious. And the others...?

Isabella gathered both Ryan and Teresa on her rapidly expanding lap. "Enrique, he made me scared. I looked at him and knew my life would change."

"And you were right."

Isabella shrugged. "Yes. It was so. And now he is gone."

"The story of a woman's life."

"But I would do it again."

Anna looked at her friend, surprised. "You have to be kidding."

"No. I would do it again. Enrique was my heart."

Later, as she and Isabella set out the potato salad and cold roast chicken Anna had bought as a treat, Anna thought about her friend's words. Ryan's father had been her pro-tector, her closest friend, but never her heart. She won-dered if she had the capacity for that kind of love after everything she had been through.

She sincerely hoped not.

Grady shoved his hands deeply in his pockets and leaned against Anna's front porch pillar. "We have some extra funds to cover this sort of thing. We'll pay your childcare costs.'' As he spoke, his gaze thoroughly swept every inch of Anna's street.

The sun had been up for a shorter time than Anna had. Now she watched Grady dissect her living situation. ''Ever been to the far West Side, Mr. Clayton?''

''We're going to be sitting on top of each other all day, Anna. At least call me Grady.''

''Grady. These people vote, you know. You should hold a rally here. There's a vacant lot on the next block that's free from three to four next Saturday. I can book it for you, if you say the word.''

Grady switched his gaze from the street to the woman. Except for her sunburned nose she looked twenty-two today. He admired her dress, which was really nothing more than a long turquoise T-shirt with a flared skirt. It made the color of her eyes even more startling. ''When you were in school, did that mouth of yours get you into trouble?''

''I was the scourge of the classroom.''

''Don't be the scourge of this stakeout.''

''I'll be the soul of self-control. I won't talk, I won't fidget.''

''You'll explode.'' He smiled. Reluctantly. There were entirely too many things about Anna to smile at.

''Is that why you're going to be there? To watch me go quietly crazy?''

''I just don't want this fouled up. It's too important.''

''You'll be dead from overwork and worry before you're forty.''

''My wife will be sure that doesn't happen.'' Grady didn't know why he'd said that. Maybe he was making a declaration of limits, but for whom, he didn't know.

Anna felt a mixture of relief and something else she didn't want to name. ''A lucky woman,'' she said lightly. ''She'll be the one to die of overwork and worry. Does she know?''

''We're not married yet.'' Again, he didn't know just why he'd said that. He was a puzzle to himself, and an irritation.

''So you're about to tie the knot. Congratulations.''

"Thanks." Grady looked at his watch. "We'd better head out. Your babysitter knows you might be back late?"

"Ryan slept there last night, he can sleep there again if he has to. But I hope he doesn't."

"Me too."

Grady watched Anna lock her front door. Then they started toward his car. The Audi was safe at home in the garage of his condo. He had borrowed a state car for the day, not only because it was less noticeable, but because he knew he would find the Audi stripped if he left it on the street near Guerrando's.

Anna's street was spiced with strong, not-unpleasant odors of frying onions and garlic and the sounds of Latin rhythms. A little girl with huge dark eyes watched them as they walked toward his car. Anna called her by name and wished her a good day in Spanish.

"You speak Spanish?"

"I wish. I have enough trouble with English, but I'm trying to learn from my neighbors."

"Trouble with English?"

"My brain does strange things with sounds. I hear them okay, but then they don't get processed exactly right all the time. It gave me fits when I was younger because I had trouble understanding instructions."

"And now?"

"I have to work harder than some people do if I want to keep up in school."

"School?"

"I take night classes at the university during the fall and spring. Just one a term, but I'm closing in on my requirements for a degree." She laughed at herself. "It should only be another twenty years or so."

"A demanding job, a kid, school."

"And you thought I was just fifteen."

"I've definitely changed my mind."

Grady opened the door of the plain white sedan and ushered her inside. They were almost to Guerrando's before they spoke again.

"What if I don't recognize anybody?" Anna asked.

"That's what we're expecting. If you do, that will be a bonus."

She settled back, satisfied.

The stakeout location was a run-down two-story office building directly across from the grocery store. The police and D.A.'s office had moved a protesting dental technician out of his laboratory for a week so that they could use the second-floor office facing the street. Cameras and other equipment were set up amid racks of denture molds. There was barely enough room for people, too.

Grady took Anna in the back way, through a twisting, garbage-strewn alley and up a fire escape. Inside he tried to make her comfortable on a folding chair strategically placed by one of the two small windows shaded with miniblinds. There was no air-conditioning because the window unit had been removed to make way for a video camera. Since the windows had to remain closed, the room was already sweltering.

Grady lifted a cola from a cooler and tossed it to her. It was unpleasantly warm. "Beats a cup of coffee in this heat."

They were alone, since the team who had been manning the stakeout before they arrived had already vanished. Anna popped the top on her can and sipped slowly. It was going to be a long day. "What time does the store open?"

"Seven. You don't use Guerrando's?"

"There's another store closer. Guerrando's always gives me the creeps."

"Smart girl."

"I haven't seen anything suspicious the few times I've been there. I just didn't like the guys hanging around out front."

"Nobody passed you little white bags with your celery?"

"If they did I thought it was cornstarch and used it to powder Ryan's bottom."

Grady unfastened the top two buttons of his shirt. He had left his tie at home. "I'd like to be out on the beach about now. Or in an ice-cold pool."

"Or sledding down a snow-covered hill."

"Or skiing at Aspen."

"Vail."

Grady watched her. "You've been to Vail?"

"In a former life."

"Where else did you go in that life?"

There was a slight hesitation. Then, "Crazy."

Grady knew he hadn't been invited into her past, but he was hopelessly intrigued. "Have you always lived in Florida?"

"In this day and age no one lives anywhere always."

"Then you haven't?"

"Did I say that?" Anna turned away from the window to meet his eyes. "I don't talk about where I've been or what I've done or who I was. I'll admit that cuts down on the small talk, but we'll just have to endure." She turned back to the window.

"Tom told me you were a runaway. You're still running?"

"Do I look like I'm running?"

"You sound like you are."

"The person I was is dead. I don't believe exhuming the body would be either healthy or profitable."

The words were brittle, but the tone was sad. Grady suffered a short bout of guilt before he pushed her again. "Can you really help the kids you work with if you can't use your own life as an example?"

"What makes you think I can't? They don't have to know my old name and address to benefit from my experiences."

"I've got no business asking you these questions, do I?"

"Tell me about you, instead."

Grady watched an old man walk to Guerrando's plate-glass display window. The old man stared for a while, then shuffled slowly down the street.

"I don't have anything exciting to tell you. I come from an old Sun County family. I grew up with old money in an old house. I went to old schools and got degrees that would keep me in the same old places with the same old people."

"And you're marrying an old woman?"

He laughed. "Hardly."

"Has everything always been that easy for you?"

"No tragedies, no turmoil," he admitted.

"What about the death of your friend?"

He had forgotten that he had told her about Travis. "That qualified," he admitted. "He was in law school with me at Stanford. The brightest star in a vibrant galaxy." He wondered about his own poetry. It hardly seemed suitable for a politician.

"And he died of a drug overdose?"

"Just before graduation."

"He died for you, you know."

"What's that supposed to mean?"

"He died to show you that the world wasn't the way you thought it was."

"Surprisingly generous, wouldn't you say?"

"It changed you, didn't it?"

It *had* changed him. He wouldn't be State's Attorney here right now if it hadn't. Travis's death had made him suspicious and watchful. He saw demons now; sometimes he even saw them when they weren't there. "I'm a different man."

"You're driven." Anna turned away from the window. "Tell me, is it power that drives you? Or is it a real desire to change things?"

She was staring at him, her lovely eyes demanding honesty. He had an overwhelming desire to reach across the cameras and the false teeth and touch her. He wanted to feel her energy flow over him, and he wanted to give her comfort.

"I'm not driven," he said at last. "I'm being driven, but either way, it's toward a goal I believe in. I have to win this election. Rand Garner is as crooked as Harry Traltor was. If he beats me, justice in Sun County will sink to an all-time low. And right now I'm the only person who stands a chance against him."

"You couldn't expose him the way you exposed Traltor?"

"There's nothing I can prove. Not yet, anyway. And probably not in time for the primary. Then, if I lose, I'll be out of power and out of chances to prove anything." He

broke eye contact to look at his watch. It was a ruse. He just
didn't want to look at her any more. She was too easy to
look at, and he was increasingly aware of how small the
room was.

"What time is it?"

"Just a few minutes to seven."

"Then they'll be opening soon." Anna leaned forward.
"Here comes a man now. If I identify someone early on, do
we get to leave?"

"Maybe."

"Then we're saved. I recognize that man. It's Mr. Guerrando."

"Unless you saw him hanging out with Paco, that won't
do the trick."

"The few times I saw him he was behind the meat counter. Can we arrest him for sanitation violations?"

"Not today."

"Too bad."

By three o'clock that afternoon the room was close to one
hundred degrees. They had opened the door several times to
try to draw in some cooler air while Grady stood guard in
the hallway. They had even cracked both windows a few
inches, but nothing seemed to help.

"This won't be good for your campaign. I can see the
headlines now." Anna held her hands up as if she were
reading a newspaper. "Prosecutor Bakes Witness in Mad
Race for Justice."

"Bakes *Self* and Witness." Grady rummaged in the cooler
again and turned up one last ninety-degree soft drink.
"Share?" He held it out to Anna.

She took it and popped the top. "Share? Why don't you
just run on over to Guerrando's and buy another six pack
or two? Some chips would be nice with it." She took a long
drink, then, as if she had weighed her decision carefully,
shoved the drink at Grady. "Here. This room is creepy
enough without sharing it with a corpse."

"Consider it a campaign contribution."

"I don't even vote."

"Why do you hate politicans so much?" Grady moved closer so that he and Anna could share the drink more easily. "Or is it just politicians?"

"Personal experience."

He imagined it was the heat that was feeding his frustration, but he was getting tired of Anna's roadblocks. He wanted to know her. He had even stopped asking himself why. "What kind of experience?"

"You're dynamite in a courtroom, right?"

"So they say."

As she held her hand out for the drink, she considered the woman with two small children going into Guerrando's. "This isn't a courtroom."

"Does it have something to do with your late husband?"

Anna decided this had gone far enough. "I have no late husband. I was never married to Ryan's dad. I wasn't old enough to be married without my parents' permission, and even if I could have been, I had no birth certificate to get a license. Neither did Matt, because he was a runaway, too. We were children. I was seventeen when Ryan was born, and Matt was dead by then."

Grady had realized she was young when she had Ryan, but he hadn't done the necessary calculations. He thought of all she had accomplished. "You have a lot to be proud of, don't you?"

She had given him that thumbnail history precisely to show him that she wasn't proud. She had hoped that if he saw the tip of the iceberg he would lose interest in seeing more. "I don't think of it quite that way."

"You've made the best out of a bad situation. You're raising a beautiful son, doing an important job, putting yourself through school. A hundred years ago Horatio Alger would have written a book about you."

She shoved the last of the soft drink at him. "Horatio Alger would have thought I was a fallen woman."

"It's what *you* think, isn't it, that's important?"

She was more than surprised he was so accepting. She covered it nicely. "What do you know about any of it, Grady? From your own account you've never had a bad situation to make the best out of. What would you know about the guilt I feel, the regrets I have?''

He moved his chair still closer, although he didn't need to. "I can make guesses. You come from a middle-class home. Maybe even better than that. You were told that life was supposed to be a certain way, and even when that turned out to be a lie, you felt guilty about it. Whatever happened to make you run away wasn't your fault, but you still blame yourself. You'll always blame yourself for everything bad that happens to you or to anyone you love. You don't forgive yourself, and you don't let go.''

"Get out of my head!"

"Wouldn't your past be easier to live with if you shared it?"

She switched her gaze from the window to him. "Maybe. But why would I want to share it with you? You're nothing to me! You're a hotshot lawyer who's moving up the political ladder so fast you're leaving a trail of dust behind you! You're passing the time right now, keeping yourself from falling asleep. What do you care about me or my life? It's a story to you. Something to while away a few boring hours! Well, it's no story to me. It's my life, my cross to bear, and I don't share it with anybody who's going to leave me behind without a second glance.''

He saw pain, naked and intense, in her eyes. He didn't even know if what she had said about him was true. He just knew that he had pushed too hard again. "I didn't mean to hurt you.''

"No?" She turned back to the window. "I'm a specimen to you. Someone different from your usual contacts. Do you think that gives you any rights?''

"No rights. But you're not a specimen. I thought we were becoming friends.''

"I choose my friends very carefully.''

"So do I.''

"You keep pushing me. What does it matter to you?''

It mattered because *she* mattered. Unlikely answer. Unfortunate answer. He tried to explain. "I'm not just passing the time. You *are* different from anyone I know. You're more alive, more excit—''

She swung her head to stare at him. He realized what he had almost said. He knew she did, too.

"How much longer are we going to stay here?" she asked after a long moment.

"Too long." Grady faced the street and tilted the blinds a little. He had moved so close to her that they were staring out the same window now.

"I don't think I can stand much more of this."

"You've been remarkably patient."

"When are you getting married?" The question was out before Anna could stop it. She kicked herself for wanting to know.

Grady thought about Susan. Quiet, undemanding Susan who would look like Palm Beach perfection when she walked down the aisle of St. Peter's cathedral in her designer wedding gown. "It's planned for September."

"A big wedding?"

"Bigger than anyone could want."

"You could elope."

He tried to imagine it. His mind couldn't conceive of Susan doing anything so hurtful to her parents or friends. Not even for love.

Did Susan love him? The question had only rarely occurred to him, usually after an unsatisfying night together. Its flip side, whether he loved her, had occurred to him with equal rarity.

Why the hell was it occurring to him now?

Anna leaned forward, her elbows on her knees. Her metal folding chair creaked as she shifted her weight. "Grady?"

"I was just trying to imagine Susan climbing down a ladder at midnight."

"Not that. There's a guy down there who looks familiar."

Grady snapped to attention. He pressed his nose to the blinds, his head next to hers. "Which one?"

"The guy in the green shirt, carrying the radio."

"Where have you seen him?"

"With Paco. He visited once or twice. He came and got Paco, and they went out together. That was months ago, and no one paid much attention. Paco wasn't at First Day long enough for us to worry about being suspicious."

"I'm just surprised you remember."

"I wouldn't. But he always carried that radio, like it was glued to his hand."

"You're sure it's the same guy?"

"Dead sure."

Grady was out of his chair by now, adjusting the video camera. In seconds the man with the radio had been captured on tape. The camera kept running. "Do you remember anything else?"

"His name was…" She searched her memory. The name, at least the first name, was just out of reach, eluding her. "Give me a minute."

"Two or even three. And keep watching. Maybe someone else will look familiar."

She stared until she had to blink. "Have you thought about my request?"

"A lighter sentence for the kid?"

"Not a lighter sentence. Rehabilitation."

"I've thought about it."

"And?"

"I'm still thinking."

"Just don't keep an open mind so long that all your humanity slips out of it."

"You may have a problem hearing sounds correctly, but you have a way with words."

"Gerard. The guy's name is Gerard, or at least that's how he was introduced."

"What a memory."

"I'm really quite bright."

Grady laughed. He wasn't foolish enough to think that Gerard could be the link that would complete the chain from drug running to sales on the streets, but he could be a clue. Suddenly he felt ten feet tall. "What about the guy who was with him?"

"What guy?"

"The guy who was leaning against the window?"

"What guy?"

Grady came over to stand beside her. "No wonder you didn't see him. There's a glare from this angle. Come on over to the other window. Maybe he'll be back."

Anna stood, stretching as she did. She was very aware of Grady's hand at the small of her back, guiding her the short distance. Then she was peering out the window over the video camera. There was still a glare, but the change in position softened it a little. She shaded her eyes, although it didn't help. "Did he go inside?"

"I'm afraid I didn't notice."

"We don't make good cops."

"I used to have that fantasy," Grady admitted.

"No. You? What changed your mind?" Anna noted that Grady hadn't removed his hand. It was burning a hole in her back.

"I don't know."

Anna thought Grady had moved even closer. Their combined body heat was enough to ignite the chemicals on the shelf behind them. "Well, a D.A. is close."

"That's why I prosecute instead of defend."

"A bring-'em-to-justice kind of guy."

"I guess."

Grady told himself he was standing so close to Anna because the situation called for it. He told himself to drop his hand...and didn't. "There's the guy. Coming out of the store."

Anna squinted, trying hard to see him in the afternoon glare. "The blonde?"

"Yep."

"He looks familiar, too."

"Thatta girl."

She tried to remember why. She had a memory of seeing him at First Day, but recently, not months before. And Paco hadn't been there recently. She had to be wrong, yet the feeling wouldn't die.

"Did you see him with Paco?" Grady asked.

She wanted to say yes, because that had to be it. Then she remembered. Too clearly. She remembered who he had been with, and when.

"No." She felt weak. Without thinking about it she leaned against Grady for support. "No, I never saw him with Paco."

Grady felt the weight of her body against his. In the intense heat it should have been unpleasant. It wasn't, although he wished it were.

"Then where?"

She shut her eyes. "I don't know. I thought he looked familiar. Now I'm not sure."

"Think hard, Anna."

"I can't think anymore. I'm about to pass out. I've got to get out of here."

He felt her slumping and was suffused with self-blame. He had asked too much of her. No one should be asked to endure this hellhole for so many hours.

Outside, the sidewalk in front of Guerrando's was clear. Both men had left, although not together. The blond man was just getting into a car. Grady noted the license number, although the video camera, which had been steadily taping, would catch it, too.

"You've done enough," he told Anna. He lifted his hands to her shoulders and turned her gently. Her eyes were shut, her face beaded with perspiration. Damp strands of hair decorated her forehead and cheeks. "Anna?" he asked with concern.

She opened her eyes and stared into his. There was something there he couldn't name, but it pushed him over the edge of good sense. He bent his head and kissed her.

Her lips were soft and moist, her body pliant. The kiss lasted only seconds, but when it ended he knew the damage he had done to them both.

"Thank you," he murmured, trying to pretend that the kiss had been about gratitude.

"I've got to get out of here," she said, turning her head.

"Go on out the back way. Here are the keys to the car. Get in, roll down the windows and turn the air-conditioner on full blast. Can you make it?"

She nodded, not meeting his eyes.

"I'll be down just as soon as I've called the station to get another team up here."

She didn't wait for more instructions.

Chapter 4

The blond man—actually, not a man, less than a man, an adolescent almost-man—was a friend of Wesley's. Pete had been at First Day for dinner twice. He wasn't a runaway—or so he had insisted. He knew Wesley from classes, not from his life before First Day. He had blinked his big innocent eyes and told Anna that he'd goofed off in high school and gotten into a little trouble. Now he was trying to make something of himself.

What a crock of...

Anna dragged herself out of bed two mornings after the stakeout and took a long, cool shower. She had believed Pete, even though she, of all people, knew how much easier it was for a street kid to lie than to tell the truth. She had wanted to believe him, wanted to believe that Wesley was making friends who wouldn't drag him back into the life he had left to come to First Day.

Of course, even now there was no reason to think that Wesley was being dragged anywhere. Wesley was as capable of being the dragger as the draggee.

Wesley had been a problem since arriving at the shelter. If he hadn't broken his arm, he wouldn't have stayed. All the staff knew it. But hustling was too hard for a kid in a cast. And there was some speculation that somebody out there was looking for good old Wesley. So to save his behind, Wesley had walked the line between staying in the program and getting kicked back to the streets. He was a master line-walker.

Anna was dressed for work in a bright red sundress before the conversation in her head progressed to the two ultimate questions. Why did she care so much about Wesley in the first place? And why had she concealed the truth about the blond kid-man from Grady?

The first was easy because she had tackled it before. Wesley reminded her of Matt, he had since the first day she had known him. Matt had been as hard, as nasty, as conniving, as Wesley. Only she had been allowed to see the sensitive, sad kid behind the tough streetwise veneer. Right from the beginning, she had believed she'd glimpsed that side of Wesley, too. Maybe it was only because that was what she wanted to see, but she couldn't give up on him until she was sure.

The second question wasn't hard to answer, either. She had chosen Wesley, First Day and the entire concept of compassion and rehabilitation over law and order justice. But if it was that easy, why did she feel so guilty? So ashamed?

Why did she feel as if she had just struck a blow for the underworld?

Ryan had been bundled over to Isabella, and she was on her way to work in her old Chevette, before she decided what she must do.

There were three men she had to talk to today. Wesley, Tom and Grady. And the last, particularly after his kiss, was going to be the hardest of all.

Anna displayed uncharacteristic patience as she waited for just the right moment to talk to Wesley. Street kids developed a sixth sense for trouble. Wesley had taken one look at her that morning and labored like a pack mule to stay out of her way for the rest of the day.

But Anna had been a street kid, too. She could beat Wesley at his own game because she was an adult now, with an adult's perceptions. She waited until after lunch, when the house was quiet. Then she struck.

"You can run, but you can't hide." Anna opened the door to Wesley's room, where she had tracked him after the meal ended.

"Did I ask you to come in?" Wesley was lying on his bed, staring up at the ceiling.

"Ask me."

"No."

"Too bad." Anna closed the door behind her.

"You makin' like somebody's mommy?"

"I *am* somebody's mommy. Not yours, though." She restrained the "thank God" rising in her throat. "What I am is the assistant director of the program that's trying to give you a new start. And what you are is a liar."

"Hey, I never claimed to be perfect." He didn't move.

"Aren't you going to ask me what lie I caught you in?"

"Does it matter?"

"We could play Twenty Questions."

Wesley didn't answer.

"I'll give the clues. The category is animal. This animal is blond, about five six or seven, and as good a sweet-talker as I've ever seen. He doesn't live here, but he visits often enough that he could be the milkman . . . or worse."

"I don't like games."

"Why not? You're better at them than anyone I've ever seen."

Wesley swung his legs over the side of his bed and pushed himself to a sitting position with his one good arm. "What's Pete got to do with anything?"

"If I call the Ed Center and ask if Pete's really enrolled there with you, what are they going to tell me?"

Wesley shrugged.

Anna went on. "How long have you known him?"

"A year or two."

"Why did you lie?"

"Because."

"Did you think we'd tell you not to see him anymore?"

"I don't care what you tell me."

Anna silently counted to ten. "Then...why... did...you...lie?"

"To save a hassle. Who needed one? Who needs this one?"

"Is your friend Pete dealing drugs to you? Are you dealing to him?"

Wesley just stared at her.

"You've got one minute to give me an answer I can believe. If you don't, we'll pack your stuff and you'll be out of here before dinner."

"You can't kick me out."

"Who's Tom going to listen to, me or you?"

"How do you know about Pete?"

"A little birdie told me."

"You think you're so smart!"

"A hell of a lot smarter than you! I used this program to get on my feet, not to take a vacation from life on the streets. I *am* somebody. You're a lying, cheating weasel."

"Then why don't you just kick me out? Don't even wait for answers!"

"You know why?" She advanced on him, hands on hips. "Because I care about you. Scare you? It ought to. You've weaseled your way into my heart, and I'm not going to give you up without a fight!"

He assessed her, as if trying to figure out how best to use that piece of news.

"And don't try to use my affection for you to get something, because I won't put up with it!" she warned.

"I don't use drugs anymore," Wesley said after a long pause.

"And do you sell them?"

"Not anymore."

"Give me the definition of anymore. This week? Today? Since you came into the program?"

"None of the above."

"When did you last use drugs?"

"I took an aspirin for a headache yesterday," he said sarcastically.

Anna wasn't sure, but she thought she detected the slightest touch of fear in his words. "I want you to be straight with me," she said. "I want to know when you last used an illegal substance."

Wesley stared at her. "When I was a little kid," he said after a moment, "my old lady asked me if I was the one who dropped an ashtray in the living room and broke it. I thought you were supposed to tell the truth, so I told her I was. She beat me so hard my father had to take me to the emergency room that night. He told 'em I'd fallen down some stairs."

Anna didn't blink. "Nice try, weasel, but I've read your files. Both your parents died when you were a baby. You lived in foster homes, lots of them, because you were hell on wheels to have around. Don't con me, Wesley. I hear your message, but give it to me straight. Don't try to make me feel sorry for you with a pack of lies!"

His expression didn't change. "It could have happened."

"Oh, please!"

"If I tell you the truth, what's to keep you from kicking me out of the program?"

"What's to keep me from kicking you out if you *don't*?" He took his time considering.

"A rock or a hard place, kid," Anna prompted.

"Pete sold me some drugs after I'd been here a week or two. Last time he was here he tri—"

"When was that?"

He calculated. "Two weeks ago."

"Go on."

"Last time he tried to sell me some more. I told him I didn't want any. He wanted me to deal drugs to the kids in the house. I thought about it."

She was sure that part was true. "And what did you tell him?"

"I told him the bed here was softer than any bed I'd had in a while, and I thought I'd stay."

"But you admit to using them what, a month ago?"

"I've been here six months."

Anna didn't fail to notice that he hadn't answered her. "Pete sold you some drugs almost six months ago. Pete's been here four or five times since, that I know about. Last time Pete came you turned him down."

"Yeah."

"And those four or five times in the middle, Wesley? Was Pete just coming here for our fried chicken suppers?"

"No."

Anna was silent for a full minute, considering what Wesley had just admitted. Then she announced her verdict. "Okay. This is what's going down. In a minute I'm calling two counselors up here to do a thorough search of you and everything you own. If you're clean, squeaky clean, you're going on probation. Any trouble, any proof that you're using or selling drugs, and you're out on your ear that minute. If you stay, any time you want to go out, you'll sign out, telling us exactly where you're going, a number where you can be reached, and when you'll be back. You'll have extra chores for the rest of the month. If Pete ever shows his face here again, I'll have him arrested for trespassing. If you're ever seen outside these walls with him, your stuff will be waiting on the front steps when you get back."

Wesley took it all in. He didn't answer, but he didn't argue.

Anna finished her speech. "Leave this door wide open. I'm calling another kid to keep his eye on you until the counselors get up here."

"Spies."

"Exactly."

Anna was almost in the hallway before Wesley spoke again. "Pete wanted me to push dope for him and I didn't. Doesn't that count for anything?"

"Yeah. It counts for a room in this house and food in your mouth. If you're telling the truth, you've made at least one good decision. Let's see if you can make some more."

* * *

The State's Attorney's office was cool and modern, with white walls, potted palms and weeping figs. The furniture was Scandinavian in design, and what wood was in evidence was lustrous teak. Harry Traltor, the former D.A., had spent a sizeable chunk of the taxpayer's money decorating it. The money he had made from his involvement in drug running had been spent for more personal pleasures.

The sophisticated appearance of the entire suite was camouflage. Inside the cool white walls, under serene contemporary oils of sunsets and beside feathery palms, muffled panic, faintly reminiscent of the mood in a stockyard, was always just ready to erupt.

Today, in the reception area, Grady watched it erupt in earnest. Two photographers were vying for his picture, a reporter was firing questions at him, and one of his prosecutors, two secretaries and the chief of police were waiting to speak to him.

The last was the easiest. The police chief was on the telephone. He knew better than to show up in person and wait in line.

Grady nodded to a reporter's question, turned his head at a photographer's request, gave his opinion into the telephone receiver about the police matter and held out his hand to sign a document that his secretary had readied for him. Fleetingly he wondered if there was any piece of him that someone hadn't claimed today.

When he looked up and saw Anna standing hesitantly in the doorway, he knew his heart had just been taken, too.

He was sure she shouldn't wear red. Her coloring was too delicate for bright colors. Yet, somehow, red was perfect on her. She was too bright, too brassy for subtleties. She would outshine pastel pink or blue. The primary colors stood an even chance of not fading into oblivion.

Anna Fitzgerald. What was he going to do about the feeling he got when he looked at her?

His private secretary turned and saw her standing there. "I'm sorry, Miss, do you have an appointment?"

Anna shook her head. Her eyes never left Grady, and she didn't smile.

"Then I'm afraid—"

Grady covered the receiver. "I'll see Miss Fitzgerald, Polly. Anna, can you wait just a few minutes?"

"Of course."

"Show Miss Fitzgerald into my private office," Grady instructed. He watched Anna trail behind his silver-haired secretary, who was tight-lipped in irritation that the flawless schedule she had arranged for her boss was going to be disrupted. He no longer felt drained, just anxious—both because he wanted to disappear into his office with Anna and because he knew he shouldn't.

Anna seated herself in the soft leather chair that Grady's secretary pointed out to her. His office was decorated much like the rest of the suite, but there was teak paneling on two of the walls and bookshelves of dark, beautifully bound volumes on the others.

His desk was remarkably neat for a busy man. There was an expensive-looking desk set, a collection of reference books between two carved walnut bookends, and a photograph in a sterling silver frame.

The photograph would be Susan. Anna debated examining it. Grady's private life was none of her business, particularly not his engagement or upcoming marriage. There was nothing between them except a lie she had to clear up and a kiss that had been nothing but gratitude.

The photograph was in her hands in a moment. The woman staring back at her had a slight smile on her flawless face. Her eyes were blue, her hair a sun-streaked brown, and her feelings a mystery. She was lovely, almost unbelievably so, but behind the face the woman was inscrutable.

Anna set the photograph back in place and went to stand at the window. Grady's view was an asphalt parking lot, reflecting shivers of heat in the late afternoon sun. It was no wonder that he sat with his back to the light.

She was just turning to go back to her chair when the door opened and Grady stepped in.

"I'm sorry I had to keep you waiting."

"Don't be sorry. I shouldn't have come without calling."

"I'm glad you did. If you had called first, Polly would have given you a firm no."

"She's a tyrant, isn't she?"

"She's about to retire." His tone made it clear he would shed no tears. "She does make a wicked glass of iced tea, though. She's bringing us some now."

Anna sat down. Instead of sitting at his desk, Grady sat beside her. There was a quick rap on the door, and Polly entered with two frosted glasses of tea decorated with a sprig of mint and a slice of lemon. She was barely polite as she set them on the small table between the chairs. She left the room quickly.

"She doesn't approve of me," Grady said. "I'm too young for the job. Even if Harry Traltor was a crook, he was an old crook. Polly could relate to him."

"She doesn't approve of me, either," Anna said.

"I imagine she wouldn't approve of any young woman I met with. She likes Susan. Maybe she thinks I'm being unfaithful." He wondered where those words had come from. What would Freud think about that kind of declaration?

"Maybe we should crack the door to reassure her."

"She works for me—I don't work for her."

Anna picked up her tea. The glass was ice-cold and beginning to sweat. She resisted smoothing it across her hot cheeks and wondered where she should start.

"You've recovered from Saturday?" Grady asked.

"I'm fine."

"I can't tell you too much about our case, but I can tell you that identifying Gerard Montego as a contact of Paco's may prove very helpful to us."

Anna sipped her tea. She had phrased her confession twenty different ways as she'd driven across town. Now none of them seemed appropriate.

Grady waited for her to speak. She seemed disturbed about something, and he imagined he knew that. He shouldn't have kissed her. He'd had no business starting anything that couldn't be finished. He had a thousand excuses, but none of them was good enough. And none of them touched the real reason. He had kissed her because she was infinitely kissable. And for the very same reason his heart had leaped to attention this afternoon when he saw her standing in the doorway. She had a hold on him, as much as he would like to deny it, as much as he *would* deny it.

"I lied about something Saturday, Grady." Anna set her tea on the table.

It took a few seconds for her words to register. "Lied?"

She played with the lemon on the side of her glass, squeezing it until there was nothing left but rind. Then she began to shred the mint.

"Lied about Gerard Montego?" Grady asked when she didn't go on.

"No. Not about him. About the blond guy he was talking to."

"The one you said you thought you knew, then changed your mind about?"

She nodded. "I did recognize him. His name is Pete Waters. And he's been at First Day half a dozen times to visit one of our residents. Not Paco, though. Another kid. It took me a minute to place him, but I'm sure now."

"Why didn't you tell me that Saturday?"

She folded her hands in her lap. "Because I had to think what to do."

"What you had to *do* is tell me the truth."

"I've just done that."

"A little late." Grady got up and began to pace the room. "So who's the kid this Pete Waters hangs out with?"

"I can't say."

He stopped and stared at her.

"I'll tell you what he told me, Grady. That's all I can do."

"What do you mean, that's all you can do? This kid could give us valuable information!"

"This kid would lie to God himself. Nothing he would tell *you* would be valuable because none of it would be true." Anna stood and faced him. "Look. I went to the kid this morning and faced him down. I suspected what had happened, so I pretended I knew more than I did. I was right on target. He admitted that he'd bought drugs from Pete Wa-

ters in the past. He said that he'd turned him down the last
time, and he'd turned him down when Pete asked him to sell
for him. We searched him and his room and belongings
from top to bottom. There were no drugs. He's on probation with us now, and he'll be watched like a baby in a
bathtub."

"That's not good enough!"

"He admitted that he'd been using drugs and getting them
from Pete. If you question him, he'll deny it, and there's no
proof to the contrary. If I turn him in to you, he'll never tell
me another blessed thing! I want this kid to make it, Grady.
You've got your information, and I've still got a chance with
him. We're even."

Grady wanted to shake her. She had set herself up as
judge and jury and social worker, too. "I can find out who
he is. I have the law at my disposal."

"I know you can. Please don't try." She moved closer.
"Look, if you have any questions you want to ask him, let
me do it for you. I'll be absolutely honest with you about
everything he tells me. And we've got a much better chance
of getting a straight answer if I'm doing the asking."

Grady's eyes narrowed. He thought about the hour he
had spent at First Day and made an educated guess. "It's
the kid with the cast on his arm, isn't it?"

"I'm not going to tell you."

He had been expecting a reaction. What he had gotten
instead was more surprising. Her face was blank, her eyes
completely neutral. It was as if the Anna he knew had disappeared behind an iron mask.

"How do you do that?"

"Do what?"

"Make it impossible for me to see what you're thinking."

"Practice."

"It's not a pretty thing to watch."

"It's not a pretty thing to learn."

"Why did you, then?"

She had told him a little about her relationship with Matt to scare him away. It hadn't worked. Now, for the same reason, she told him a little more.

"I learned it because that's the only way to survive when you're lifting wallets from strangers or standing off street gangs who want you out of some dark alley they think they own. I learned it for lots of reasons, none of which makes pretty listening. It works, though. And I'll use it every time you ask me a question I can't answer."

"I've seen convicts with more emotion in their eyes."

"Maybe that's why they got caught and I never did." She thrust out her chin. "Make no mistake who you're dealing with, Grady. I'll fight for the kids I work with. I was one of them once, and I'm not so far removed now. I've done everything they've done, been everything they've been. Somehow I survived, and I'm going to make sure they do, too!"

He didn't even want to think about what she was telling him. She had already admitted to stealing when she was a runaway. He knew the other things girls like Anna had to do to survive. They prostituted themselves, made pornographic movies, danced in topless nightclubs. He wanted to shake her, demand that she reassure him. He wanted to kiss away the pain she had so carefully hidden.

Instead he kept his voice neutral. "I'll be in touch with you if I have any questions for the mystery kid."

She took a deep breath and released it. "Fine. I hoped I could count on you."

"Can I count on you to tell me the truth from now on?" he asked with just a touch of cynicism.

"I didn't want to lie to you. That's why I'm here today." She went to her chair and picked up her purse.

"Would you have turned this kid over to the police if you'd found drugs in his possession?"

"We would have notified the authorities. He's a ward of the court."

"Good." Grady walked her to the door, reaching around to put his hand on the knob before she could open it. "Just one more question. Did Tom Schneider insist you come here today?"

"I told you before. I have my own reasons for hating drugs. I didn't want to do anything that might keep you from making arrests. Tom knows about all of this. I talked to him today. But it was my idea to come here."

"Pete Waters is a kid, and you're not protecting him."

"Pete Waters needs a good scare."

"There's actually a kid you don't want to rehabilitate?"

"I'll work with him. After a good scare." Anna met his eyes. "I really am sorry, Grady."

He couldn't let her off so easily. She had lied, and she was still concealing evidence. He gave a noncommittal grunt and opened the door.

Susan stood on the other side of it, talking to Polly.

Unwittingly he had compared Susan and Anna in his mind. Now, in living color, the contrast was even more obvious. Susan was dressed in a lightweight summer suit of palest mauve. Her long hair was tied back at her nape with a patterned chiffon scarf, and the same subtle shades were picked up in her striped blouse. She looked cool and correct and polished to a fine sheen. Her eyes flicked over Anna before they went to Grady's face.

"Hi. I know I'm early. I'll wait."

He searched his memory. He couldn't imagine what she was early for.

"We were going out to dinner," she reminded him. "Unless something's come up?" Her eyes flicked back to Anna.

"No, of course not." Grady debated introducing the two women. Under the circumstances he wasn't required to, but it felt impolite not to. "Anna Fitzgerald, this is Susan Powell. Anna and I have been working together on a case," he explained to Susan.

Polly gave an unmistakable sniff.

Anna examined the image, not the woman. Susan was everything she would never be. Susan would be the quintessential politician's wife. Anna usually gave as little thought to what she was wearing as she did to the brand of dishwashing detergent she picked up at the supermarket or the number of bristles in her toothbrush. Now she felt distinctly underdressed and overexposed. She wished she had slipped her white blazer on over the sundress.

Susan extended her hand politely. "I'm glad to meet you."

Susan's handshake was firm and short. Anna nodded. "I'm glad to meet you, too." She turned back to Grady. "I'll be back in touch if I find out any more information. But don't expect to hear from me. I think I've found out everything I will."

"All right. Thank you for coming." Grady watched Anna stride toward the door. She walked with the same boundless energy that characterized everything she did. He realized she was probably walking out of his life. Their business was completed unless there were new developments. He wished he had told her she was forgiven.

He realized Susan was watching him. He looked down at her and managed a smile. "Well, where would you like to go for dinner?"

"Your place."

He wasn't sure he had heard her right. "You want to eat my cooking?"

"Let's pick up something and take it with us. We'll have a quiet evening."

Her voice held a promise he had seldom heard there. "You're sure?"

"Absolutely."

It was only when they were on their way home that he realized that Susan understood him better than he had realized. She had seen him looking at Anna. She had guessed what he was feeling.

Chapter 5

Sleeping late was one of Anna's rarest joys. On the days when she was working, she rose at six-thirty in order to get Ryan up, fed and dressed before taking him next door to Isabella's house. On her days off, Ryan's internal alarm clock still rang at six-thirty, and she was immediately in demand as a cereal fixer or television tuner. There were only infrequent exceptions, mornings when Ryan woke up but could be convinced to go back to sleep if he was allowed in bed with her, or, most infrequent of all, mornings when Ryan overslept on his own.

Saturday morning was one of those. Anna and Ryan had been up late the night before with Isabella and Teresa. They had splurged and taken the children to a pizza theatre, where a life-sized, animated menagerie sang old songs and told older jokes, and where pizza was second in importance to rooms filled with arcade games. Ryan had stuffed himself with pizza and overdosed on repeated video games. He had gone to bed an exhausted but happy little boy and slept right through his normal waking time.

Anna blissfully reveled in the unexpected luxury. She awoke once, just long enough to appreciate the miracle that was occurring, then fell immediately back asleep to take advantage of every second.

She was deep in slumber when she heard the loud buzz of her doorbell. She tried to ignore it, working it into her dreams as an annoying insect, but when it sounded again, she pushed herself off the sofa bed and padded to the door, her eyes only half open. Her single goal was to tell the early morning interloper to hit the road before he or she woke Ryan and spoiled Anna's chance of going back to bed.

She threw the door open to stare at Grady Clayton.

He was dressed in brown shorts and a green plaid sports shirt, and he carried a child-sized fishing rod. "I could have been a burglar," he pointed out.

Anna stared at him through heavy-lidded eyes. "What?"

He stepped past her and closed the door behind him, setting the fishing rod beside it. "I could have been a burglar. Or a rapist. Or an ax murderer."

"If you'd had an ax, you would have just chopped the door down."

"This isn't a good neighborhood to be so trusting." Grady took in the picture she presented. Her hair was tousled into irresistible golden tufts. Her legs were bare halfway up her thighs, and the rest of her was covered by a huge T-shirt of brightest orange. He averted his eyes. "That T-shirt would keep me awake."

"I don't sleep with my eyes open, and I don't sleep with you." Self-consciously, Anna pulled the T-shirt down. It crept right back up like a window shade with an overwound spring. She scanned the room for her robe, but it was nowhere in sight. For once she had hung it in the closet in Ryan's room, where it belonged. "What are you doing here?"

He took in the soft peach on the walls, the furniture, which was natural rattan and upholstered in soft floral prints, the seashell collection framed over the sofa. "I'm wondering why you sleep on the sofa."

"Because there's only one bedroom and Ryan's old enough to need privacy." She dared him to comment, but he just nodded his approval.

"Cute place, even if it's tiny."

Since she had worked hard with very little money to make the house attractive, she softened. "You're here to get ideas on decorating your condo?"

"How do you know I live in a condo?"

"An educated guess." Anna yawned and motioned Grady to a chair. "You may have noticed I'm not dressed. I was sleeping."

"I noticed."

"I'm going to get my robe. Want some coffee?"

He trusted himself to say nothing more until she had another layer of clothes on. He just nodded.

"Cream and sugar?"

He shook his head.

Her robe was a brilliant purple, and it covered her to the turn of her slender ankles. The coffee was dark and rich, some of the best he had ever had.

"This is my day off." Anna sat camp-fire style at the end of the sofa bed, rather than taking the time to fold it up. "I used my last day off to play cops and robbers. Don't ask me to do it again."

Grady swirled his coffee. "I'm not."

"I don't have any more information for you. My source had nothing more to say."

"I'm not looking for information."

There was a noise in the next room, something scraping across the floor. Then Ryan appeared in the doorway carrying his ragged blanket with one hand and dragging a toy rifle with the other. "Is there a bad guy here?" he asked hopefully.

Grady wondered why he had never given having children much thought. "No bad guys," he told the little boy. "Remember me?"

"You're Grady. My balloon popped."

"That's the trouble with balloons."

Ryan headed for the sofa and climbed up on Anna's lap. "Park your weapons at the door, partner." She removed his rifle and set it on the floor.

"Can I have pizza for breakfast?" he wheedled.

"Didn't you have enough last night?"

"No."

"I'll warm some up in a minute."

Grady couldn't help himself. "Pizza?"

"Why not? It's got everything cereal's got and more. Almost a balanced meal."

"You're a lucky kid," Grady told Ryan. "I grew up on scrambled eggs and whole wheat toast."

"Yuck," Ryan and Anna said in unison.

Grady's laughter rumbled through the room.

"What's that?" Ryan pointed to the fishing rod sitting beside the door.

Anna had almost forgotten its existence. She lifted an eyebrow to second the question.

"A present." Grady got up and brought the rod over to the little boy. "Do you like to fish?"

"Sure!"

"He never has," Anna said cautiously.

"I have a cabin not too far from here on a fresh water creek. I was hoping you'd both come with me to try your luck off my dock."

Anna just stared at him.

"Could we?" Ryan began to bounce up and down, jolting all the breath from Anna's lungs.

Grady took pity on her. He reached out and lifted the little boy into the air, then set him down on the floor with the rod. "There's no hook on it yet. You can practice with it here." He showed him how to release the catch and reel it in.

Ryan was in the corner happily reeling in imaginary fish before Anna spoke.

"Why?" she asked quietly.

"I need to get away for a day. I owe you a thank you for helping last Saturday." He paused. "And I wanted you to know I understand why you didn't tell me right away about Pete Waters."

He thought of all the things he could have added. How she had been on his mind all week. How her unseen presence had made him plead exhaustion and take Susan home early the night they had gone to his place for dinner. How

he was beginning to question everything he had ever believed he wanted.

"You don't owe me anything." Anna folded her arms
across her chest. "I didn't do it for you. I did it because I
don't like drug dealers any more than you do."

"I'd still like you to come."

Her next question was inevitable. "Does your fiancée
know you've invited me?"

"Susan's in California at a friend's wedding."

"While the cat's away?"

"I'm not asking you for an affair. I thought we could
spend a day together as friends. And I thought it would be
fun to teach Ryan to fish."

She was no coy young miss. She knew he wasn't telling
either of them the truth. On the other hand, she knew how
foolish it would be to blow simple physical attraction out of
perspective. Grady was nothing if not ultimately honorable. He hadn't invited her with any intentions other than
those he had named. And they were both adults. They could
control themselves, particularly with a four-year-old chaperon. Both of them had too much to lose if they didn't.

"I want to go fishing!" Ryan reeled in with difficulty, as
if a six-foot tarpon were on the line.

She knew she ought to say no, but Ryan so rarely had a
chance to leave the city. And, if she was going to be truth-
ful, she wanted to spend the day with Grady. Maybe it really
was possible for a man and a woman to simply be friends.
She and Matt had been, and there was nothing in her life
except Ryan that she treasured more than that brief, shining relationship.

"We can stop for fried chicken to take along," Grady
said.

"Extra-crispy." She unfolded her legs and stood,
stretching as she did. "I've got to warm up some leftover
pizza for breakfast first. Care for a slice?"

"Pepperoni?"

She nodded.

"Anchovies?"

She made a face. "Only after noon. Please."

* * *

Grady's cabin was tucked away on a wide, spring-fed creek so clear that in places you could count the scales on the silver fish darting along the bottom. The cabin itself wasn't much larger than Anna's house, but sturdier and built high off the ground in case of flooding. Its most interesting feature was a huge screened porch built almost to the tree line at the water's edge. A stairway led down to a brand new dock parallel to the riverbank.

Ryan was like a Great Dane puppy who'd been cooped up all his life in a city apartment and finally set free. Wearing a child-sized life jacket, he ran from deck to porch and back again, exploring everything in sight. Grady had given him a friendly lecture on water safety, on the variety and danger of the snakes that sometimes sunned themselves on the riverbank, on the perils of getting a finger near a friendly-looking turtle who lived under the house, and on the appearance and hazards of poison oak and fire ants. The lectures, delivered with the competence of a boy scout leader, had all made the proper impression. Which didn't mean that Grady and Anna took their eyes off Ryan for even a second afterward.

"Do you supposed he'll slow down enough to fish?" Grady asked, watching Ryan practice jumping from the river's edge to the dock and back again.

"Do you suppose there'll be any fish left in the river if he does? He's making enough noise to scare them upstream to Tallahassee."

"I saw a nice sized bass jump right over there a minute ago." Grady pointed to the middle of the river.

"If he caught a nice sized bass, he probably wouldn't know what to do."

"I'll stay right beside him."

"You're enjoying him, aren't you?"

Grady hadn't given it much thought. The trip up had been noisy and eventful. They had stopped for chicken and twice for the bathroom, then once more to explore the tackiest souvenir store Anna had ever seen. They had eaten ice cream cones and bought Ryan bright plastic sunglasses and a hat with a stuffed alligator perched on the top. Then, while Anna had taken Ryan to the bathroom yet again, Grady had bought her a hat just like it.

He hadn't thought about whether he was having fun because he had been too busy having it. "I've never thought much about having kids," he admitted now. "I don't know why."

"You and Susan haven't talked about it?"

"I think she'd like to have them. I guess she just expects to." He thought about the children he would have with Susan. Quiet, well-bred children. Children whose preschool would be chosen before they were born, children who would be on the list for an exclusive private academy as soon as their gender was determined.

"I never thought about having them, either," Anna said, walking to the edge of the porch to get a better look at Ryan. "Which is why I got pregnant, obviously."

"You could have had an abortion."

"And kill the only part of Matt left in the world? Not a chance."

"You loved him very much."

"He was my best friend. If it weren't for Matt, I probably wouldn't be alive right now."

He wanted to know what she meant, but he knew what she would tell him if he asked. He waited, hoping she would go on, but she didn't.

"It looks like Ryan's getting bored," she said instead. "He hasn't moved in five seconds."

"Can't have that." Grady joined Anna at the porch's edge. "Ready to fish, Ryan?"

Ryan began to jump up and down.

"That means yes," Anna interpreted.

"Then let's go."

An hour later, the fishing had been less than successful. Ryan liked to cast, and he liked to reel in. Sitting quietly to wait for a bite was beyond his capabilities.

Anna watched as Grady, with infinite patience, untangled Ryan's line once more and rebaited the hook. Ryan had little contact with men. The boys at First Day were as close as he usually got, and she always had to spirit him away before they taught him the things *they* knew. Now he was lapping up everything Grady taught him. He was even copying Grady's expressions.

"Now you have to sit still," Grady instructed. "See, if the fish hear you jumping around up here, they'll swim away."

"Fish don't have ears."

"They have something like ears."

"But they're under the water!"

"They can hear under the water."

"I can't, and I have ears."

"But you're not a fish."

"I can swim."

Grady laughed. "Got me there. Maybe you are a fish."

"I'm not!"

"Then you'll have to sit still."

Ryan frowned thoughtfully, but while his mind tried to make the next leap in logic, he sat without moving a muscle.

"Five more minutes," Anna mouthed.

Grady nodded.

Anna thought how lovely both the place and the day were. There were huge moss-draped live oaks and palms shading the riverbank, trees that had seen generations of people come and go. There were birds of all sizes and description, water birds skimming the water to dive and retrieve a meal, songbirds of bright colors and brighter melodies. Grady's cabin was only two hours out of Ponte Reynaldo, but it might as well have been halfway around the world. Moss Run Creek was Florida as it had been before the developers saw its potential. Ponte Reynaldo was an example of both the best and worst of their schemes.

Anna was glad she had come. Surely there could be nothing wrong with a day spent with Grady. She had discovered that he had a surprisingly offbeat sense of humor that nicely complemented her own. He seemed to genuinely enjoy Ryan and all the details of being with a child, from shoe-tying to answering riddles. He was considerate and easy to talk to, and he treated her with appropriate nonchalance. There was no reason to think that this day would lead to any complications for either of them.

She turned her head to look at him and found that he was looking at her. There was a half smile on his face, as if what he saw pleased him. There was warmth in his eyes, not the warmth of a man thinking about fishing, but the warmth of a man thinking about a woman. His smile widened, and he reached around Ryan to take her hand.

At that moment, Ryan's bobber ducked under the water. "I got something. I do!"

Grady quickly dropped Anna's hand as if the fish was somehow retribution for that small act of intimacy. "Reel it in slowly," he instructed, his attention all focused on Ryan now.

"It's big!"

"A whale," Anna affirmed. "At least."

"Don't jerk, Ryan," Grady said. "Slow and steady. You're doing great. I've never seen anyone do better."

"Fish for supper," Anna said. "I can almost taste it."

Ryan's head swiveled, and he looked at her, his eyes wide. "Eat it?"

"Look, Ryan, you can see it now." Grady pointed to the water. "There it is. You caught a shiner. A real honest-to-goodness shiner!"

Anna forced herself not to laugh at Grady's glowing description of the just-larger-than-a-minnow fish that was now at the water's surface. "Reel it all the way in," she told Ryan.

Ryan peered into the water. "It looks like Fin."

Grady squinted at the fish. "Fin?"

"One of his guppies," Anna explained. Actually, the two fish had nothing in common except their species, but she wasn't going to argue.

"Reel it all the way in," Grady said again.

"We're not going to eat it, are we?" Ryan asked, his lower lip beginning to tremble.

Grady misunderstood. "Sure we are. It'll be a good mouthful for a good fisherman."

"No!" The trembling lip gave way to tears. "I want to put it in my 'quarium."

Now Grady was the one who looked startled. Anna started to intervene, then realized this was between the two males. She waited.

"You don't want to eat it?" Grady asked.

"It's alive!"

Grady looked to Anna for help, but she just smiled encouragement. "People fish to eat," he explained.

"I want to put it in my 'quarium. With Fin!" Ryan sobbed.

"It will eat Fin and any other fish you have." Grady put his arm around Ryan. "Tell you what, though, it's not really big enough to eat, is it? And it looks like a very smart fish. You're a smart boy to have seen that. Smart fish don't make good eating."

"They don't?"

Grady shook his head. "No. And only smart people can see that. So, I'll tell you what. Let's reel him in and put him in this bucket for a little while so you can see him and touch him, then we'll put him back in the creek and let him swim away. Smart fish belong in schools."

Anna groaned.

"Okay!" Ryan was all sunshine again. In a minute the tiny fish was on the dock. Grady took the hook out without damaging the fish and dropped it in the waiting bucket.

Ryan stood over it crooning reassurances.

"Next we try a baseball and bat," Grady said, holding out his hand to Anna to help her up. "He doesn't have a pet baseball, does he?"

"I cried the first time I caught a fish," Anna said. "My sister told me it was a wicked witch in disguise, and if we didn't take it home and eat it, it would turn back into a witch and cast a spell on us."

"What did you do?"

"I ate every bite of it and wished there was more."

Grady didn't drop her hand once she was standing. "So you have a sister?"

She hadn't thought about what she was revealing. "Once upon a time."

"Older than you?"

"Right."

"As pretty as you?"

"Beautiful."

"Did she die?" he asked gently.

"No, I did." Anna pulled her hand away. "I don't know about you, but I'm getting very hungry. Since the chicken's not alive, we should be allowed to eat it, don't you think?"

"Didn't I tell you? They were out of extra-crispy, so I got extra-alert." His smile bathed her in warmth. "When are you going to trust me?" he asked, lifting his hand to cup her cheek for a moment.

"We've been through this."

"We've never been through *this*." Grady dropped his hand. "We've never just had fun together."

"So?"

"It changes things." As he said it, he knew it was true. Today had marked a new landmark on the road map of their relationship. He was afraid it blockaded the easy way back to the time when they weren't important to each other.

Anna didn't want to feel what she was feeling. "You're going to be married, and I'm going to be busy raising my son, doing my job and finishing my education."

"We're going to be important to each other."

She didn't know how to answer, because she didn't know exactly what he was trying to say. She suspected he didn't, either. "I'll lay out the food. Will you bring Ryan up after you've thrown the fish back in?"

Grady knew when it was wise to stop pushing. "After lunch we'll go for a boat ride. Maybe we can even find a gator for Ryan."

They found not one alligator but two, and a host of sun-sated turtles lying on dead logs at the creek's edge. The creek, which was as deep as a small river, meandered and twisted through woods and meadows. Grady told Anna that almost four square miles of the area had once belonged to an eccentric millionaire who had counted his net worth in Spanish moss and large-mouthed bass rather than cold, hard cash. Upon his death, his heirs had parceled the land out and sold it with severe, iron-clad restrictions on development. Grady's father had bought one of the parcels many years ago but had never found a way to break the restrictions. The result was Grady's good fortune.

Back at the cabin, in the hottest part of the afternoon, they practiced energy conservation by sitting under the ceiling fans that cooled every room and drinking gallons of ice tea made from the boiled sulphur water of Grady's well. Grady taught Ryan to play a simplified game of Hearts, and Ryan taught Grady to play Old Maid. Anna tried not to let the sight touch her, but she didn't succeed.

They had planned to leave before dinner time, but the beckoning promise of a cool breeze from the creek and a laser show of fireflies held them captive. Grady drove into the nearest town for provisions and came back with steaks and all the accompaniments. Anna made a salad while he grilled.

By the time dinner was finished, Ryan—whose day had been momentous—was sound asleep.

"If we put him in the car carefully, he'll probably sleep all the way back," she said as Grady laid Ryan on the double bed in the cabin's bedroom and covered him with a sheet.

"That's what we'll do, then. But let's wait a little while. The fireflies are just starting to come out."

"I can't believe you don't have commitments tonight. Don't you have a meeting to speak at or hands to shake or something?"

"I did. I canceled." Grady let that sink in before he added, "I had to have a break, Anna."

"How many votes did you lose?"

"I wasn't the only one on the program, or I never would have skipped out. But I just couldn't face one more banquet meal and impassioned speech. Let Rand Garner and the candidates for the other offices tug the heartstrings of the Sun County Pompano Club. I just didn't have it in me."

"Do you really want the job?"

"The correct question is do I want Rand Garner to have the job. The answer is no."

"Is Garner involved in the mess at Guerrando's?"

"I can't talk about it."

Anna followed Grady out on the porch and sat on a hanging wooden swing beside him. "Then tell me this. Suppose Garner were involved and you could prove it before the primary so that he was disqualified. Would you still want the State's Attorney's job?"

"You specialize in pointed questions."

"No more than you."

He wanted to deny his passion for politics. Somehow it seemed more noble just to be a lowly junior prosecutor, doing his job for love of justice. But the truth wasn't that simple.

"Running for office is exhilarating," he admitted. "I think I can do a good job if I'm elected. I'm doing a good job now."

"You're well respected."

"A compliment, Anna?"

"A little heavy on the law and order, though."

He laughed. "I need someone like you around to remind me."

"Does it do any good?"

He stretched his legs out to stop the swing's rhythm. "I took your advice. We're looking into rehabilitation programs for Paco Hernandez."

She was amazed. "Really?"

"Our jails are too crowded to give him the help he needs."

"You're really not completely hard-hearted, are you?"

"Nope. Just a guy looking for a better way to run the world."

"Then abandon politics."

Grady was silent for a while. They rocked back and forth again, watching the night mists close in around them. He could feel the warmth of Anna's body beside him and the long length of her legs just inches from his own. The day had meant more to him than a break from routine. He hadn't just relaxed; he had recharged. And the woman to his right was the reason.

His future was firmly cemented into the expectations and plans of others, but since meeting Anna he had been questioning the seeming inevitability of it all. Why hadn't he questioned it before? Why had he always assumed that what others believed was best for him really was? Was he truly at fault, or was he just having a momentary lapse from responsibility? Was he falling under the power of a turquoise-eyed witch who would cast a spell on him if he didn't devour her—or if he did?

"We probably ought to be heading back, don't you think?" Anna asked.

"Who are you, Anna?" Grady knew the question had been building inside him. It didn't surprise him. "I have to know."

"No, you don't."

"Do you feel what's happening?"

"I don't feel anything."

"You're lying."

She pushed herself out of the swing and went to stand at the screen. "I'm not *going* to feel anything. You're as good as married. What is it you want from me? A little fun? A little sex before you settle down for good with someone else?"

"Damn it, I don't know what I want, but I don't want that!"

"Why not? I'm perfect for that kind of an affair, aren't I? I've got a child out of wedlock, so I'm obviously an easy woman. I've got no relatives to come after you with a shotgun. I even live in a part of town where no one would think to look for you late at night."

He choked back angry words and thought about what she *hadn't* said. "Suppose you tell me why you feel that way about yourself."

"What way?"

"Like you're something dirty instead of a wonderful, warm, intelligent woman who makes me feel alive when I'm with her."

"I am something dirty, or rather, I was. Maybe I still am!" she flung back at him.

"Never were, never will be."

"How do you think I supported myself on the streets, Grady?"

He took a deep breath, but the rush of oxygen did nothing to ease the sudden sharp pain in his gut. Truth might, although what it would do for Anna, he couldn't say. "I don't know what you did, but obviously it means a lot to you. So spill it, Anna, and let's get it out from between us."

She bit her lip. She had gone too far to turn back now. Her past wasn't really a secret, at least, not the part of it after she had run away. The staff at First Day knew her story, and some of the kids did, too. She told it to them to make them see how far they could come. She wished it were a secret, though. She wished she could pretend that none of it had ever happened.

She felt Grady's hand on her shoulders. "Anna, it's not going to make a difference to me."

"I ran away when I was sixteen."

"Why?"

She lifted her shoulders to dislodge his hands. "I'll never tell."

"Then tell me what you can."

It had been a night as dark as this one, and she had been just this scared. Anna swallowed hard and tried to make herself tell him it was none of his business. She couldn't.

"It won't matter to me," Grady said gently.

She shut her eyes. "I left home at night. I took some jewelry to sell that a great-aunt had left me, and about a hundred dollars in cash. And I took the bus to New York City, to the Port Authority bus terminal."

She wanted to tell the story objectively, not to feel its horror, but as she talked, she began to relive her memories. She smelled the sour odor of the bus station, felt the stares of strangers and the crush of bodies as she waited in line to find out about a city bus or subway to take her somewhere, anywhere, else. "Do you know that pimps hang out in bus stations, waiting for girls like me?"

The pain in his gut doubled. "I know a little." His hands settled at the base of her neck again. He stroked them along her shoulders. "Was one waiting for you?"

"I'd been protected, and pimps are smart. This guy came up beside me while I was reading the schedules for the city bus. He was good-looking and well-dressed. He made some comment about how the buses didn't run very often late at night. He just made a comment, not even necessarily to me. I responded like a duck to a hunter's call. I was tired and scared and on the verge of tears. I asked him where the different buses went. He bought me coffee."

"When did you realize he was a pimp?"

"When he took me back to his apartment, instead of the hotel he'd recommended, and attacked me."

"Anna." His pain was in his voice.

If she acknowledged his feelings, she knew she wouldn't be able to go on. "There are two kinds of pimps. Those who psychologize and seduce, and those who beat and rape. I got the second kind."

"God."

All she could do was continue, because then, eventually, this would end. And it had to end, because she couldn't bear it much longer. "He called himself Gray Moon, probably still does, for all I know. He had four girls working for him, and I was supposed to be the fifth. But I didn't cooperate. After three days of hell he tried to turn me out—put me on the streets, if you don't know the lingo—and I ran away. He caught me and convinced me in his own sweet way not to run anymore." She was hurrying now, because nausea was welling inside her, although her eyes were achingly dry.

"You don't have to—"

"Sure I do. You wanted to know. You were curious, remember?"

"I don't want you hurt."

"You're a little late for that. Years late. The next time Gray Moon turned me out, I went with one guy, then another, who wanted to pay the price that had been set for me. I thought anything would be better than what Gray Moon would do to me." She shuddered. "I was wrong. When the third guy came along I knew I'd rather die than live this way. We went up into this filthy hotel room with Gray Moon keeping watch in the hallway, and I started to cry. I knew the guy would tell Gray Moon and that this time he might beat me to death, but I didn't care anymore. I pleaded with him to help me."

"Anna—"

"You want to know something funny? I'd picked a winner. He helped me escape. He was somebody's father, out for a once-in-a-lifetime thrill. When I started to cry, he started to pray for forgiveness. He prayed like a man who'd had lots of practice. Finally he started an argument with Gray Moon in the hallway while I went out the fire escape. I ran for blocks. The guy had given me some money, so I took a subway as far as the end of the line. That neighborhood was worse than the one I had just left, but at least Gray Moon was miles away. I was hysterical by then. I couldn't stop crying. So I ducked into a dark alley. There were already people there."

She took a deep breath and let it out slowly. "The alley was a gathering place for street people because there were two restaurants that threw their garbage into the Dumpster there. One of those people was Matt Fitzgerald. He was a runaway who'd been on the streets for a year by then. He had done everything a boy can do to survive except sell his body. A couple of bums going through the Dumpster thought I might make a tasty meal, but Matt felt sorry for me. He fought them off and took me to his place. It was the basement of a burned-out tenement. He even had somebody's old mattress that he'd dragged in to sleep on."

She felt Grady's hands on her arms. Until that moment she hadn't realized she needed the support. She had told the story before, but never like this. "Matt took care of me after that. He taught me all the things I had to learn to survive. I went to a runaway shelter the next day with him. They made me see a doctor after I told them everything that had happened. A couple of weeks later I went back and found out I'd been one of the lucky ones. I didn't have any deadly souvenirs of my days with Gray Moon. I was left with hideous nightmares, but that was the worst of it." She paused, then her voice dipped dangerously. "I still have the nightmares sometimes."

Grady's hands clenched spasmodically.

"Eventually Matt and I got out of the city. No one knows how dangerous a city can be until they're on the other side of the law. One night I saw one of Gray Moon's girls. She'd been nice to me before, even tried to make Gray Moon let me go. She told me that he was looking for me, that he had others looking for me, too. Pimps don't take kindly to being made to look foolish, so she warned me to get out of New York before he found me. She was from somewhere down South, I don't remember where, but she thought I ought to go to New Orleans. I could dance in a club there, and Matt could find work on the wharfs."

Anna knew it was time to face Grady, to see what his eyes would tell her. Once she was facing him, she couldn't make herself look at him. She stared at her feet. "I tried, but I couldn't make myself dance. I'd learned to pick pockets and locks and run a con game to survive, but I couldn't make myself stand up on a table wearing nothing but a G-string. Matt couldn't find work, either. We left and drifted all over the South. Sometimes we found work . . . we always tried. Sometimes we didn't and we slept on beaches, in parks, ate out of garbage cans."

"Why didn't you stay at runaway shelters?"

"I was afraid to." She didn't elaborate.

"Afraid you'd be sent home?"

"Something like that."

"Could anything have been worse than what you were already going through?" Gently, Grady lifted her chin.

"Yes." Anna met his eyes, but they gave nothing away.

He wanted to push her, but he knew her limits. She would not talk about what had made her run in the first place. "You told me that Matt was killed in Miami."

"I was pregnant by then." She hesitated, then decided to tell him the truth, although she didn't know why. "Matt and I were together for a year before we became lovers. We were young, and after Gray Moon I was terrified of being touched. Anyway, sex was at the bottom of our list of needs, with food and a place to sleep a lot higher. When we finally did make love, it was just the next way of comforting each other. We didn't think that we might have a child.''

"But you did." Grady put his arms around her and drew her against him.

She rested her cheek against his shoulder. "When Matt found out I was pregnant, he decided we should go to Miami. He was almost eighteen by then, almost old enough to get legitimate jobs. The city seemed big enough to lose ourselves in, warm enough to survive in until we could afford a place to live. Only there were no jobs. There were so many poor people there already to take the kind of jobs Matt could have gotten, and they were older and more experienced than he was.

"Matt got involved with some guys who said they were working for a loan shark. He decided to tag along and see if there was anything he could do. The last thing he said to me was—" Her voice caught, and for a minute she couldn't go on. "Was that this would be the last time he did anything illegal. The day he turned eighteen he was going out to find a real job because he didn't want his kid having a criminal for a father...."

She took a deep, shaky breath. "He was killed that night. I found out later that he'd discovered these guys were selling drugs, not loans, and he'd tried to get out. Before he could, some other guys who were selling, too, came in with guns."

"Anna." Grady stroked her hair.

"I left Miami, but I didn't have anyplace to go. I made it as far as Ponte Reynaldo on the money I had. I had the baby to think about, and I knew I couldn't make it on my own. So I went to First Day and asked Tom Schneider to take me in." She fell silent.

Grady continued to stroke her hair. He felt as if he had just lived through hell with her. He couldn't conceive how she had survived. "And Ryan was born there?"

"Amazingly healthy. And so was I. After everything, we both came through unscathed."

Except that he knew she hadn't. Her body had survived the onslaught of life on the streets, but her opinion of herself had not. She blamed herself for every horrible thing that had been done to her and everything she'd been forced to do. She blamed herself for Matt's death, too. He'd heard it in her voice.

She had told him her story to scare him away. He knew that, too. But more than anything in the world, she needed him to tell her that none of it mattered. He searched his heart and knew that none of it did. The only thing that mattered was that he was holding her now.

A question came easily. "Did you think anything you said would change the way I feel about you?"

She pulled away a little so that she could see his face. "You don't have to pretend, Grady. I know who I am now, but I also know what I was."

"So do I. Very brave. Very scared. And very determined to survive. That's all you were, Anna. And you did survive. That wonderful little boy sleeping on my bed is proof."

"I lived outside the law you value so much!"

"I value you alive and here in front of me more!"

She tried to think of another way to tell him that he was wrong, but she had run out of ways. His feelings were in his eyes now, and they told her that nothing she could say would change his mind. He pulled her closer and bent his head.

There was nothing comforting about his kiss, and nothing gentle. If anything, *he* needed comfort after the ordeal of hearing her past. He needed to prove to himself that she had survived hell and come out of it alive and in his arms.

He didn't think once about Susan or his career. He thought only of the woman he held and the strength of his feelings for her. She was life, strengthened and nourished by hardship, honed to a razor-sharp awareness, courageous and foolish and passionate. She was everything he had long valued and somehow forgotten.

Anna's resistance was only momentary. She kissed him back with the strength and intensity that made up the most integral part of her.

Chapter 6

The Powells' Palm Beach home was built around a two-story atrium that was filled with rare, exotic rain forest vegetation and a retinue of screeching wildlife. Grady always hated the moment when Pim, the Powells' butler, ushered him into the atrium to wait for Susan. Mrs. Powell was convinced that everyone was as fascinated by a rain forest as she was, and she left standing orders that guests—particularly beloved ones like Grady—be given the privilege of waiting there.

Grady always had the feeling that either a giant Venus flytrap or one of Mrs. Powell's macaws would mistake him for dinner. Pim would come back to find that nothing was left of him but a particularly stubborn bone and, with studied nonchalance, would throw it into the shrubbery for fertilizer.

Mrs. Powell labored intensively to save the rain forests. In some ways she was a misfit in a society where causes were excuses for social gatherings. Mrs. Powell marched, wrote letters and lobbied her legislators. While friends planned teas for the local hospital, she was rafting down the Amazon, taking photographs of endangered species and the slash and burn agricultural method that was destroying their habitats.

She was absolutely traditional in one way, however. She expected Susan and Grady to behave in the accepted manner befitting a couple about to be married. She wanted the proper parties and the proper announcements at the proper times. She was a stickler for doing their wedding by the book.

Today, as Grady waited for Susan in the atrium—one lone macaw circling his head like a buzzard—the list of wedding guests was on his mind, as he knew it was on Mrs. Powell's. He and Susan had set this date to go over the final version. Invitations had to be ordered during the next week for the wedding to stay on schedule.

Grady had never felt less like preparing for a wedding. He was tied in knots at the thought of wanting one woman despite his approaching marriage to another. Just weeks ago he had never questioned the strength of his commitment to Susan. Now he knew it for what it was. Susan was his friend, much as Anna had described her relationship with Matt. And Anna? Anna was fast becoming his heart and soul.

Grady was an honorable man. He could not marry Susan feeling as he did about Anna. Yet he knew that honor could be another word for foolishness. He had only known Anna a short time. Surely the strength of his attraction to her would fade. He had never experienced anything like it, so he had nothing to help him compare. But a current of feelings as swift, as dangerous, as those he felt for Anna could only wash him downstream. By the same token, his relationship with Susan was slow and steady, guiding him toward the goal and the life he had always believed he wanted.

"Pim just told me you were here." Susan stepped into the atrium. "I think he likes to make you wait in Mother's forest as long as possible. He knows you hate it so."

"Nice guy, your butler."

"He doesn't think you're good enough for me," she explained. "No man is. I'm Pim's little sweetheart. He's never noticed I took down my pigtails."

Grady had to agree that Pim's assessment of him was correct.

Susan approached and reached up to kiss him. The kiss was brief and lukewarm. "Been busy since I've been away?"

"Very. How was the wedding?"

"Perfect. Bloodless. They each married for money. Cass confided that she's got enough to see Jerry through the rest of medical school. Then she's going to let him support her in the style she wants to become accustomed to."

"That's not really your idea of a perfect marriage."

"At least they can't do anything to hurt each other."

Her tone was surprisingly bitter. Grady realized that somehow Susan had heard about Saturday and his trip to the cabin with Anna. "Let's sit down."

"No. Let's go for a walk. I'd like to be away from here when we talk."

Neither of them said anything more until they were a distance from the house. The sky was gray with thunderclouds that temporarily shaded the summer sun. Just beyond the edge of the road the ocean crashed against concrete breakers, like a mighty lion barely restrained by the bars of its cage. They walked along it without noticing.

Susan was the first to break the silence. "I understand you took Saturday off instead of campaigning."

"I went to my cabin. And yes, I took a woman with me. We also took her four-year-old son. How did you know?"

"Someone saw you heading out of town. She couldn't wait to tell me."

He didn't even ask who it had been. It didn't matter. "You met Anna the other day in my office."

"The pretty blonde in red."

"She helped me identify some suspects."

"And you were so grateful you took her away for the weekend."

"Not the weekend. One day. No nights. And it wasn't the way you're making it sound."

"Wasn't it, Grady?"

"No."

Susan was quiet for a while. "How was it, then?" she asked as they turned onto the next street. They began passing houses that were clearly architectural gems. It didn't matter.

He wished he could lie. He wished he could say something to take the hurt out of her voice. But his lying would hurt her more. "I don't know how it is," he admitted. "She came into my life like a whirlwind. I'm still suffering from shock."

"Do you love her?"

"I hardly know her."

"I'm told that sometimes that doesn't matter."

"I don't feel the same things for her I feel for you."

She gave a short, bitter laugh. "Maybe she's lucky."

"You're my best friend. You're everything a man could want in a wife."

"But not in a lover."

There was nothing he could say to that.

"Maybe we've made a mistake," Susan said. "Maybe we both wanted this because it seemed right, but maybe it wasn't right after all."

He couldn't mouth the excuses, the reassurances, that most men would have been comfortable with. He wasn't comfortable with anything other than the stark truth. "Maybe we have," he said, regret in his voice.

"When I was at Cass's wedding all I could think about was ours. How different our marriage would be, how honest we would always be with each other. But we've never been honest, have we?"

"I don't know, Sus. The major thing I'm feeling is confusion." He glanced at her. Her eyes were dry. She didn't even look particularly upset. Either she had shed her tears before or she would shed them later. But she was too poised, too controlled, to do it now.

"Would you like your ring back, Grady?"

"No."

"Then do you want to order wedding invitations?"

He thrust his hands in his pockets. "Let's wait."

Susan laughed a little. Grady knew what it had cost her. "That will be difficult to explain to Mother. We'll have to have them printed if we go through with the wedding, and Mother will die if they're not properly engraved."

"Do you love me?"

The smile she had forced died. "I always thought I did, but I don't feel like the bottom's dropping out of my heart now. Maybe there's something wrong with me."

"Maybe I'm the something wrong."

"It's possible we'll both thank this Anna person someday. We can still be friends if we break the engagement, but it would be hard to stay friends after a divorce."

"Don't think about that yet. We both just need a little time. Apparently we haven't thought this through enough. And the date is closing in on us."

"Prewedding jitters?" Susan linked her arm through Grady's. "Maybe so. We've done everything else by the book. Why not that?"

The two weeks after the trip to Grady's cabin were the busiest Anna had ever known. The conference First Day was sponsoring occupied most of her time at work. She was proud that she had succeeded in finding an even better hotel at a cheaper cost to participants. She had confirmed times and topics with all workshop leaders and scheduled them in appropriate meeting rooms. She had even planned the menu of the farewell banquet on the final night.

In addition she had tried to do most of her usual jobs because there really wasn't enough staff at First Day to absorb her responsibilities. She had secretly welcomed the work, because it had kept her from thinking about Grady.

He hadn't called, and he hadn't come to see her. One day while she was at First Day he had stopped by Isabella's to give Ryan a beautiful gourami for his fish tank, but even though she had called to thank him, he had not returned her call.

She knew why. She had been a pimp's property, and she had only escaped that life through a lucky draw of the cards.

She had lived out of garbage cans, lifted wallets and told lies to get money from strangers. She had roamed the country with Matt and borne his illegitimate child.

It was not exactly a story you could run in the newspaper.

Grady was a politician. His personal life had to be squeaky clean—or at least appear that way. His friends had to be people who could help him up the political ladder, his lover a woman like Susan Powell, who had been born to be a politician's wife.

He had kissed her once in gratitude and once because he had been deeply moved by what she had told him. He was a good man, a compassionate man, and he had felt her pain. But he was also a practical man, and when the pain had lessened he had looked at his life and known that Anna Fitzgerald could never be a part of it again. Not even as a friend.

Which was just as well, since they had progressed to the far brink of friendship and had been teetering on the edge of something else, anyway. And that something else had been disaster.

So she understood why Grady hadn't called. There was a funny kind of honor in his silence. She imagined he was trying hard to think of a way to keep from hurting her. And she imagined that he hadn't yet found an answer. She took some comfort in the knowledge that he might be suffering, too. It was the equivalent of a Band-Aid after an amputation.

On the Monday morning a week before the conference, Anna walked into her new office on the third floor of First Day to find Grady waiting for her. He was thumbing through a copy of *Children of Darkness*, a riveting work on runaways by a well-known journalist, Jess Cantrell. The book, which was two years old, had caused quite a sensation and shot up the nonfiction bestseller lists days after its publication. It had also been responsible for changes in the laws of several states. Anna had it on her desk because she was sure it was going to be a topic of discussion at First Day's conference.

Anna had almost preferred Grady's silence to his presence. Now she would no longer be able to tell herself lies about why he hadn't called. She was going to find out the truth, and he was going to make the goodbye official.

She tried to be casual, as if nothing had happened. "It's a good book," she said, closing the door behind her. "The best in the field."

Grady stood, staring at her. Anna knew what she looked like. She was taking half a dozen kids to a water park later that afternoon. She had on black-and-red flowered surfer shorts and a lavender crop-top T-shirt with a black lightning bolt pointing dead-center at her navel.

"You've reached a new level of workplace chic." His smile was warm enough to send the window-unit air-conditioner into a flurry of activity.

"I wouldn't have been so formal, but I heard the boy-wonder prosecutor was up here waiting for me." Anna stood by the door, her hand still on the knob.

Grady noticed. "Planning to make an escape?"

"If necessary."

"Do you have a moment to talk?"

"A moment."

"How's Ryan?"

Anna walked to her desk and pulled her chair out so that she was facing him without the desk between them. "Bouncing off the walls, as usual. I found him fishing in his aquarium the other day. Without a hook, of course."

"I saw him last week."

"I know. I called afterward to thank you for the gourami."

He tilted his head. "You called?"

"And left a message with your secretary."

"I didn't get it."

From his tone Anna knew that his secretary would hear about it when he went back to the office. "I just wanted you to know how much Ryan appreciated the gift. He named it Whiskers."

"He's everything a kid's supposed to be."

"Thanks." Anna didn't quite meet Grady's eyes. She wished he would get to the point. She wasn't sure she could bear much more small talk.

"I've had a lot to think about, Anna."

She wondered why she had wished he would get to the point. Something perilously close to fear was blooming inside her. She didn't want to hear this. She knew, at that moment, what she had refused to recognize before. Grady Clayton mattered to her. A lot.

She stood, because sitting still was suddenly unbearable. "So have I. Look, I know what you're going to say. I understand, and I don't blame you. I told you the truth about myself so that you'd stay away from me. I'm dangerous to your political health. And nothing that I told you is a dark secret. I share it anytime I think it will help one of the kids who comes through here. There are dozens of people who've heard my story. Anybody who wanted to find out what I told you could do it by making a few phone calls."

He watched her pace. She didn't look at him, so she didn't see the grim set of his mouth. She continued.

"I don't like politics, and I don't like politicians. But I like you. I think you're one of the rare birds, Grady. I think you're going to be on the side of justice and honor. You are now, and you will be later, when the people make your job more or less permanent. But to get to that point you're going to have to exercise a lot of care."

"This is all variations on a theme so far. Unless you're planning to change the melody, may I say something?"

She stopped pacing and looked at him for the first time. She realized he was furious.

In a moment he was towering over her. "What kind of a man do you think I am, anyway? The last time we were together you thought maybe I was after you for a little sex on the side. Now you think I'm here to tell you you're not good enough for me." He lifted his hands to her shoulders, as if to shake her. "What in God's name has happened to you to make you so gun-shy of politicians? Is it just that the law never came to your rescue when you were out on the streets?

Did you try to get help at some point and get turned away instead?''

She didn't answer. Couldn't.

"I'm really sick of this game, Anna. Sure, I was upset by what you told me. Who wouldn't be? Did you think I'd like to hear about you being raped and savaged by some maniac pimp when you were barely old enough to know such things happened? Did you think I enjoyed knowing that you spent more than a year of your life eating out of garbage cans and sleeping on the streets with only a boy between you and violence and starvation?"

"Grady—"

He raised his voice. "Did you think I wanted to know that your precious little boy will never know his father? That a truly heroic young man never got to know his son? Your life has been worse than a soap opera. It doesn't make pretty listening, but who the hell cares if I enjoyed it? It made me sick, but it made me respect you more than I've ever respected anyone! I don't respect you right now, though, because you have so little faith in yourself that you think you're not worth a thing. And you think so little of me that you believe I'd trade our relationship for flattering ink on a sheet of newsprint!"

She stared at him. Then her temper ignited. "Who are you to criticize me for what I thought? What was I supposed to think? You disappeared for two weeks! No phone calls, no visits. As far as I knew you weren't even on this planet anymore. I told you the story of my life!" Tears welled inside her, and she couldn't fight them down. She gasped the rest. "I told you the story of my life and you left me, like so much stinking garbage you didn't even want to throw away!"

He grabbed her and pulled her close. She was shaking with sobs. He cursed softly and held her tighter. "I'm sorry, Anna. My God, I just never thought you'd see it that way. I had to have time to think, not because of what you told me or who you used to be, but because of who you are now. Don't you see what's happening? You've changed my whole life. I don't even know who I am anymore or what I want. I have to find out, and soon."

"I'm not asking you for anything. I don't want anything."

"I know that. I know." He stroked her hair. It slid through his fingers.

"We can be friends. But *after* the election, Grady."

"Don't start that again, damn it."

"I know more about this than you think. The public can be swayed by bad publicity. They can change their votes over one headline."

She tried to move away, but he wouldn't let her. She felt too good in his arms. Too good, and his own reaction was too obvious to deny. "Then let them. I'll never do a song and dance for anybody, for any reason. You might think about making that your motto, too."

She looked up at him, hurt apparent through the tears.

This time he didn't comfort her. "You've got a ways to go before you free yourself from the past. How are you ever going to help these kids if you don't really believe that today's supposed to be the first day of the rest of your life? Isn't that the saying this place is founded on? Maybe you'd better give it some thought."

"It's so easy for you to say," she said softly.

"No, it's not easy. Not easy at all." He bent the few necessary inches and brushed his lips across hers. "I'll see you soon."

"I'm going to be busy."

"So am I. I'll still see you." He traced the trail of one teardrop on her cheek. Then he was gone.

With utmost graciousness, Susan cancelled her participation at a campaign barbecue at the Ponte Reynaldo Yacht Club that night. Grady's parents, charter members, discussed it with him all the way there and all the way back. The situation was particularly compelling to them because Melissa Clayton was a close friend of Kathryn Powell. Melissa meditated and Kathryn protested, but the two women were both different enough from their terribly-correct friends that they had formed a close bond the first day they met.

"You *are* going to call her?" Grady's mother asked for the fifteenth time as his father drove his Mercedes into the driveway where Grady had parked his own car. "Kathryn says that Susan seems unhappy. And she didn't give me any reason for cancelling when I talked to her. She just said she was tired. I wonder if she's sick?"

"You might consult the stars," Stan Clayton said acidly. "Or you might just ask Susan the next time you see her."

"Grady should do the asking." There was a slight pause. "Kathryn says that you haven't yet presented her with our list of guests for the wedding. She's frantic that there might not be time to have the invitations engraved."

"We would be drummed out of proper society," Stan said in the same acid tone.

"You've never taken anything seriously," Melissa said to her husband. "Grady, why haven't you given Susan our list?"

Grady had suspected it would be a mistake to ride to and from the barbecue with his parents. In addition to the inevitable conversation as they drove, it presented him more as the yacht club's favorite son and less as a serious candidate. He had done it at their request, however, because, quite simply, he loved them. Now he wished he loved them a little less, because he knew he was about to hurt them.

"Susan and I aren't sure we're going to go through with the wedding," he said.

His mother, who was never at a loss for words, fell silent.

Surprisingly, it was Grady's father who protested. "She's perfect for you, son. What in blazes has gotten into you?"

"I'm not going into reasons. I don't know what we're going to do." As he said it, Grady knew it was a lie. He did know what they were going to do. He'd known since his last conversation with Anna.

Melissa Clayton found her voice. "It's just jitters. I had them before I married your father. I was sure he would never take me seriously."

"And I never did," Stan muttered.

"I wanted to warn you." Grady opened his door and stepped out of the car.

Grady was sure his parents would have said more, but as they opened their doors to follow him, a figure materialized on the edge of the front porch.

Susan leaned against a pillar, her arms folded in front of her. "How was the barbecue?"

"The ribs were tough and I was long-winded." Grady reached the porch before his parents did. "You were missed."

She smiled sadly. "By whom?"

Melissa and Stan stepped up on the porch. "By all of us, dear," Melissa said, leaning over to kiss Susan's cheek.

"Come on, Missy." Stan tucked his arm through his wife's and began to pull her toward the door. She resisted long enough to say, "If you're not feeling well, Susan, I have a new friend who heals with crystals."

"It's nice of you to think of it, but I'm fine."

The elder Claytons disappeared into the house.

"Crystals?" Grady said.

"So many of the women I know are bored." Susan continued to lean against the pillar. "They throw themselves into parapsychology or ecology or charity balls so they'll feel like they've got a reason for living."

"Those aren't exactly bad pursuits."

"That's not the point though, is it? They shouldn't have to make up reasons to get up in the morning. They should get up because they feel good about themselves, because they know they're valued and loved. Then, when they go out and pursue their interests, it's *from* that energy."

"I'm not sure I follow you."

"I'll put it simply." She smiled a little. "I don't want to marry you."

It took him a moment to respond. "If we had married," he said at last, "you would have been valued and loved."

"Not the way I need to be." Susan pushed herself upright. "Grady, we were turning into carbon copies of our parents. You were growing, becoming someone important.

And I was standing on the sidelines making it easier for you.
Your career would have been my rain forest, my metaphys-
ics. I would have made a crusade out of being sure you always won every election. And I wouldn't have done it
because our relationship gave me that strength and energy,
but because I needed energy. I would have done it because I
needed to feel important. *You* don't make me feel important. Your career does.''

He thought about what she was saying and knew it was
true. "I'm sorry. Maybe there's something wrong with me."

She shook her head. "No, sweetheart. There isn't. At
least, no more than what's been wrong with me. We were
easy for each other to fall in love with. Too easy and too
comfortable. Nothing has ever really sizzled between us.
Now you've found someone who gives you energy. I don't
know if I'll ever find someone like that, but at least I'll never
settle for less again." She reached down and stripped off the
oriental-cut diamond that had been his grandmother's. "I
want you to take this back."

"You're entitled to keep it."

"*I'm* breaking the engagement." She reached for his hand
and wrapped his fingers around the ring. "You would have
broken it, too, I know, if I'd given you the chance. We're so
terribly alike in so many ways."

In that moment he felt more for her than he ever had. It
pointed out everything that had been missing all along. "I
love you, Sus. I always will."

"I know that, too." She lifted herself up on her tiptoes
and kissed him. "Will you tell Anna for me that she's got
herself quite a guy?"

"I don't know what will happen with Anna."

"Go for the gusto, Grady."

He laughed, although his throat had a peculiar lump in it.
"What are you going to do now?"

"I'm not sure. But you'd better believe I'm going to go
for the gusto, too." She squeezed his hand and turned away.
Her voice quavered. "Be happy."

In a moment she was gone.

Chapter 7

Isabella was waiting for Anna on the front porch that night when she came to pick up Ryan. Teresa and Ryan were digging in a new pile of sand placed beside a plastic wading pool in the tiny front yard. They dug, jumped in the wading pool, then got out to dig some more. They looked as if they had been cast in concrete.

Anna noted how tired and sad her friend looked. Anna had no air conditioner in her house. Isabella was only slightly luckier. Her bedroom and Teresa's had antique units that wheezed lukewarm air twenty-four hours a day, just taking the edge off the heat. Isabella was almost eight months into her pregnancy, and the hot weather was unbearable for her.

Anna felt a pang of guilt. She had been leaving Ryan for longer hours because of her work on the conference. She had paid Isabella more, but right now it looked as if Isabella needed rest more than money. In addition to Ryan, she also provided morning care for a baby who was just beginning to toddle and the baby's cousin, who was only a few months old. She loved children, and she was endlessly patient. But she was only human.

"Why don't I take Teresa to my house tonight?" Anna offered, taking the chair next to Isabella's after she'd gotten sandy welcoming hugs from both Ryan and Teresa. "She's old enough to sleep over. That way you can have a whole night to baby yourself."

"I want her with me tonight."

Anna knew immediately that it was more than fatigue that was causing the sadness on Isabella's face. "What's wrong?" She put her hand on Isabella's knee.

"I come here so I can have a better life. I know I will miss my family, but I come anyway, for my children. Then I lose my husband. Now I have no one. I even have no letters from home. My family, they are all dead. I know."

Anna was unsure what to say. Living so intimately with Isabella she had learned much about the horrors of war in Central America. Isabella, Enrique and Teresa had escaped those horrors, but no one else in their families had. Their town had been caught in the crossfire of opposing political forces, and everyone's chance for survival was just the luck of the draw.

"No letters doesn't mean they aren't alive, Isabella. It only means they can't get mail through."

Isabella reached down and picked up an envelope, passing it to Anna. It was graced with colorful foreign stamps. "Enrique did. Read."

Anna opened the envelope, and a bank draft in Spanish fluttered to her lap. The enclosed note was two lines. Anna could only decipher the second, the signature. "What does it say?"

"For the baby."

"Then he's thinking about you."

"This thought, it's cheap, no?"

"The money will help."

"A little. He sent me the same before."

"How could he go back there, just for another woman? Isn't his life in danger? Isn't that why he came here in the first place?"

"Who can understand a man's heart? He was silent after we came. He was not the Enrique I knew. Then he was gone."

"And you're sure it was another woman?"

"He wrote me and told me that, yes."

"It doesn't make sense."

"Today nothing makes sense to me. Tomorrow?" Isabella shrugged. "Tomorrow I go on."

A week later Anna walked into First Day to find Tom Schneider grinning like the cat digesting the proverbial canary. "Take care of what you have to, then come up to my office," he said, still grinning.

"For good news, obviously."

"Terrific news." He strolled off, grinning away.

Anna wasn't grinning by the time she made it to his office. She had been forced to collar Wesley. As part of his probation he had been given the task of overseeing a thorough cleaning of the First Day residence before the conference. At first it had seemed that he might do a good job. Then, halfway through, he had stopped working. Now, with the conference only two days away, the house was still in need of scrubbing and polishing. Wesley hadn't even bothered to assign the chores.

Anna had just finished delivering an ultimatum. He was either to finish his assignment or be placed on total house restriction for the next six weeks. The scene hadn't been a pretty one, but at that very moment, Wesley was rounding up a work crew.

She knocked on Tom's door and went in.

Tom looked up from a letter he was typing. "Did you hear Jill had her baby last night?"

"One of the kids told me. So that's why you were grinning away down there."

"That was part of it. A little girl. She's named her Anna. Did you know?"

Anna shook her head, afraid to speak past the sudden lump in her throat.

"She's giving her up for adoption. The agency let her see the profiles of several couples. She's chosen one with a horse ranch somewhere in central Florida. It was a hard decision, but she seems relieved. She wants to do what's best for everyone."

"Jill's going to make it."

"And Wesley?"

Anna drummed her fingers on his desk. "Fifty-fifty at best."

"You're optimistic," he warned.

"I thought I was coming in here to be cheered up."

"I do have some good news."

"Let's hear it quick, then. I need an antidote anytime Wesley's our subject."

"Our keynote speaker cancelled."

She waited for the punchline. When he didn't go on, she lifted a brow in question. "Was he so boring that his can-celling was something to celebrate? Is silence going to be more interesting?"

"He would have been okay. His replacement will be spectacular."

"You've gotten someone else on such short notice?"

"Jess Cantrell."

Anna just stared.

"Surely you know who Cantrell is," Tom prodded. "He wrote—"

"*Children of Darkness.*" Anna sat down.

"You don't seem pleased."

Anna's mind was miles away. Years away. She was re-membering another time, another life. And a long conver-sation with Jess Cantrell.

"Are you going to tell me what's wrong?" Tom asked.

Anna barely heard him. In her mind she was at a Wash-ington, D.C., cocktail party she had been forced to attend. She had been just fifteen, the only nonadult in the room. Attending social and political functions was just a part of who she had been. She had resented this party, and she had headed straight to a corner to escape her stepfather's no-tice.

Jess Cantrell had found her there. He had made his name as an investigative reporter, and at that time he was still doing occasional articles. He was at the party, he'd confided, to look for news. He hadn't confided that news was the only reason he was there, that he detested the social scene as much as she did, but he had made it clear all the same.

They had talked for a long time, not about anything he could use in an article, but just about her and about Washington and what it was like to be a teenager in these difficult times.

She had never forgotten, because it had been one of the few times an adult had treated her like a person. She had thought of him, too, when *Children of Darkness* came out. The irony of knowing the man who had written with such depth and understanding about the problems of runaways hadn't escaped her.

Now he was coming to First Day.

"When does he arrive?" she asked.

"Tomorrow morning. I'd like you to pick him up at the airport. You know he and his wife operate a program in Virginia for runaways, don't you?"

Anna shook her head.

"It's small, but quite a good one. She may be joining him here at the end of the conference, but he's bringing his daughter with him tomorrow. She's nineteen, and apparently she's majoring in psychology at college. He thought the conference would be good for her."

"I can't pick them up."

"You mean you don't want to."

"I *can't*."

"Anna, what is it?"

She ran her hand through her hair. "Look, I just can't, Tom. Please trust me on this. I can't say why."

"You know Jess Cantrell, don't you? Does this have something to do with his book?"

"Nothing to do with it."

Tom seemed to be weighing his options. He picked up the beat that Anna had been drumming on his desk. Finally he seemed to have made his decision. "I'm sorry, but I'm not going to let you get away with this," he said. "You're too old to keep running. You will pick up Jess Cantrell tomorrow and resolve whatever he has to do with your past."

Anna had only rarely heard Tom speak with such absolute authority. "You don't understand...."

"If I don't understand, it's because you've never told me."

"You've never pushed before."

There was compassion in his eyes, but determination, too. "I've never been in this situation before. You are the assistant director of this program. You can't let the past interfere with how well you do your job. For your own sake or ours."

No matter how hard she stared at herself in the mirror, Anna still saw traces of the fifteen-year-old she had been. Seven years ago her hair had been long, falling straight and sleek past her shoulders. She had seemed to grow an inch every day, and she had been thin and awkward. Had she still been wearing braces, or had they already come off? She couldn't remember. She did know that her eyes were the same odd blue-green now that they had been then, and that nothing she had suffered on the streets had somehow rearranged her features. She still resembled the girl she had been at that Washington, D.C., cocktail party. And if anyone looked hard, that girl was still apparent.

There was a chance Jess Cantrell might recognize her tomorrow.

"Mommy?"

But if he did, she could tell him that he was mistaken. No, she wasn't Rosie Jensen. But isn't it funny, she would say, how much strangers can resemble each other? She'd never been mistaken for a senator's daughter before. She was honored.

"Mommy!"

"Yes, bunny-nose." Anna switched off the bathroom light and went to check on Ryan.

"There's a knot in my fishing line."

Anna wasn't sure when Ryan had added his fishing rod to the collection of treasures he kept at the foot of his bed. They were all things that made him feel secure. His blanket, a one-eared donkey, his favorite storybook. And now the fishing rod that Grady had given him.

"You're supposed to be asleep," she scolded. She took the fishing rod out of his hands and set it in its place of honor.

"But it's got a knot!"

"Did that bad knot wake up my boy?"

He giggled.

"I'll fix it for you tomorrow."

"Grady can fix it gooder than you can."

"Of that I have no doubt."

"Let Grady fix it."

"We'll see." Anna didn't want to tell him that Grady had disappeared from their lives again. She'd spoken to him once, briefly. He had been very closemouthed, just telling her that he would talk to her again soon when he had a real break. That had been four days ago.

He didn't owe her anything. She told herself that every day. He was running for office, building a case against drug runners, doing all the other myriad chores of his position—and planning a wedding. He had already given generously of himself. No matter his protests to the contrary, there wasn't room in his life for her, anyway.

And she was sick to death of such noble thoughts! She wanted to see Grady. He meant more to her than she wanted to admit, even to herself. His acceptance of her past—or at least what he knew of it—had gone a long way toward cleansing her of self-doubt and blame. Their friendship—and she refused to let herself think of it as anything more—would have to end after his wedding. For now she wanted to use the short time left learning to know him better. And she needed him, although she wouldn't be able to tell him why. She needed him, and she wanted the comfort of his presence.

Anna shut the door to Ryan's room and washed the few dinner dishes they had used. Despite fans in every window and a breeze blowing through the screen door, the house was still close to ninety. Even though she was assistant director of First Day, her paycheck was small. Social service agencies paid notoriously low salaries, and First Day was always scrambling for every dime they could find. By the time she took care of her bills, paid Isabella and put aside what she needed for tuition the next semester, there was nothing left over for a savings account. She had dreams of buying air-conditioning units for two rooms, but so far, they were only dreams.

She was just climbing into her orange nightshirt after a long, cool shower when someone knocked on her front door. She pulled on her robe with a grimace, because it was heavy and hot and would undo all the good the shower had done. Still toweling her hair dry, she went to answer the door.

Grady stood on the other side of the screen. He was dressed in a tan suit, as if he had just gotten off work. His tie was unknotted but still hanging around his neck.

As he waited for her to unlatch the door, he slipped out of his jacket. "If I carried a knife, I wouldn't even have had to knock. I could have just slit the screen and unlatched the door myself."

"Complain, complain." Anna opened the door. "Come on in and swelter with me."

"Did something happen to your air conditioner?"

"It disappeared."

"It was stolen?"

"By the previous tenant. Before I moved into the house. My landlord refuses to install another because every time a tenant leaves, the air conditioner leaves, too."

"I don't know how you stand it."

"The heat seems worse if you're going in and out of air conditioning. The one in my car is broken, and we keep the thermostat at First Day set high to save money. So I'm more used to it than you, silver-spoon-in-the-mouth pussycat that you are."

She smiled at him, flashing two deep dimples. Grady wondered how he had managed to go so long without seeing her. His reasons had been unassailable, but now he wondered why he hadn't managed to find a way.

Anna stood several feet from him, wishing she had the right to take the necessary steps to put her arms around him. She needed Grady tonight. She needed him to tell her that everything was going to be all right, even if he didn't know why she was upset.

He breached the distance and put his arms around her instead. He rested his cheek against her wet hair. "I've missed you."

Anna tried to move away, but he wouldn't let her. She felt a thrill of fear, because she doubted she would be able to resist him, and she would hate herself if she didn't.

"Don't pull away yet," he murmured.

"We shouldn't be doing this."

"I'm not getting married. Susan and I have broken the engagement."

She felt so many things, but she couldn't identify a single one. She succeeded in lifting her head. "Why?"

"Because, despite appearances to the contrary, we weren't really right for each other, and we both finally saw it. And because I met you."

She shut her eyes and shook her head. "I never tried to take you away from Susan. Tell me I didn't."

"You never did," he affirmed.

"We still have no future together."

He touched her cheek. "We'll worry about the future some other time if you'd like. Look at me."

She did.

"My relationship with Susan is over now. And ours is just starting. Everything that's happened has been right, even if it's been painful. Let go of the past and just be with me in the present."

"Grady?" Ryan came to the living room door, rubbing his eyes.

Grady let go of Anna and held his arms out to the little boy. "What are you doing up so late, bunny-nose?"

Ryan went to him to be picked up. "My fishing line has a knot!"

"We can't have that, can we? Jump down and get it, and we'll fix it right away." He set Ryan down and watched him run through the kitchen to his room.

"I don't know what woke him," Anna murmured.

"Good feelings. He felt them all the way in his bedroom."

She met his eyes. He was smiling at her, and it was seeping through all her defenses. She tried to joke. "That and the heat."

"Tomorrow I'm going to do something about that."

"No you're not. Don't come in here and start messing with my life, Grady Clayton."

"I've already messed with your life, Anna Fitzgerald. And I plan to keep right on messing with it, too." His fingers brushed her cheek. "Maybe I'll mess with it slowly, and maybe I won't. Whatever I do, though, it's for the long haul. I don't take this lightly. I don't take *you* lightly."

She shut her eyes and felt his fingers trace the curve of her mouth. Then she felt his lips brush hers. When Ryan came back with his fishing rod, her cheeks were flushed from more than the heat.

In southwestern Virginia, in a big, rambling white house, Jess Cantrell stood in the doorway of his bedroom and watched his wife stare at the framed photograph of a teenage girl.

"What made you think of Rosie?"

Krista turned, setting the photograph back in its place of honor on her desk. "Did you meet the girl who dropped Tate off this afternoon?"

"I was upstairs talking to one of the kids."

"She looked so much like I envision Rosie looking now. Her hair was the same gold, and she was tall and slender and lively."

"Don't torture yourself, Kris."

She smiled sadly. "Do you remember when you stopped calling me Krista and just shortened it to Kris? It was October of our first year here when the water pipe broke and flooded the cellar."

"And Tate ran away again."

"And the authorities told us what we were doing was illegal and threatened to haul us all off to jail."

They laughed together, remembering.

Jess crossed the room and took her in his arms. "Shall I call you Krista again, then?"

She snuggled against him. "I don't even remember who that other woman was. I've been Kris too long."

"And Mom."

"It's still hard to believe I've got a daughter almost as old as I am."

"Tate tells her friends that you were only nine when you had her, and that the birth is in *The Guinness Book of World Records*."

"Tate enjoys causing a commotion."

Jess let Krista's white-gold hair sift through his fingers. "Will you be all right here for the rest of the week while Tate and I go to this conference?"

"I've got plenty of help."

"I want you to join me afterward. Tate's got to fly back to school, anyway. You and I can have a few days alone in Florida lying on the beach and soaking up the sun."

"If I can make the arrangements, I will. I promise."

There was a knock on their bedroom door. Very few of the kids in residence had the courage to disturb Jess and Krista there. Tate had no such qualms.

"Come in," Jess called.

A black-haired, blue-eyed nymph poked her head into the room. "There's a fight downstairs about who gets to choose what the kitchen crew is going to cook for dinner tomorrow. They're divided evenly between hamburgers and roast chicken."

"Tell them to stuff the chicken with the hamburger," Jess said.

"Don't listen to your father." Krista held out her arm and Tate came over to be included in their hug.

"This house is even more zooey than my dorm." Tate hugged them both. "Ah, for the relative peace of life on the streets."

They all laughed, because they knew Tate didn't mean it. There had been a time when she had, though. Jess and Krista had met in one of New Orleans's seediest bars. Krista had been posing as a runaway, looking for her sister Rosie, who had left home more than a year before. Jess had been interviewing runaways for the book he intended to write about them. By a strange coincidence, he had met Rosie several years before.

He and Krista had teamed up to find Rosie, and along the way they had found Tate, instead. Now, four years later, Tate was their adopted daughter, and they were the administrators, house parents and official peacekeepers of a small rehabilitation program for street kids. Stagecoach Inn, as it was called, catered to the weariest of travelers. Jess and Krista took kids that no other program would willingly accept. Their success rate was high, considering the difficult kids that they worked with. One in three made it off the streets for good.

Tate was one of those kids who had made it. But it had been a long, hard haul for all of them. During her first year with Jess and Krista, she had run away three times. Twice they had found her and brought her back. The third time she had come home on her own and announced that she was never leaving again. Together they had sloughed through the mountain of paperwork necessary to terminate her mother's legal rights so that they could adopt her. They had finally managed to make the system work for them. Tate had stayed, graduated from high school and then begun college, where she had nearly a four point average.

Tate had truly been found, but Rose was still missing. All of them felt her absence, even Tate, who had never known her.

"Did you notice that Charlie, the girl who dropped me off today, looks a little like your sister?" Tate asked Krista now. "At least, she looks like the picture you have of her."

"I noticed." Krista gave them both another hug, then stepped back to go downstairs and settle the dispute. "I'll see what I can do with the kitchen crew. At least they're thinking ahead."

Tate and Jess watched her go. "This house has a ghost," Tate said when the door shut behind Krista.

"I haven't told Kris yet, but I heard today that her stepfather's been given an endorsement by three key senators. They'll swing a good portion of the rest of the delegates he needs for the nomination."

"He doesn't really have a chance at the presidency, does he?"

Jess looked his daughter straight in the eye and saw that she already suspected the answer.

"Hayden Barnard has more than a chance. Unless a miracle happens and I can finally expose him for the man he really is, he's probably going to be the leader of our nation."

Chapter 8

Anna dressed carefully the next morning. Grady hadn't stayed late, although she suspected that might not have been the case if Ryan hadn't been awake to chaperon. She'd had a long, sleepless night to worry about Grady's desire to pursue their relationship—and about Jess Cantrell. Sometimes just before daybreak she had realized that both problems were out of her hands. There was nothing she could do about Grady. And all she could do about Jess was plan to look her most professional.

Now she appraised her efforts. She was wearing her white blazer and a white pleated skirt. Her blouse was the one pastel piece of clothing she owned, a pale peach that made her look suitably demure. Her hair was swept back over her ears, and she wore dainty gold hoops in her earlobes. She was even wearing makeup to hide the childish freckles that never seemed to fade.

Fifteen-year-old Rosie Jensen stared unflinchingly back at her from the mirror.

She reminded herself for the hundredth time that Jess Cantrell was a world traveler. In the course of his research he had probably interviewed thousands of people, a number of them teenagers, since his last book had been about runaways. He wasn't going to recognize her, and he wasn't going to remember.

And she wasn't going to feel safe again until Jess Cantrell was back on the plane leaving Ponte Reynaldo.

She made the trip to the airport through rush-hour traffic. For once in her life she was glad to be hemmed in by irritable commuters. As she crept slowly toward her destination, she visualized what would happen if she just passed the airport exit and kept right on going. Running was a temptation. The problem was that she was now an adult, with an adult's responsibilities. For the first time since she had closed the door of her Washington home behind her, she wondered if the time had come to face her past. Jess Cantrell probably wouldn't recognize her.

But someday, somewhere, somebody might.

"Is somebody meeting us?" Tate asked, as she pulled her overnight bag out of the compartment over her head.

"Tom Schneider said he was sending their assistant director. It should be interesting being here a day early. We'll get a chance to see how their program runs." Jess stretched his legs out and bumped into the seat in front of him. He would be glad to get off the plane. He no longer flew first-class. His book royalties were more than respectable, but every cent he made went into Stagecoach Inn. Even with federal and state grants and a healthy number of charitable contributions, there were always more bills than income.

"Why do you always wait until everybody else is off the plane before you get up?" Tate demanded.

He reached for her hand. "To irritate my pushy, high-spirited daughter."

"It's working." Tate flashed him a grin to soften her words.

Jess admired the effect. Tate had been a skinny, dirty, ragged street kid when he had first met her. He had seen her potential, but no one could have foreseen the beauty she would turn into. Her hair was thick and shiny, and it fell arrow-straight to her shoulders. Her eyes were almost the same deep blue as Krista's, startling with her pale skin and black hair. Her cheekbones were high but not gaunt, her nose straight and narrow. But it was her smile, the same fetching grin she was giving him now, that catapulted her from pretty to outstanding. The grin was as full of life as she was.

"Are you finally ready, old man?" Tate asked. "The only people left on board are the crew."

"I guess we can go." Jess followed Tate out into the aisle. Despite what she had said, they had to wait in line as the crew said their polite goodbyes.

In the airport, Jess scanned the crowd for the woman who was to meet them. Tom had said she was blond, with unusual taste in clothes. Jess didn't see anyone of that description.

"Mr. Cantrell?" A pretty young woman stepped out of the crowd. She fit Tom's description, except for the outfit she was wearing. It was simple and feminine, much like something Krista would choose. In fact, she resembled Krista. He stared at her.

"I'm sorry, you are Jess Cantrell, aren't you?" she asked. "I'm Anna Fitzgerald, from First Day. I recognize you from the photograph on your book jacket."

Jess wondered if he was going crazy. After years of searching, it couldn't be this easy. He repeated her name. "Anna?"

She didn't quite meet his eyes. "That's right." She turned toward Tate. "And you must be Tate Cantrell. We're glad to have you both with us."

Tate was looking at her father. She stole a glance at Anna, then looked back at Jess. "Dad?"

Jess took a deep breath. "It's good of you to come for us...Anna. We've been looking forward to this. More than you could guess."

"Well, good. Why don't you go get your luggage while I bring my car around?"

Jess considered for the briefest moment. "Tate, you go with Anna and keep her company. I'll meet the two of you outside."

Anna had expected anything from no reaction to a point blank question as to her identity. She hadn't expected the shared expression of shock on father and daughter's faces. It made no sense. Even if Jess had recognized her, Tate certainly wouldn't have. And if Jess had remembered a certain cocktail party, it would have been curiosity she saw on his face.

She wondered if she was losing her mind. Maybe she was just imagining the whole thing. "It'll only take a minute to get my car."

Tate was at her side in a moment, almost as if she were afraid she was going to get lost . . . or Anna was. Anna tried to shake off the feeling that something momentous was occurring.

She was still trying to shake it off half an hour later when she closed Tom Schneider's door, leaving Jess and Tate to chat with him.

"I can't tell you what an honor it is to have you here," Tom said, after Anna had left his office. "To have someone of your stature as keynote speaker will be such a bonus for our attendees."

Jess leaned forward. He was a large man, dark and intense. And he was famous for cutting right through to the heart of any matter. "Tom, you don't know me, and I don't know you. But you know my reputation. So when I ask you to tell me about Anna, remember that discretion's responsible for half my royalties."

Tom sat back in his chair, almost as if he were trying to put a safe distance between himself and the man in front of him. "Oh, brother."

"Do you want me to go keep an eye on her?" Tate asked her father. "I can tell her I'd like to see the program through her eyes."

"She's already wondering what's going on. Neither of us hid our shock very well." Jess turned back to Tom. "Will Anna run?"

"Run?"

"If she feels threatened."

Tom considered. "I don't know," he said after a long moment. "It depends on how threatened, and whether Ryan's threatened, too."

"Ryan?"

"Her son."

"She has a child...." Jess smiled a little. "I'll be damned. One minute she's as good as dead, the next she has a son."

"Suppose you tell me what this is all about," Tom said.

"I'd rather hear what you know about Anna, first," Jess answered. "I'm not asking you for anything confidential. Just whatever you can tell me."

Tom was obviously considering whether he should speak at all. But finally he shrugged. "Anna came here four years ago, pregnant and alone. Her baby's father was killed in Miami. She was so depressed I don't think she would have survived if she hadn't had the child to think about. She'd been on the streets for almost two years, apparently, under the protection of her boyfriend, another runaway. She asked us to take her in, but she wouldn't tell us who she was and where she came from."

"And did she ever?"

"Never has. Other than that, she was a model resident. She worked hard to get her G.E.D. and to be a good mother to Ryan. When it came time for her to leave and get a job, she stayed on here running errands and doing night watch at minimum wage. A year later we made her a counselor. Six months ago she became assistant director. She's a living example of what a program like ours can do."

"I'll be damned," Jess said again.

"Now it's your turn."

"She's my sister-in-law." Jess looked satisfied with himself. "She doesn't know it, though."

Tom had heard enough stories in his work with runaways to write a book himself. Nothing surprised him anymore. "She knows you have some connection to her," he said. "She didn't want to pick you up at the airport."

"I met her a long time ago, before I met her sister, actually. Her real name is Roseanna Jensen. She used to go by Rosie."

"Then she doesn't know you're related?"

"I think she would have left town if she had." Jess leaned forward again. "There's a lot more to this than I've told you. She has every right to be hiding her identity. I'm afraid her life's been in danger from the day she left home. I don't want her to know the truth until I've had a chance to get to know her a little and she trusts me. Otherwise she may run again."

Tom didn't ask any more questions. That was one of the things he was best at. "I won't say anything to her."

"Good."

"She's my aunt," Tate said.

Jess smiled at her. "Yeah, I guess she is."

"I have an aunt." Tate shook her head wryly. "And a cousin. All this family. I don't know if I can stand it."

"Get used to it, toots. Hopefully, when this is settled, Ros—Anna is going to be in your family for a long, long time."

Anna sat in the large audience and listened to Jess Cantrell close his speech. Like many of the people there, her eyes glistened with tears. He had just told the story of his nephew, a runaway, who had died on the streets of Atlantic City.

"I have another reason for my passion for this problem," he said, stacking his notes neatly in front of him. "My wife has a sister who's been missing for over six years. No one knows better than we do what it's like to wish and hope and search every passing face. No one *can* know unless they're in that position. There are more victims here than just kids on our streets. There are parents at home, sisters and brothers who will always carry with them the anguish of a grievous loss. When we shelter a kid and provide him or her with services, we are serving those families, too. Let's never forget that when we extend our hands, we're reaching out to a chain of people stretching far beyond those we'll ever see. When you get discouraged, remember that. And remember how important you are, how special. Everything

you do in your shelters makes a difference. You may never
know how much."

He sat down to thunderous applause. Anna looked down
at the end of her row to see how Tom had enjoyed the
speech. He was looking at her. He smiled. Tearily. For that
moment she did feel special, and very, very vulnerable.

The crowd began to break up for workshops. Anna stood
and stretched. Through a gap in the row ahead of her she
saw Tate approaching. In the twenty-four hours since she
had met Tate, she had grown fond of the younger woman.
Tate was outspoken and exuberant. Her comments were in-
sightful and her sense of humor keen. Anna had spent most
of yesterday with her, showing her the program and listening to Tate compare it to Stagecoach Inn.

"Are you heading for a workshop?" Tate asked.

"I'll be in workshops all afternoon. Right now I've got to
get back to First Day and be sure it's spic and span. They're
dong a tour at noon, and I don't want anybody to see it the
way it really is."

"Can I tag along?"

"Sure. You don't want to go to any workshops?"

"There are two this afternoon I want to attend. I think I'll
learn more this morning just watching how you do things."

"Fine. Let me tell Tom I'm going. Then we'll head out."

On the trip from the hotel to First Day, Anna took the
opportunity to get to know Tate better. There had been no
more awkward moments since their meeting at the airport.
Both Jess and Tate had treated her casually, although it did
seem that one or the other of them was always around.
Anna had pretty well convinced herself that Jess hadn't
recognized her. Whatever else had been going on at the airport, she was sure he didn't suspect who she was.

"Tell me about Stagecoach Inn," Anna asked. "How did
you feel when your mother and father suddenly started taking in runaways?"

Tate laughed. "I'm a runaway myself, so what could I
say?"

Anna turned onto the interstate leading to First Day.
"What do you mean?"

"Jess and Kris found me on the streets. I'm not their natural child. Kris is less than ten years older than I am. And Jess would have had to be a pretty active young stud."

Anna had privately thought the same thing. "Then they adopted you?"

"Sure did. And they tell me they don't even regret it."

"How on earth did they find you?"

Tate hedged. "Well, it's a long story. You might say I just kept getting in their way. Anyway, they started Stagecoach Inn about six months after I went to live with them. Jess had bought this huge old house in Virginia, and it really was a stagecoach inn at one time. He and Kris just started filling it up with runaway kids. Everybody else comes and goes. I stayed."

"That's a pretty wonderful story." Anna was curious. "What's this Chris like?"

"She's gorgeous, and she's good with the kids. She and Jess play good guy, bad guy. Jess lays down the discipline and Kris softens everybody up. They both love the kids who come through, though. And the ones who are able see that."

"I'd like to visit someday."

"I'm sure you'll be invited."

Anna glanced at Tate, because her last comment had sounded as if she were strangling. Tate was looking out the window.

At First Day, Wesley and crew were putting the final touches on the house. Even Anna had to admit that they had surpassed her wildest expectations. A subdued Jill was back from her hospital stay, and Anna paired her up with Tate for a while to try to cheer her up.

Anna was just completing some paperwork in her office when there was a knock on her open door. She expected Tate. She got Jess.

"May I come in?"

She was wary, but she wasn't sure why. The vital moment for "Aren't you Roseanna Jensen?" had passed. Jess hadn't asked her then, and she doubted he would ask her now. Her wariness grew anyway. It had something to do with the warmth in his eyes.

"I was just finishing some work here. But it can wait. Is there something you need?"

"Well, as a matter of fact there is. But it's confidential. May I close the door?"

She debated, then nodded. The warmth in his eyes wasn't the variety that meant Jess was planning to chase her around her desk. It was far more personal, and even scarier. But keeping her door open wasn't going to make a difference.

Jess seated himself across from her. "Did you like my speech?"

"It was outstanding."

Jess leaned back in his chair. He still looked like a tiger about to spring. "I'm curious. Have you read my book?"

"Cover to cover."

"Am I sincere, Anna, or am I just another smooth-talking journalist?"

She had no idea where he was heading. She could only answer from her heart. "I think you're sincere. What would you have to gain by championing the cause of runaways? There can't be any money in it."

He smiled wryly. "Not a cent."

"What's this about, Jess?"

"I need your help. And I wanted to be sure you trust me, because I'm going to be asking for information."

She was thoroughly confused now. And wariness was growing toward fear. "Why are you talking to me? Why not Tom?"

"I've already talked to Tom. He thinks you're the one who might be able to help me."

"I really doubt it."

"Let me tell you my story, then we'll see."

She searched for a way to tell him no, but he was already moving on.

"I talked a little about my wife's sister in my speech. Do you remember?"

"Just that she's missing."

"For six years. She would be twenty-two now. Your age."

"That's a long time to be gone."

"We think so, too. About six years too long."

"Do you want to check our files? Is that what you're after? Because Tom will have to give you permission to do that."

Jess shook his head. "No. I just wanted to see if anything in our story rang a bell with you."

"But she ran away so long ago...." Anna paused. "Oh, you think I might have met her when I was on the streets."

"Just let me tell you, and we'll see." He was carefully searching her face. "This will have to be confidential, though, because, you see, Krista and Rosie, her sister, are the stepdaughters of Senator Hayden Barnard."

As clearly as if Tate were in the room, Anna heard her voice. *Jess and Chris found me on the streets. Chris is less than ten years older than me. Chris is gorgeous. Chris. Chris. Kris. Krista.* Anna shut her eyes. She knew what Jess was going to say. She knew what he already *knew.* "Jess, I'm not feeling very well," she murmured. "I think this may have to wait."

"It can't wait any longer," he said gently. "Six years is already too long."

She wondered why she hadn't made the connection before. Yet why should she have? She had been worried that he would remember her from a meaningless cocktail party. She had never in her wildest imagination guessed that he had married her sister.

"Maybe it's the heat up here." Anna stood. "I'm going to have to get some fresh air."

He stood, too. "I'll come with you."

"No, I don't want company."

"I'm sorry, but I think we both need fresh air."

She wanted to run and knew she'd be caught if she did. "Can't you just leave me alone?"

"Rosie, nobody's going to hurt you."

Her head snapped up. "Don't call me that!"

"It's going to take me some time to know you as Anna."

She left the room without looking back. Now she knew why Jess and Tate had trailed her every footstep since they had seen her at the airport. She half stumbled, half ran to the back stairway and took it two steps at a time. She knew Jess was right behind her.

Outside she found her way to the old citrus grove that bordered the gardens. The air was heavy with humidity, and the sun beat down mercilessly through the trees. The air was no fresher than that inside. She felt as if each breath was being torn from her lungs.

She leaned against an orange tree and fought for self control. Jess stood beside her, his hand on her shoulder. "Krista has mourned you for six years," he said.

"You have me mixed up with someone else."

"I came to you today for a reaction, and I got one."

"I'm not feeling well. It's the heat and a headache."

"Krista has your picture on her desk. The day before I left I walked in our room and found her holding it. No day goes by that she doesn't think of you, mention you. Tate says you're the ghost who haunts Stagecoach Inn."

"You have me mixed up with someone else."

"I don't think so."

Anna knew that nothing was going to change Jess's mind. She wasn't going to admit her identity, but there were some things she could say. "I'm sorry, but you definitely have me mixed up with someone else. I can prove it. I'll tell you about my sister. She was older than me. From the day I was born she pretended she was my mother. My own mother didn't really want me, so my sister took care of me. I grew up trusting her. I even thought she loved me. Then one day I found it had all been a lie. I told her something she didn't want to hear and begged for her help. She told me to go back home and face my fate like a big girl. For *my* sister, knowing the truth wasn't as important as pretending that everything was just great. That's when I disappeared, and it was the smartest thing I've ever done."

"Do you know how she regrets it?"

"I have no idea. And neither do you, because I'm not the person you wish I were." She began to walk, randomly, aimlessly. Her legs felt as heavy as weights; her eyesight was blurred.

He walked beside her. "Your story's just like the one Krista told me."

"Funny coincidence."

"Then I'll tell you the rest of it. Maybe that will be a co-incidence, too."

"I'm not interes—"

"Krista hired a detective after Rosie ran away. She spent every bit of her money on it. When the detective found only one lead, she went to New York herself and walked the streets of Times Square looking for *her* sister."

Anna wished she could cover her ears.

"We met when she was out on the streets of New Orleans looking for you. She was pretending to be a runaway be-cause she'd gotten a tip from a girl in New York that you'd been seen in the French Quarter. Krista was hanging out in bars, pretending that she belonged. I found out the truth later, and we started looking for you together."

"Not *me*."

"*Her* sister, then. For Rosie. Anna, we found out the *whole* truth together. And our lives were threatened. Ro-sie's life was threatened, too, and we had to stop looking. But we've never stopped searching."

"That doesn't make any sense!"

Jess stopped and put his hands on Anna's shoulders. "Look at me."

She shook her head, but she didn't try to break away.

"We found out that even after Rosie ran away, she might have been under surveillance. There was some proof that her whereabouts were known, photographs of her that were obviously taken after she had run away. We were told that if we kept looking for her, or if we tried to publish anything we learned, she would die, and no one would ever know. So we stopped looking, at least as far as anyone could tell. But I've been working for most of four years to find enough scandal to force the one man who can bring her back to us to do it."

She raised her eyes to his. The question cost her every-thing. "And did you find it?"

"There's enough scandal to bury the man, and not a bit of concrete proof. Except the woman standing in front of me."

She didn't flinch. "I have a son. Did you know?"

He nodded.

"He is my life." She shook off his hands and began to wend her way through the grove.

"Anna!" Jess came after her. "The only way to completely protect yourself and Ryan is to tell the truth. If the world knows what you've suffered at Hayden Barnard's hands, you'll be safe. He wouldn't dare touch you."

She kept walking.

"He's running for president, and he's probably going to win the nomination," Jess said, lowering his voice.

Anna stopped. She didn't turn around. "I know. I pity the nation."

"Do you think he'll take chances with his reputation?"

Anna was silent, but she felt a thrill of alarm.

"Men like Barnard don't negotiate. They assassinate. I found you, Anna. Purely by chance. Barnard could find you, too."

She shuddered at the thought, then told herself what she always did. She was invisible. She had made herself invisible. None of what Jess was saying was true.

"What do I tell your sister?" he asked when she started walking again.

"I have no sister. The day she told me to face hell alone was the day my sister died."

"And you've never made a mistake?"

"My biggest mistake was trusting her in the first place!" The trees blurred in front of her, and her throat burned as if scalded. She began to run.

She didn't stop until she was safely in her car, driving toward the interstate.

Grady heard the angry buzzing of his intercom, angry because Polly always leaned on it too long when she was irritated. He wondered what had gone wrong to spoil her morning. A crowded bus? A long line at the post office?

"Miss Fitzgerald is here to see you."

Grady smiled. Having Anna there was the first ray of sunshine in a chaotic, difficult day. "Send her right in."

"You have an appointment in five minutes."

"Ask them to wait, and hold my calls."

"The appointment's with Judge Patrick. You're supposed to be in his chambers."

Grady ran his hand through his hair. He had forgotten. "Show Miss Fitzgerald in and call Judge Patrick's secretary. Tell him I'll be delayed five minutes."

He stood to open the door for Anna and saw immediately that she had been crying. He took her in his arms as if it were the most natural thing in the world. "What is it?"

"Grady, I've got to have a place to get away for a few days. Can I use your cabin?"

"What on earth is wrong?"

"I can't tell you. Trust me, please."

He felt her trembling against him. Whatever had happened had devastated her. He wanted to push her to tell him what was wrong, but he was afraid to, for fear she might crumple completely. "Can you find your way up there all right?"

"My sense of direction is perfect."

He felt in his pocket for his key ring and pulled it out. He held the keys behind Anna's back so that he wouldn't have to let go of her and slid the cabin key off the ring. He hesitated, then slid the Audi key off, too. "Here's the key, and the car key, too. My Audi's parked on the third level in the building garage. Take it. I don't want you driving your car that far."

"I couldn't—"

"You have to. Give me your key and I'll have someone take your car home after work. Are you parked on the street?" He waited for her nod. "Are you taking Ryan?"

"I was going to. But Isabella's going to keep him. She insisted."

"That's wise. You're not in any shape to have to worry about him out there." He held her at arm's length and lifted her chin so that she was looking at him. "Can't you tell me anything?"

She shook her head. Her eyes were wild.

"Are you going to be able to drive?"

"I'll go slowly."

"Be careful. The Audi's a power machine."

"Thank you." She felt in her pocket for her car keys and thrust them at him. Then she burst into tears again.

He didn't want to let her go, but he knew he had little choice. "Call me," he said. "There's a phone in town, but none at the cabin. Call me tomorrow. Promise?"

She nodded.

He pulled out a handkerchief and gave it to her. "Don't drive until you've calmed down."

"I won't." She wiped her eyes with a trembling hand. Still clinging to his handkerchief, she turned and opened the door. "I'll call you tomorrow."

"I'll be waiting. Whatever is wrong can be fixed, Anna."

"You have no idea how impossible that is."

Grady put his hands on her shoulders. "I mean it. Whatever it is, I'll help you."

She didn't turn. "Nobody can help me, Grady. This one is all on me."

Chapter 9

Anna watched dense black thunderheads creep slowly across the darkening sky. The wind had picked up as she sat on the screened porch, until now the orange and lemon saplings that Grady had planted on the side of his cabin danced with frantic energy. One egret, who had stationed himself on the dock, had left minutes before for safer quarters, and now a flock of ducks was following his path.

In recent years storms had not held the threat for Anna that they had when she was living in parks and doorways. She could revel in their savage majesty, because now she was safe from their effects. Today the storm matched her mood. She was filled with pent-up energy waiting to explode. She had been at the cabin for two nights, and she was no closer to knowing what she should do about Krista than she had been when she came.

She had also, undoubtedly, lost her job. Tom was an understanding man, but she had left without a word while he was in the midst of trying to run a conference. She had called and left a message at First Day telling him that she wouldn't be back for a while, but she knew that her call wasn't going to be good enough.

She had called Ryan, too, on both days. He had told her that he was having fun at Isabella's and promised a surprise for her when she got back. There had been considerable background noise both times, as if Ryan were talking from a Times Square phone booth on New Year's Eve. With a mystifying ability to keep secrets, he had told her that the noise was just part of the surprise.

As promised, she had also called Grady. She'd had to speak to his answering machine, but at least she'd been able to leave a message telling him that she had arrived safely and settled into the cabin.

The conference would be over tomorrow at noon, but Anna knew her problems were just beginning. Jess Cantrell knew her identity, and by now Krista knew where her long-lost sister was living. Krista, who had denied Anna help at one of the most desperate moments of her life. Krista, who had forced her onto the streets and into the arms of Gray Moon.

According to Jess, Krista regretted her part in Anna's disappearance. If what he said was true, Krista had struggled to find Anna, emptying her back account and putting her own life in danger. Which, by anybody's standards, was enough penance to pay for forgiveness.

Except that Anna couldn't bring herself to forgive. Apparently now Krista knew that Anna hadn't lied about their stepfather and was guilt-ridden that she hadn't believed Anna's pleas. But Anna tried to imagine telling Krista she was forgiven. There were no words inside her to do it. She had suffered the existence of the damned. The person she had loved and trusted most in the world had condemned her to hell.

There were other memories, though. They filtered in through the anger and pain. Memories of Krista slipping into bed with her at night after she had suffered a nightmare. Memories of Krista attending her school plays, her softball games. Krista drilling her before spelling tests and defending her from other little girls who told her she was stupid. Krista who had been the one to explain about boys and moods and growing up.

She had no such memories of her mother. After her father's death, Anna had been little more than invisible to Sonya Jensen. Then, after Sonya's marriage to Hayden Barnard, Anna had been nothing more than an inconvenience, best swept under the rug and pulled out and dusted off for social occasions.

Her mother was dead now. Anna had seen an article in the paper after Sonya's fatal heart attack two years ago. Anna had been curiously numb for days, but when she had finally mourned, it had been for the mother she had never had, the woman who would have protected and nurtured her. The woman who *should* have protected her from Hayden Barnard, and hadn't.

All her warm memories, then, were of Krista. She had loved Krista, and the love she had felt had made Krista's betrayal so terrible that now she couldn't forgive her.

Forgiveness, or lack of it, was only part of the problem, however. She had been in such a state of shock that Jess's story had only made partial sense to her. He claimed he and Krista had searched for her, then stopped because Hayden Barnard had convinced them that he would kill her if they continued.

How much could she believe? How much could she afford not to? She was established in Ponte Reynaldo. She had a job she loved and a place to live. She had wonderful child care for Ryan and a university nearby where she could slowly complete her education. Those opportunities wouldn't be waiting for her anywhere else. She would start again from zero.

And she would lose Grady.

She needed Grady now. She needed his wisdom and his cool head. She needed his comforting arms around her. How could you grow to need someone so quickly? She had known him for just a month, yet now he seeemd the only person who could help her make sense of her situation. She couldn't drag him into it, though. Knowing her identity would put him in danger, and it could have far-reaching effects on his political career. After all, the next president of the United States was bound to have some clout. Even in Sun County.

In every way she was the worst woman in the world for him.

Rain began to splatter the porch with giant drops. The storm was a typical Florida cloudburst. The air was already redolent with ozone and the dark, vital fragrance of rain-nourished foliage. Lightning split the sky overhead, and Moss Run Creek leapt and tossed in wild abandon.

She watched intently. The storm would depart as suddenly as it had blown in, yet while it pelted the earth with rain and tortured the creek with wind and lightning, it was hard to imagine that it hadn't always been there, or that it would ever disappear.

She heard a long bang coming somewhere from the back of the house and remembered that the door didn't always fasten securely when it was closed. Since she had been out to call Ryan this morning, she had probably neglected to shut it tight, and now it was being tossed by the wind.

Halfway through the house to fasten the door, she found a rain-soaked, cursing Grady. The cursing stopped when he saw her. "Anna. Are you all right?"

It was a question with no answer. She stared at him and longed to fling herself into his arms.

There was only a short distance separating them, but Grady looked unsure he would be welcome if he breached it.

Anna found her voice. "Why are you here?"

His eyes devoured her. "I was worried about you."

She went to him, telling herself as she did that she just wanted to help him with his raincoat. Instead she went into his embrace. Her arms slid under his coat and around his waist. He held her tight, dripping water all over her. "I was worried," he repeated softly. "I got your message, but you hardly said anything."

"I didn't know what to say." She clung to him, moaning a protest deep in her throat when he finally moved far enough away to shrug out of his coat.

"I knocked before I came in. Were you out on the porch?"

"I was watching the storm."

"It's a bad one. I've been in it all the way from Ponte Reynaldo."

"Shouldn't you be at work?"

"I canceled my appointments." He held her close again. "Are you all right?" he repeated.

"I don't know."

"You've got to tell me what's wrong."

She burrowed closer. "I can't drag you into this."

"I'm already there." He brushed her hair with his fingers. "But I've got to know what's going on if I'm going to help."

"There's nothing I can tell you."

His patience deserted him. "You're going to tell me everything! Right from the beginning! And you aren't going to leave anything out. I'm sick of all the secrets, and whether you know it or not, you're sick of them, too. They're poisoning you. You've got to talk to somebody!"

"I've talked! Or rather, I've been talked to. That's the problem!" Anna pushed away from him. "This is more than my need for secrecy. Your future could be at stake. My life could be at stake."

He struggled to be calm. "I'm in your life. If you're in trouble, I'm already involved. Can't you see that? How can *not* knowing the truth protect me? The best kind of trouble is the kind you can plan for!"

Anna realized he was right. She'd seen it herself in her brief moments of clear thinking. And she'd seen what she had to do about it. Unless she moved a thousand miles from Ponte Reynaldo, Grady's future, maybe even his safety, could very well be destroyed. As long as she stayed nearby he would continue to seek her out. They were already walking the tightrope between love and friendship.

If Hayden Barnard knew her whereabouts, he also knew the people she was close to.

"Anna. You've got to tell me everything."

The truth hadn't been this clear to her before. Grady might already be in danger. Even if she was gone, the wheels of injustice might already be turning, and his career, even his life, might be ground beneath them. Keeping the truth from him would ensure that he couldn't fight. He wouldn't even suspect who his opponents were.

She had no choice. She had to tell him the truth.

But she couldn't bear to begin. She delayed. "I'll make you some coffee." She started toward the kitchen. Grady followed right behind. Anna detoured by the bathroom and got him a towel. "If you're going to hear the story of my life, you ought to be dry."

"Then you're going to talk to me?"

"I have to."

He sat down at the table and toweled his hair dry as Anna moved nervously around the kitchen, brewing coffee. She brought two mugs to the table, then thought better of it. The storm was still raging, and it suited her emotions better than the silent kitchen. "Let's take this out to the porch. Unless you're too chilled?"

Grady noted the way she had distanced herself from him. But there was something besides politeness flickering in her eyes. Desperation. Despair. Fear. He wanted to force the truth from her in a rush, but he knew better than to try. She would have to do this her way and in her own time. All he could do was wait.

He followed her to the porch. Waves from Moss Run Creek were washing over his dock, and the rain was eroding the creek banks.

"The storm will move on," she said softly. "And everything it touched will recover."

"Not recover. Grow. Improve."

"Not if the storm's been bad enough."

He knew they weren't talking about the Florida cloudburst. "Tell me about your storm."

Anna sat on the swing. Grady joined her.

She tried to think where she would begin. Somehow it seemed important to tell him everything. Some things were important for him to hear, and some were just important for her to share.

She began at the beginning. "I was born in Minnesota. My father died when I was just a toddler. My mother was a woman who believed she had to have a man to take care of her. When she had to go to work after Daddy's death, she couldn't cope very well. She withdrew from my sister and me. Krista was six years older than I was. She just about raised me."

"Krista. A Scandinavian name?"

"My real name is Roseanna Jensen. I was always called Rosie." Anna felt such a flood of emotion at just admitting that fact out loud that she had to stop to gather her forces for the rest.

Grady suspected what it must feel like to utter her own name after all these years. In a way, saying it out loud was taking it back. "It's lovely."

"It doesn't belong to me anymore. Roseanna Jensen died." She stared at the rain swollen creek and wondered how she could tell the rest.

Grady sat silently, waiting until she began again.

"I was a handful for Krista to raise. I'm sure she must have resented such a big burden. She was an *A* student in school, and everybody loved her. On the other hand, I never could seem to learn what I needed to know. I was the scourge of the classroom. Early on I decided I was just stupid and worthless. Krista tried to help, but she was only six years older than me. She was a kid, too."

Grady hoped he would never be forced to be in the same room with Anna's mother. He knew better than to try to comfort Anna now, but he draped his arm over the back of the swing, just to remind her that even immersed in bad memories, she wasn't alone.

"Krista went away to college just when I hit my teens. I probably would have gone through adolescence with no supervision except that my mother remarried." She pushed herself off the swing and walked to the edge of the porch. It didn't matter that rain was filtering through the screens. She couldn't sit still. She felt sick, as if a festering sore was being drained. There would be no turning back after she told Grady who her stepfather was. Her secret would be exposed. She shut her eyes. Indecision made her hesitate. Outside, lightning split the black sky.

"She married Hayden Barnard." The words were uttered in little more than a whisper.

"Anna?" Grady came to stand beside her. He couldn't believe what he had heard.

"You heard me right," she acknowledged. "My stepfather is Hayden Barnard."

Gently, he turned her face to him. "If your stepfather is the most powerful senator in Washington, how in God's name did you end up out on the streets?"

"He put me there."

He searched her face and silently cursed the pain he saw.

She shrugged off his hand and turned back to the storm. "He seemed the perfect stepfather at first. Kind, considerate, interested in me. He sensed how detached my mother was from my life, and he took up the slack. Somehow he pulled enough strings to have me admitted to one of the best private schools in the city. They took one look at me and sent me for two days of testing. That's when someone finally figured out that I was a smart kid who had learning disabilities."

She began to talk faster, as if speed would make the rest of it easier to say. "They worked out an individual education program for me. They bombarded me with speech and hearing therapists, special tutors and techniques. For the first time I began to really learn. I improved by leaps and bounds. The whole world opened up to me. I started feeling good about myself."

Grady sensed she was telling him this because, somehow, the achievements she had managed had made the rest of the story worse.

She went on. "I saw everything good that was happening as Hayden's doing. Finally I had a parent who cared enough about me to try and see beyond the bad grades and the bad attitude. Hayden had my undying loyalty. I would have walked over hot coals for him." She laughed, and the sound twisted Grady's heart. "Unfortunately, Hayden didn't want anything that minor. He had something else in mind."

Grady knew what she was going to say. Sometime during the first year of his career as a prosecutor he had lost his belief that all people were basically good. Some weren't, and some of *them* were in charge of the nation. He tried to say something, anything, that might comfort her, but no words came.

"Hayden's fatherly pats and hugs gradually became more intimate," Anna said, no emotion in her voice. "I was very naive. He made me uncomfortable, but I told myself that he just cared about me, like he'd care about his real daughter if he had one. I hadn't had a father since I was out of diapers. I just didn't remember how fathers acted."

Grady found his voice. "The bastard."

"It finally got the point where I couldn't pretend anymore. And Hayden stopped pretending, too. He told me in no uncertain terms what he wanted from me and what he would do if he didn't get it." She put her hand against the screen to steady herself. If there was no emotion in her voice, it was still inside her, tearing her to pieces. "I got away from him that night. I ran to Krista's. I told her everything that had been happening. She had always been the one to protect me. I believed she would again." Her voice broke, and all the emotion came pouring through. "She told me to go home! She even called my mother and told her to come pick me up. Krista said that Hayden Barnard was the best thing that had ever happened to our family, and she wasn't going to let me destroy him or my mother with lies."

She put her face in her hands and began to sob. "She didn't believe me!"

Grady's arms went around her, and he turned her so that she could sob against him. "Anna."

She heard sorrow, but she also heard fury at the man who had abused her. "She didn't believe me!"

He tried to imagine what that had done to the vulnerable teenager Anna had been. "What did you do?"

"My mother came to pick me up. She...she was livid with anger. She told me I was an ungrateful brat. I...I broke down and told her the truth. I was desperate! Of course she told me she didn't believe me. She told me if I breathed a word of my lies to anybody, she'd have me put in a psychiatric hospital. She wasn't going to let me ruin Hayden's career."

He stroked her hair, her back. "Did she know the truth?"

Anna had asked herself that question over and over. "I don't know." She almost left it at that, but she wanted him to know the worst. "I think she suspected."

He held her tighter and thrust his own anger away. There would be time to deal with his feelings about Anna's mother later. "Was that when you ran away?"

"I barricaded myself in my room, but I knew it was only a matter of time before Hayden found a way to get me alone. That night I waited until everyone was sleeping and I left."

He remembered the rest of the story all too clearly. "Did you ever try to go back home?"

"Never!"

Grady tried to digest what she had told him. He was no fan of Hayden Barnard's, but he had a certain expectation that senators, even senators whose political stance was contrary to his own, were men and women of high moral standards—even if that expectation had been proved wrong more than once. It was hard to imagine Hayden Barnard with such a crucial, visible fault. But it wasn't impossible. How could her mother and sister have condemned her to suffer at his hands?

"What stirred this up now?" he murmured into her hair. "You've lived with it all these years. Is it because Barnard's so close to winning the presidential nomination? He was a candidate for nomination last election. You must have suspected he'd have a good chance this time."

Anna couldn't answer until she knew one thing. "Do you believe me?"

He held her away from him. "Of course!" He still saw doubt in her red-rimmed eyes. "Anna, I don't doubt your integrity. Doubting Barnard's isn't hard at all."

She tried to smile, but couldn't manage it. "Do you know just how powerful he is?"

"I have a good idea." He hesitated, then told her the truth. "I've met him. He's charming, but there's something not so charming behind the facade. I know he can be ruthless."

"I know how sick he is. I wish I knew how ruthless." She swallowed more sobs.

"What brought all this up?" he asked gently.

In as few words as possible she told him what had occurred with Jess.

He tried to put her life together in seconds. He understood her despair now. And he was just beginning to understand something else. "Then your life could be in danger."

"If Hayden knows where I am. But it's worse than that. Ryan could be in danger, too. That's how Hayden would get to me. I know how he works. You could be in danger, too. What if he suspects that you know my past? He won't want you telling anybody."

"You told me your story to protect me." He realized for the first time what telling him had cost her. And she had told it to him so that he would know what he might be up against.

"And so you'd know why I have to leave Florida." Anna swallowed another sob. "I see that now. I have to leave and hope that I can run far enough and fast enough to escape him. And I have to get out of your life, Grady. Can you see what he might do to you?"

"You're not going anywhere." He tightened his grip on her arms. "You're not going to run again. If you do, it won't just be Barnard looking for you."

"Don't be a fool! Hayden can say the word and your career will be a memory!"

"Better my career than you!" He pulled her close again, but not to comfort her. He kissed her, denying her choice.

She struggled until she knew it was futile. Even as she sagged against him, she knew she hadn't struggled against the kiss or the man, she had struggled against the fate that doomed her to leave him.

"We'll work this out," Grady said, his lips soothing, healing, everywhere they touched. "But you're not going to leave. Do you hear me?"

Anna wrapped her arms around his neck. The secrets that had been a wall separating them were secrets no longer. Her burden was shared.

He kissed her again, and this time she responded with all the desperation she felt. The future was an unknown. No matter what Grady said, she couldn't be responsible for putting him in danger. For this moment, though, she was hungry for the comfort, the love, she felt in his touch. She'd had no comfort since Matt's death. And love was something she'd never known. Not this kind of love. Not love that filled her with such force it threatened to burst its bounds.

Grady forgot where he was. He forgot that the storm was spraying them with rain through the screens. He forgot that he had told himself to go slowly with Anna, to let their relationship develop and grow before he asked anything of her. As he kissed her, he remembered the torture he had felt the first time he'd touched her, the longing unlike any he'd ever known. Now she was in his arms again, and he knew that whatever else their future held, she was going to be his.

His hand slid under her T-shirt from her waist to the soft, smooth skin of her back. She was as pliable to his touch as clay to a sculptor's hands. She moved against him, letting him know in every way that she wanted him, too. He slipped the shirt over her head, and only when it was off and her skin wet with raindrops did he remember the storm.

He lifted her easily, still kissing her. Lightning split the sky as he carried her inside to his bedroom. He laid her on the bed, falling down beside her as he did.

Anna fumbled for the buttons on Grady's shirt. Her life had been made of lightning and thunder, yet she had never felt the storm inside her before. There had always been thought and the slow suffering of icy rain. Now there was no thought, just the blazing heat and shock of lightning, the mind-numbing roar of thunder.

Some part of her knew that she was making Grady a promise. She had given up her secrets; now she was surrendering her body. Her heart would go with it. She was binding herself to him, but she felt no fear. When his chest was bare, she greedily stroked her hands over him, and when they were both naked, she breathed and absorbed and consumed the very essence of him.

He was heat and strength and mysterious male. He was hard where she was not, strong in ways that surprised her. He was elemental, primitive urge and need, and she bent to him as she made her own needs known. She explored her own body through him, shifted and moaned and gave back the pleasure he gave her.

Grady knew without conscious thought that they were moving too quickly toward that which should be savored. He guessed that Anna hadn't been with a man since before Ryan's birth, yet going slowly was out of the question. All he could do was assuage the terribly empty ache inside him with the feel of her flesh, the scent of her, the taste.

Her breasts were full and rose-tipped, her waist narrow, her hips gently rounded. He followed her contours with his hands and lips, thrilling to her responsiveness. They were new lovers, yet it was as if they had always been together, always known what pleased each other.

Anna wanted no part of patience, no hint of restraint. Restraint was thought, and she wanted nothing but feeling. Grady was hers for this moment. She wanted the moment, wanted to freeze it and capture him forever.

She wrapped her legs around him, shuddering at his groan of protest. She circled him with her arms and captured the groan against her lips. When he finally made them one, she was more than ready for him. She had been ready for him forever.

Through all the lonely, hellish years, she had been waiting for Grady. And in the moment when he became part of her, she knew that she would choose to suffer those years again if they would lead her to this place and time.

The storm had passed by the time Grady awakened. Sun filtered through the blinds, and judging from the music outside the window, the birds had returned. Anna lay beside him, her head pillowed against his shoulder, her leg curled intimately over his.

Grady thought about the person he had always been. He had prided himself on doing what was right, on being rational and objective. He had almost married Susan because it had seemed the right thing to do. He had exposed Harry Traltor for the same reason, and now he was challenging Rand Garner because that, too, was right.

His life had been led without passion, except for a passion for justice. But all this time there had been a stranger living inside him. That stranger had taken control with Anna.

Long live the stranger.

Anna shifted restlessly. Even in sleep she was constantly moving. She was filled with energy; she gave him energy. When he was with her he felt as if he could move mountains and charge windmills.

Hayden Barnard was a windmill in need of charging.

She shifted once more. Still snuggled against her, he could feel her body coming awake by degrees. She stiffened slowly, as if she was just beginning to realize what she had done and where she was. When she began to move away from him, he captured her with one arm.

"You're not leaving," he said.

The confident, powerful woman who had made love to him was gone. "Didn't you hear anything I told you? What are we doing?"

His voice was a caress. "I can explain it to you if you really need to know."

She tried to move away. "I can't jeopardize your life or your future."

He kept her close. "If you leave, I'll come after you. And I'll find you."

"I told you about Hayden to protect you!"

"Now let me protect you."

"That's impossible."

"Anna." He turned so that they were face to face. It was a struggle. "You've got to think carefully. Start with what you know. Hayden Barnard has every reason to want you dead."

She shuddered.

He was filled with remorse, but he had to continue. "And according to your brother-in-law, at one time, at least, Barnard knew where you were. He found you. Didn't Cantrell say that Barnard even had photographs to prove it?"

"What are you trying to say?"

"He should have had you killed to keep you quiet. He knew where you were, and we know he's powerful enough to arrange the murder of a street kid and never be suspected." He paused for effect. "You're still alive."

"Don't you think I've thought of that?"

"And what did you conclude?" He tipped her head to his. Her face was still flushed with sleep, her hair a rumpled golden mop. He felt a wave of desire and knew that he would never have enough of her. But he intended to make the effort.

"I don't know!"

"There are two possibilities. Either he lost track of you before he could have you killed, or he still has some scruples."

She stared at him.

"We know he's a sick man," Grady said. "We don't know that his sickness reaches so deeply inside him that he would murder his own stepdaughter because she might be a threat."

"He would do anything!"

She said the words with such venom that Grady knew she believed them. "Think about this, then. Cantrell and your sister are still alive."

"That's no proof that he still has some kind of conscience. Jess Cantrell's a famous man and nobody's fool. He must have protected himself somehow, and protected my sister, too.'' For the first time Anna thought about all the danger Krista had placed herself in, not only the danger of the streets, but the danger from Hayden. And despite the threats Hayden must have made against them, Krista and Jess had still searched for evidence. For four years they had been trying to find a way to force Hayden to find her.

Grady watched Anna trying to make sense of something that was senseless. Her emotions were clearly visible. She was no longer the woman who hid her feelings behind a wall built with years of hard-earned wariness. She trusted him. ''I can guess how he protected himself.''

''How?''

''Cantrell has this entire story on file somewhere, with his attorney, probably. If he and your sister die, the attorney has instructions to reveal what he has and begin an inquiry. Barnard knows it.''

''But what would be gained? What proof would there be that Jess had been telling the truth?'' Anna answered her own question, almost before it was finished. ''It wouldn't matter, would it? There'd be such bad publicity for Hayden, he'd lose every election, even if there was no proof.''

''Men have gone down to defeat on less.''

''Jess wanted me to go public with my story.'' Anna sat up, then suddenly realized that she was wearing nothing. She pulled the sheet around her breasts.

''I liked you better the other way.''

She didn't look at him, but her cheeks heated. She continued as if he hadn't spoken. ''I didn't understand why. Not really. But I do now. It would give me a measure of protection if I did.''

''It might.'' Grady sat up and wrapped his arms around her, pulling her back against him.

''My sister's life was in danger.'' Anna turned her face to his chest. ''She spent months looking for me. She could have been killed.''

''From what you've told me, she's never really stopped looking.''

''Why did she send me away that night?''

He knew he was hearing the Roseanna Jensen who had never really died, no matter what Anna claimed. "Because she hadn't lived what you had. Maybe, like most of us, she didn't want to believe something so terrible."

"It was true."

"You're as old now as she was then. Is it always so easy for you to tell the truth from a lie? It seems to me that Krista made a tragic mistake, but not because she didn't love you. When she sent you back home, it was because she believed that was where you belonged. I can only guess, but maybe she was thinking that you had to face whatever was wrong and learn to deal with it. Isn't that what you try to teach the kids at First Day?"

"Not if what's at home is so bad it'll destroy them."

"But how do you determine that? How can you? Sometimes you have to make guesses, based on what you know. Krista probably never saw the side of Hayden that you did."

"I *know* she didn't."

Grady heard Anna defending Krista, even if she didn't realize it. "Then she didn't have much to go on, and she made a bad guess. But not because she didn't love you. It was a bad guess based on love. And later when she realized that, she gave up everything to try to find you."

"I trusted her."

"You trusted her to love you. She did. The problem is, you also trusted her to be perfect, and she wasn't."

"I *loved* her."

"You still do." Grady turned her face to his. "You have to see her."

"I can't."

"I'll be with you."

"I can't drag you into it!"

"Haven't you noticed I'm already involved?" He kissed her until she was pliant in his arms. "We'll fly to Virginia and face her together."

"This has to be my decision."

"I know. I've already made mine."

Anna searched his face, trying to read his thoughts. "What decision, Grady?"

"I'm not going to let you run away again. I'm part of your life now, and I'm not going to let you leave me. We'll find a way to keep you safe and keep you here."

She had no more strength to argue. She had been alone with her fears and torment since the day she had left her stepfather's home. Even Matt hadn't known her full story. Now, in spite of everything she had told him, Grady was standing beside her.

She didn't want to leave Sun County, and she didn't want to leave Grady. As he kissed her again, she knew that the time for running had ended. And maybe, just maybe, the time for trusting had begun.

Chapter 10

Grady parked the Audi outside Anna's house. The morning air was already scalding. Four doors down on the other side of the street, a nearly naked toddler played in a sprinkler while her mother watched from the porch.

"I'd like to see Ryan." Grady laid his hand possessively on Anna's shoulder. "Unless you want some time alone with him."

Anna was in no hurry to say goodbye to Grady. They had spent the night together, then, reluctantly, driven the Audi back to the city this morning. The car Grady had borrowed from his parents to drive to the cabin would be picked up later by someone from his office.

Anna wasn't really ready to be back in Ponte Reynaldo, but she hadn't wanted to be away from Ryan any longer. She also knew she had to face Tom Schneider to give him an abbreviated account of why she had left so precipitously. Grady had to be at his campaign headquarters by one.

"He'd like to see you." Anna smiled. She wanted to lean over and kiss him, but they weren't at the cabin anymore. They were in the city Grady served, and Anna didn't want their relationship to be public.

"Isabella knew you were coming?"

"I hope so. When I called from the service station this morning, I left a message with the man who answered."

Grady raised an eyebrow. Anna had told him Isabella's story. "A man? Is she getting back at Enrique?"

"That wouldn't be like her. I'm guessing that it was a relative. She's got a large family, and they've been trying to immigrate. Maybe someone made it through."

"Maybe I'd better not go in."

"Why not?"

"I'm the law, remember?"

It took Anna a moment to understand. "You think they might be illegal?"

"They wouldn't be the first."

She considered. "Would you have to ask?"

He considered. "No."

"Then don't." Anna put her hand over his and squeezed. "Come on. We'll get Ryan and take him to my place. You can stay outside on the porch if you'd rather."

"I just might."

Grady followed Anna up the steps and stood beside her as she knocked on Isabella's door. There was a low buzz of voices from the house. "Has she ever told you how many relatives might try to come?" Grady asked.

"I don't think she can count that high in English."

The door was flung open. A man with dark curly hair and a heart-melting smile stood on the other side of it. "You're Anna." His voice was pleasantly accented.

Anna recognized him immediately, both from the photograph that Isabella kept on her dresser and from their nodding acquaintance when he had first moved in next door—before he deserted his wife and child. She drew herself up to her full height and nodded coldly. "Enrique."

"Isabella!" He made music of his wife's name, then turned back to Anna. "Please come in."

She did, with Grady following, and she was immediately attacked by two small, warm bodies. Teresa clung to one leg and Ryan to the other.

"Teresa's daddy is home again," Ryan announced.

Anna looked around. Teresa's daddy wasn't the only one home. The small house was filled with people, and obviously none of them was paying a social call. They had moved in. There were sleeping bags in neat rolls on the floor and makeshift luggage in every corner.

"Anna!" Isabella came from the kitchen, drying her hands on a dish towel. Her eyes were shining.

"I told you there was a surprise," Ryan crowed.

"Anna, meet my family," Isabella said proudly. As if on cue, people began to line up for introductions. Isabella reeled off their names and status. There were her brother and his wife and baby son, two of Enrique's sisters, a cousin of both of them with three stair-step children but no husband, and two of Enrique's aunts. At the end of the line was a middle-aged woman with short silver hair and Isabella's features. "And this is the woman Enrique has been living with," Isabella said, tears coming to her eyes. "My mother."

Anna's gaze flew to Enrique's face. He looked both sad and proud, a combination she would have believed impossible. "Your mother?" she asked.

"Enrique brought them out. He couldn't tell me why he went back. He knew I'd try to stop him because it was so dangerous. And there are..." She searched for the right word. "Spies here? People who might have learned what he was doing. So he lied."

"Not really a lie," Enrique said, going to stand behind Isabella to rest his hands on her big belly. "Just not the whole truth."

"How did you get them all out?" Anna asked.

Before anyone could answer, the door clicked shut behind Anna. She turned and saw that Grady was gone.

"Is your friend all right?" Enrique asked.

Anna understood. Grady had not wanted to hear any details of their trip over the border. She felt a glow of warmth, because she knew how he valued the law. She explained to the others.

"We were some of the lucky ones. We can prove that our lives would be in danger if we stayed. We are all going to

Canada," Enrique told her when she had finished. "There is an organization helping us. We are just here temporarily. Tell your friend that the paperwork is already begun, and we are in this country as visitors."

After she had congratulated them all, the impact of what Enrique had said finally hit. "Isabella, you're going, too?" Anna asked.

"After the baby is born, yes."

"What will I do without you?"

"You will come and visit, no? You will bring Ryan so that he and Teresa can play."

Anna stifled the urge to wallow in self-pity. She didn't begrudge her friend her happiness, and it was clear that Isabella was beyond happy. For a while she had stopped believing in Enrique, but she had never stopped loving him.

"I'll miss you, but I'll come and visit. I've always wanted to see Canada." Anna hugged Isabella; then, on impulse, she hugged Enrique, too. The relatives were all chatting in Spanish, and despite her lessons with Isabella, Anna couldn't understand a word. If Isabella's leaving was a devastating blow, at least it kept Anna from having to fumble with a language she would probably never learn.

Outside, Grady was waiting on the porch with Ryan. Anna realized she was interrupting a man-to-man talk about fathers and why some kids had them and some didn't. Grady had lifted Ryan to the porch railing, and the two were eye-to-eye.

"Your father died before you were born," Grady was saying.

"Then he can't be my father. Fathers live with you."

Anna waited to see how Grady would handle that one without explaining the birds and the bees.

He managed neatly. "Was Enrique Teresa's father when he was away?"

Ryan screwed up his face in thought. "Yes."

"Your father is still your father, even though he died. In a sense, your father is just away, too."

"I don't want him to be away. Will he come back like 'Rique did?"

"No. He can't."

"Then can I have another one?"

"Sometimes that happens."

Ryan caught sight of Anna. "Can I?"

"I don't know."

"Maybe for Christmas?"

She managed a smile. Whenever Ryan wanted something she couldn't afford just then, she always told him, "Maybe for Christmas." Now she tried to explain. "Father's don't come in boxes with ribbons, bunny-nose."

Ryan might have pursued the subject, but at that moment Teresa wandered out on the porch carrying a flour tortilla wrapped around a filling that immediately permeated the air with a mouth-watering fragrance. Without another word, Ryan disappeared inside to claim his share.

Anna watched him go. "I'm going to have to get all Isabella's recipes before she leaves."

"Leaves?"

"They're all going to Canada. Don't worry. They're here legally. At least, sort of."

"I'm glad to hear it. What will you do with Ryan?"

"He's old enough for a day-care center. He could use the enrichment if I can find a good one." She leaned against him and put her arms around his waist. "I'm going to miss Isabella."

"Are you going to leave Ryan here now?"

"He'll throw a fit if I try to remove him before he has lunch. I'm going home to unpack."

"I'll walk you over."

They covered the short distance arm in arm. Anna had unlocked the door and gone inside before she noticed a change had been made. A brand new air conditioner perched cheerfully in the window. If she had been paying attention she would have seen it from Isabella's porch.

"Did you have anything to do with this?" she asked Grady.

"Not as much as you think."

Anna walked through the tiny house and found another air conditioner in Ryan's bedroom. "How much?" she asked.

"A phone call."

"To who?"

"Your landlord."

Anna was more intrigued than irritated. "How did you know who he was?"

"I had an assistant look it up in the records at city hall."

"What did you say to him?"

"I just told him who I was. I told him a friend of mine lived in one of his houses and desperately needed air-conditioning. I told him if he wasn't willing to have two window units installed, I was going to do it and I'd need a key." He paused. "Then I just happened to mention that I'd be sending an inspector in first to be sure the wiring was up to code before they were installed."

Anna could imagine her landlord's reaction. "He was probably out the door and at the store before you hung up."

"I've got an electrician scheduled to come tomorrow, anyway, just to check things out." He held up his hands to ward off her retort. "Anna, please don't argue. If anything happened to you or Ryan, I don't know what I'd do. I'm going to have a locksmith coming, too."

She knew her revelations about her stepfather had prompted the second. She wanted to be angry, but she couldn't be. "You're messing with my life."

With some guilt, Grady reflected that Anna had no idea how *much* he was going to mess with it, but he knew that now wasn't the time to tell her. She would find out soon enough. "What are you going to do now?"

"I'm going to call Tom and tell him I'll be in to talk to him tomorrow."

"You'll be around for the rest of the day?"

"I want to spend some time with Ryan."

"Why don't you fix me dinner tonight?"

She gave him a slow smile. "You like my cooking, don't you?"

He did, as a matter of fact. She had a natural flair that made even ordinary foods special. But he liked the woman even more. He pulled her into his arms and kissed her with a hunger that had nothing to do with dinner.

"You're sure you can spare another night away from the campaign?" she asked when he had reluctantly stepped away.

"The next few weeks will be grueling. Let's grab what time we can."

"Just be careful. The papers have already picked up your broken engagement. I don't want to be fingered as the other woman. Especially now."

Grady understood what she was saying. Not only did she believe her past would be a serious detriment to his winning the primary, she wanted to be certain that nothing drew attention to her. The threat from Hayden Barnard was too great.

"Tonight." He leaned over to kiss her again, then left her staring at the air conditioner.

At his campaign headquarters, Grady closed his door on three people with urgent messages, then consulted his phone book and dialed the number he had sought.

Five minutes later he hung up the phone, his business completed. Then, with effort, he put Anna out of his mind. His evening would be consumed with her. Right now, somehow, he had to try to campaign for State's Attorney again.

Krista emerged from the jetway at the Ponte Reynaldo airport and scanned the crowd at the arrival gate for Jess. He was behind a group of chattering teens. His latest book was a departure from his previous ones. Instead of an exposé, he was writing about the values American society imparted to the young. She guessed that he was listening intently to what the kids were saying. If Jess were locked away in a padded cell, he would come out of the experience with a book about the effects of mattresses, window bars and institutional food on the human psyche. And it would be a bestseller.

He left his teenage subjects behind as soon as he saw her and wrapped his arms around her for a welcoming hug. The hug was longer and fiercer than she had expected.

"I guess you missed me." Krista hugged him back.

"Yeah. I guess I did."

"Where's Tate?"

"She took a flight out this morning. She had to get back to write a term paper. I came over with her and rented a car to use while you're here."

"I'm sorry I missed her."

Jess led Krista through the crowd; then, arms around each other's waists, they started toward the baggage claim. "So how was the conference?" Krista asked. "Learn anything we can use?"

Jess wasn't about to tell her what he'd learned. Not here, anyway. "It was good. I could take you over to First Day for a look sometime over the weekend if you're interested."

"I think I'm going to forget about business while we're here and concentrate on my man."

"It's a short ride to the hotel."

"Not short enough."

Later, after a drive that had been decidedly over the speed limit and an hour's introduction to the blissful freedom of making love without a dozen squabbling teenagers nearby, they lay in each other's arms, replete.

"I guess you did miss me," Krista said sleepily.

Jess looked at the clock beside their bed and knew he couldn't delay telling her about Anna any longer. He had been practicing silently since the moment he had realized who Anna really was. He still didn't know what to say.

"Kris, I've got something to tell you." He sat up and pulled her against his chest. Her hair fanned over him like a pale golden cape.

"Sounds serious."

"Yeah." He could feel her body becoming more alert. He locked his arms around her to keep her against him.

"Is this going to spoil our day? Because if it is, I don't want to hear it."

"It's about Rosie." He heard and felt her quick indrawn breath. "She's here," he went on, before she could think the worst. "She's very much alive. In fact, she's the assistant director of First Day."

Krista sat up, pushing his arms away. "When did you find out?"

"The minute I got off the plane. She was there to meet us."

"Why didn't you call me?"

He pushed a lock of her hair behind one ear. "She doesn't want to see you, Kris. She wouldn't even admit who she was." He watched her expression change by degrees. He wanted to shut his eyes to her agony.

"Are you sure it's her?"

"There's no question." He told her what he'd learned from Tom Schneider, finishing with the fact that Rosie had a four-year-old son.

"And she knows you know?"

"I confronted her. She was upset." He thought about how inadequate that word was. "She left town right afterward, but she's back now."

"How do you know?"

"A friend of hers called me today." He suspected that "friend" was another inadequate word. Grady Clayton had sounded much too concerned to be a friend. "He wanted me to go to her house with him tonight. I told him you'd be here, too. He wants us both to go."

"Does Rosie know?"

"No."

"What should we do?" Krista was obviously distraught.

Jess didn't know what to say to make her feel better. "I think it has to be up to you."

"I don't know what to do!"

"Kris, less than a week ago we didn't know if Rosie was even alive. Now we know she's not only alive, but well and happy, too. No matter what happens next, you've got to remember that."

Krista's mind was racing full speed ahead. "If you found her, my stepfather could find her, too. What if he's having us watched? What if he finds out Rosie's living here?"

"Even Barnard doesn't have the resources to have us watched every day for five years. I think he gave up long ago. If anything, he has us investigated periodically. But there's no reason to think that he followed me here. I found her purely by accident. And after all, this wasn't a mystery trip. My reason for being here was perfectly legitimate."

"Unless he knew Rosie was here already." Krista put her head in her hands. "She doesn't want to see me!"

Jess put his arms around her. "She was shocked. I'm sure that remembering the past is difficult."

"I know what she remembers!"

"By now she's remembered good things, too."

"Do you think we should go?"

He debated silently. "Grady Clayton thinks we should," he said at last. "I think we should trust him."

"She's alive. I've waited so long to know." Krista felt sobs begin deep inside her. In a moment she was weeping against Jess's chest.

He held her tight and hoped that Grady Clayton knew what he was doing.

Anna put the finishing touches on spaghetti sauce made with ground beef and smoked sausage, fresh tomatoes and her own combination of herbs and spices. At the kitchen table Ryan buttered French bread, getting most of the butter on the table.

"Grady should be here any time now," she said, glancing at the clock on her stove.

"I hope he brings ice cream."

"It would be a good day for it." Grady had called to tell Anna he was starved. He had promised to bring dessert.

"Why don't I have rel'tives?" Ryan asked.

Anna knew what had brought that question up. It was the same thing that had made him question Grady about fathers. Teresa had had no father and no relatives that Ryan had known about until two days ago. Now her house was overflowing with family. Ryan was wondering when his would be, too.

The question was a strange coincidence considering that Anna was now faced with the possibility of a reunion with Krista. She was no closer to making a decision as to what to do about her sister than she had been a minute after Jess told her who he had married.

"Why don't I?" Ryan repeated.

She couldn't tell the little boy that his father's family refused to acknowledge his existence. After Ryan's birth she had contacted them at Tom's urging. They had told her that since there was no proof the child was Matt's, they wanted nothing to do with him. As far as they were concerned, Matt had been dead since the day he left home, anyway.

And how could she tell Ryan that she couldn't take him to Minnesota, where she still had family, because if she did, his life might be in danger? Or that he had an aunt who reportedly wanted to meet him, but that Anna was too confused to allow it? Or that her stepfather would like her better dead?

There was nothing she could say that Ryan would understand. She tried a watered-down version of the truth. "You have relatives," she said, as calmly as she could. "They live far away, and we're not friends."

He appeared to think about that, scraping butter off the table and slapping it on the bread as he did. "That's bad," he said after a while. "You're s'posed to be friends."

She thought of Krista, who had always been more than a friend. Except once. One mistake. One mistake she had tried to atone for ever since. Krista who would be the kind of aunt a little boy needed.

Ryan put the French bread on the pan Anna had given him and carried it to the oven for her to heat.

"You should say sorry," he told her, lifting the pan to her outstretched arms. "That's what I do when Teresa and I fight."

She set the pan on top of the stove and stooped to give him a fierce hug. "Why don't you go out on the porch and wait for Grady?"

"Can I fish?" One of Ryan's favorite pastimes was using the rod Grady had given him to pretend-fish over the porch railing. He had been known to catch whales and sea serpents.

"Sure." Anna ruffled his hair and stood.

She was putting the bread in the oven when he ran by with the rod. The front door creaked open, and she heard the sound of voices. There was no way to make out what Ryan was saying over the noisy buzz of the living-room air conditioner, but she guessed that Grady had arrived. Deciding to give them a few moments alone together, she turned the water on the stove from medium to high and went to the cupboard for spaghetti.

She was waiting for the water to reach a full boil when she heard a noise behind her. There was a welcoming smile on her face when she turned.

Krista stood in the doorway. Alone. Anna stared at her.

Krista was the same, and yet not the same. Her hair was the remembered pale gold, still long, still wavy. She hadn't gained or lost more than a pound or two, and she still had a figure that any man would notice. She wore a soft yellow knit dress; yellow had always been her favorite color, probably because it suited her so well.

The differences were subtle. She was almost seven years older than she had been the day she had forced Anna to go back to her abusive stepfather. There was a new maturity about her, an elusive quality that had more to do with who she was than with the subtle changes of aging. She had once been soft and pliable. Now Anna guessed that she was formed of steel.

Anna looked her fill, then turned back to the stove. Her hand was shaking as she dropped the spaghetti in the boiling water. She took a deep breath, but it didn't calm her. "I don't remember inviting you here."

"I know. May I stay anyway?"

Anna reached for a spoon and began to stir the sauce—too fast. "Let me guess. Grady brought you. Is your husband here, too?"

"He and Grady took Ryan for a walk."

"Does Ryan know who you are?"

"No. I didn't think I should tell him."

Anna realized that the sauce was splattering the stove; she forced herself to stir slower. "It's funny, Ryan was just asking me about family and wondering why he didn't have any except me."

"What did you tell him?"

"I told him that I had family, but we weren't friends." She didn't add Ryan's answer.

"In all the years you stayed away, did you ever think how I must be feeling?"

Anna had expected an apology. Krista caught her off guard. "I imagined you were relieved," she said bitterly. "You didn't have to listen to my *lies* anymore."

"I was never relieved."

"Is guilty a better word, then?"

"Terrified."

"Well, I'm here, safe and sound. You don't have to be terrified anymore."

"Rosie, I'm still terrified. I'm terrified I've really lost you for good."

Anna turned just long enough to answer her. "My *name* is Anna."

"When you were little, I used to call you Anna sometimes. Do you remember? It was a game we played. You were Anna and I was Louise. We'd pretend we were society ladies having tea."

"I don't remember."

"Do you know I still pay an answering service in Maryland?" Krista walked across the room and leaned against the sink so that she could see her sister's face. Avidly she drank in all the changes. "When I moved in with Jess in Virginia, I was afraid you might try to call my Maryland number some night when you were lonely or desperate. So I had my number transferred to an answering service. Just in case."

"I was lonely and desperate plenty of times. I never thought about calling."

"What did you think I'd say if you did?"

Anna faced her. "I *knew* what you'd say. You'd say what you said to me the night I told you about Hayden. 'Go home, Rosie,'" she mimicked. "'You've had a fight with Hayden, but that's no reason to tell such hateful stories. You're going to have to grow up and take some responsibility!'"

Krista spoke softly. "I made a terrible mistake."

Anna set the spoon on the stove. Her hand was trembling too hard to stir any longer. "I know about mistakes, Krista! Shall I tell you about mine? The biggest was that I trusted Hayden. The next biggest was that I trusted you. When that didn't work, I hopped a bus to New York and trusted a guy named Gray Moon. Now that was a really big mistake!"

Krista was already pale, but she turned paler at Anna's words. "I met one of his girls when I was in New York looking for you. She showed me the jacket you had left there and told me you'd gone to New Orleans."

Anna knew there would be no pleasure in making Krista suffer through the details of what she had endured. "I ran away from him when I could. I met another runaway, Ryan's father, and we traveled together until he was killed. We were only in New Orleans for a week. We were through there a few times after that, but never to stay."

"I would do anything I could to give you back those years."

"You can't."

"What about the years ahead?"

Anna knew what Krista was asking. They stared at each other, two women in pain. Anna wanted to forgive. She believed in forgiveness, taught it to Ryan and the kids she worked with. Yet she couldn't find the words to forgive Krista. She had suffered too much, and she was suffering still. Suffering still.

"I think I was alone too long," she said at last. "I have Ryan now, and maybe even Grady. But I don't think I have room in my life for you."

"Room in your heart?"

Anna shrugged.

"Are you punishing me, Rosie?"

Anna didn't react to the name. She hardly noticed it. "I don't know."

"I have room in my heart for you because you've always been there. Even the night I told you to go back to Hayden, you were there. I was young and naive, but I thought I was doing what was best. Can you believe that?"

Anna wanted to believe it, but everything was still too new, and she was still too wounded. "I don't know what I believe," she said, turning back to the stove. "But right now I think it would be best if you left." She felt a hand on her arm, and her head snapped up.

"Will you be in touch?" Krista asked. There were tears in her eyes.

Anna's eyes flicked to the fingers lightly resting on her arm. Her skin and Krista's were an identical shade of ivory. She lifted her arm so that Krista's hand dropped away. "I don't have any answers."

"I'll be waiting for you to find some." Krista turned to go, and then, as if afraid she might never have another chance to say what was in her heart, she turned back. "You've grown into a beautiful woman. And Ryan is a beautiful little boy. You're so lucky to have him." Her voice caught.

Anna didn't want to know anything about Krista. Knowing about her, knowing about her life, would make her that much more real. But she couldn't stop herself from asking, "Do you and Jess have any children besides Tate?"

Krista smiled sadly. "I've been afraid to. A child would just be another weapon Hayden could use against us."

Anna hadn't given much thought to the way Hayden had threatened Krista's life, too. And it was only because Krista had searched for her.

How much penance did one person have to do to merit forgiveness? Anna stared at her sister, but through her own confusion and pain, the words just wouldn't come.

"Take care of yourself...Anna." Krista crossed the room. Anna heard the front door close.

She was staring out the window over the sink when Grady came into the kitchen a few minutes later. He put his arms around her waist, and she leaned back against him. "Did I make a mistake?" he asked.

She couldn't be angry with him. "You've appointed yourself my guardian."

"Your lover."

She struggled for control. "I didn't know what to say to her."

"Now that you've talked, maybe it will be easier to know what to say next time."

"She's suffered, too."

Grady laid his cheek against her hair. "If you can see that, then you've come a long way."

"I have a lot farther to go. Too far, maybe."

"Jess wants you to go public with your story about Barnard. He thinks it will protect you."

"Maybe that's part of it, but he also wants to stop him politically." Anna rested her hands on Grady's. She needed his arms around her right now, more than she wanted to admit. "I'm not going public, Grady."

"Why not?"

She turned so she could see his face. "I have no proof of anything I would say. Hayden's career might be ruined, and I might be protected, but my whole sordid background would be dragged out, too. I don't want to live with that kind of publicity. And I don't want you to live with it, either."

He knew she was thinking about his career. If she was worried about the effects on him, she was beginning to believe she might be a part of his life. He cupped her face in his hands. "You've got to do what's right, whatever you decide that is. My political career isn't the only thing to consider. Your safety and Ryan's have to be top priority."

"I've lived here since Ryan's birth. I've never been threatened. I'll be careful, but I'm not going to run, and I'm not going to give an interview. I'm just going to take each day and see what happens."

"If Barnard knows where you are, then he knows about me, too. He may or may not guess that you've told me who you are, but I don't think he'll take any chances. You're not a faceless runaway anymore. You have friends and a job, and you have the Sun County State's Attorney as your lover. I don't think he'll take the risk of harming you."

Anna's thoughts were back on Krista. She spoke, as if to herself. "Krista used to be so full of life. Tonight she was so..."

"Sad?"

"She asked me if I'd ever thought of what she must be suffering."

"And did you?"

"I thought she'd be glad I was gone."

"You were wrong."

"There was one time." Anna had never shared this with anyone; now she was grateful to be able to share it with Grady. "In Georgia somewhere, when Matt and I were traveling together. I was feeling ill because we hadn't eaten anything for two days, and I was just beginning to suspect I was pregnant. It was a weekend, and we found the shell of a new building to sleep in. Matt left me there to go out and find some food. He didn't come back that night because the cops picked him up. I didn't know what had happened, and there was no way to look for him. I stayed where he had left me because I was afraid I'd miss him when he came back. It took him two days to find a way to get out and come back for me. I almost phoned Krista then. I couldn't get her out of my mind. I kept hearing her call my name."

The last word trembled.

Grady wrapped his arms around her back and pulled her tight against him. "Maybe she *was* calling you."

Anna knew enough about his parents to try to joke. "You have more of your mother in you than you think."

He heard the tears in her voice. "Krista loves you. And you love her. Take some time. She'll be waiting for you."

The front door slammed, and jackhammer footsteps sounded through the living room. "That lady's nice! She gave me a present.'' Ryan came to a screeching halt at the stove. "Can I keep it?"

Anna looked down and saw a transparent carrying case filled with a dozen tiny cars. It was exactly the kind of gift Ryan liked best. "You can."

"I've got more cars. Wanna see?" Ryan grabbed Grady's hand to drag him into his bedroom.

Anna had backed away from Grady when Ryan came into the room. Now Grady tilted his head in question.

"I'm fine," she told him. "I'll just drain the spaghetti and we can eat."

Grady followed an excited Ryan. No one was there to see the tears Anna had wanted to cry from the moment she saw Krista in her doorway.

Chapter 11

Tom understood why Anna had needed to leave town. One lapse in dependability was no reason to take action against her. He told her he had been more worried than upset. The kids, on the other hand, had been more upset than worried. Particularly Wesley.

Anna went to find Wesley after her talk with Tom. She was still feeling raw from her encounter with Krista. Her life had changed dramatically in the last weeks. There was little left of her past and only uncertainty in the future. She wasn't sure she was up to this confrontation.

Wesley was at the back of the house, weeding azaleas. It was a dirty job that someone had to do, and the someone who did it was usually Wesley. His parents had worked a small family farm until they lost it shortly after his birth. They had become migrant laborers and had died en route to another harvest when he was still a baby. Wesley had been thirteen when he'd tired of yet one more rural foster home and decided he could do better on his own.

Because of frequent moves, Wesley's education had been sporadic, but he was highly intelligent. He had quickly learned the skills he needed to survive on the streets. The kids who managed best were the ones who had no morals about who they trampled along the way. Wesley had quickly learned the score. He had been a runner for a Miami pimp before coming to First Day. His job had been to procure runaway girls by befriending them and gaining their trust, then, when they were ready, turning them over to his boss.

He had been very good at his job and was capable of strenuously defending it as part of the "helping profession." If First Day could convince Wesley to turn his life around at least 180 degrees, he had a future as a shyster attorney.

Another strong possibility for future employment was in a landscaping firm. The feel for the soil was something Wesley had obviously inherited. Perhaps if his parents had never lost their farm he would have grown up happy and secure raising corn and hogs and griping about the weather and the price of pork. As it was now, although he complained when garden chores fell to him, Anna noticed that he spent longer hours and was more thorough than any of the other kids in the shelter. Even with one arm in a cast.

Today, by the time Anna found him in the midst of the azaleas, there wasn't a weed in sight and he was carefully spreading fertilizer around the perimeter of each bush.

She lowered herself to the grass and watched him. "Hi."

"I'm busy."

"You're mad at me."

"Why should I be?"

"Because I was supposed to be around the last few days and I wasn't."

"Were you gone?" Wesley carefully measured fertilizer into the hollow he had scooped out, then covered it and mulched with pine needles. His left arm was nearly useless, but he managed anyway.

"I'd like to be perfect, but I was having some personal problems and I had to get away."

"Nice place you chose."

Anna leaned back against a tree and plucked a long blade of grass to chew on. "How do you know where I was?"

"Candy took your message. Told me you were staying at Grady Clayton's cabin."

Anna realized she should have know better than to leave a message with a resident instead of speaking to Tom. But at the time she had been upset, and Tom, with his connection to Jess Cantrell, was one of the last people she'd wanted to speak to.

She tried to explain. "He has a cabin a couple of hours away. He let me borrow it for a few days so I could do some thinking."

"Sure."

Anna sucked on the grass stem and searched for a reason why Wesley would care where she had been. "Did I miss something important?" she asked finally.

"No."

Anna heard "yes" in his voice. "Did you get bad news about your arm when you saw the doctor on Friday?"

"Cast's coming off this afternoon."

"Great." Anna continued to probe. "Did you hear whether you passed your basic skills test?"

Wesley scooped fertilizer into another hole. "I passed."

Anna let out a whoop of joy. "That's wonderful! Why didn't you tell me right away?"

"You weren't here."

She'd meant as soon as she sat down, but his answer was revealing. In Wesley's eyes, she hadn't been here when he'd finally had something good to share with her. She had, effectively, deserted him, just as everyone always had. The message went even deeper. He was beginning to care about her; she was important in his life. As far as she knew, Wesley had never before cared about anyone.

"I'm here now." She rose and went to him, kneeling between two azaleas. "Look, I'm sorry I wasn't here when you found out. I wish I had been. I'm absolutely thrilled. I just knew you could do it."

"Yeah." He didn't look at her.

"Have you thought about what this means? It's the first step to a real future, Wesley. It shows you can choose what you want to do with your life and work toward it now."

"I want to be a millionaire."

"Let's start a little smaller than that, okay? Next step's a high school diploma."

"Did you and Clayton have a nice vacation?"

"I was by myself most of the time." Anna wondered if Wesley was jealous of Grady. Boys his age often had crushes on older women. It was possible, but she suspected it was more that he would be jealous of anyone she spent time with. She understood that the sort of reaction he was having was a very delicate step toward maturing. How she handled it could make an important difference in his life. "Look, Wesley, you're special to me. You're not just one of about a billion kids. You're Wesley, and what you do matters."

"Don't let it matter too much. You might be dis-sapointed, Annie babe," he sing-songed.

She ignored the threat. "But I've got a life, too," she continued. "You're part of my life, but I've got other parts. So I can't always be here the minute you need me."

"I don't need you."

"But that doesn't mean I don't care," she finished, continuing to ignore him. "How about if I take you out for pizza this afternoon to celebrate? My treat."

"I'm busy."

"Too busy for pizza?"

He looked at her for the first time. His eyes were carefully blank. It was like looking in a mirror. "I don't need you."

She smiled gently. "Sure you do. And I need you. We're important to each other. Someday there are going to be a lot of people who are important to you."

For just the briefest moment his eyes showed fear, or something like it. She suspected that he was just beginning to realize she might be right. And it scared him to death. He looked down. "I don't need you, and I don't need your pizza."

Anna knew who he was trying to convince. She stood, dusting off her knees. "Okay," she said, injecting all the warmth she could muster into her voice. "But this is an open invitation. You can cash it in anytime you want. And I'm still proud of you.''

Wesley's face was blank again. He leaned over and began to dig another hole.

Anna silently prayed that someday he would learn to treat people the way he treated azaleas.

Ryan went to bed that night with a minimum of fuss. The new air conditioners made it easier for him to sleep, and now that he had scads of playmates at Isabella's, he was worn out by the time bedtime came.

Once he had fallen asleep, Anna went outside to sit on her porch. She lived in a neighborhood of porch sitters. Porch or stoop sitting had always been a treasured tradition among the nation's immigrants. She could visualize her Swedish ancestors sitting on the porch of the Minnesota cabin they had built with their bare hands, watching night close in on the land they had wrested from forest and thicket. Here, in the city, porch sitting was more of a social occasion, a way of keeping a finger on the pulse of the neighborhood.

She loved the sounds from her porch, the exotic rhythms, the laughter, the cries of babies before Mom or Dad arrived with nourishment. She never felt alone here. Tonight she needed that feeling that she was part of something. Tonight it didn't come.

She missed Grady. Less than twenty-four hours had passed since she had seen him, but she missed him already. How could she have grown to depend on him so quickly? She prided herself on managing her own life. She had learned the hard way that she had to take care of herself, and she had taught herself not to need anyone.

She needed Grady.

She had never thought of herself as a passionate woman. Her first experiences with sex had been with the devil himself. Then loving Matt had cleansed her of Gray Moon's violence. But lovemaking with Matt had been just another way of holding him, of letting him know she cared. She had always believed her traumatic background would keep her from the passion, the ardor, that other women swore they felt.

With Grady she had been more than passionate. He had touched her, and she had become a woman she didn't know. How could she have lived this long and not known that woman was inside her? How could she not have known what it was like to burn for a man, and how could she not have known the dangers that would ensue? She was trapped by what she felt, trapped as surely as if Grady had bound her to him. She could no longer run, and she could no longer hide.

There was only a smattering of traffic on the street. A car full of teenagers passed, driving over the speed limit but not fast enough to worry Anna. One of them hooted at her as they passed.

The next car to pass had one lone occupant, but he was definitely more her type. Grady pulled his Audi into a parking place several houses past hers, got out and started toward her.

Anna hadn't expected to see him. He had told her that he would be swamped with work and campaign demands for the next two weeks. Now, here he was, and before she thought about it, she was halfway down the sidewalk to meet him.

He grabbed her at the waist and swung her around twice before he set her down. It was almost midnight, but he was obviously, outrageously exuberant.

She laughed because his excitement was contagious. "What is it?"

"We got them. The whole ring of drug smugglers. Top to bottom."

"The ones operating out of Guerrando's?"

"Yep!" He pulled her back into his arms and gave her a long, enthusiastic kiss.

"That's wonderful."

"The news or the kiss?"

She laughed. "Don't make me choose."

With their arms around each other's waists they started toward her house.

"Caught them in the act," Grady said when they reached her porch. He sat down and pulled her to his lap.

She waited for the biggest piece of news, and when it didn't come, she prompted him. "Did you get Rand Garner?"

Grady buried his face between her breasts and thought he could stay that way forever. "No."

"No?" Her blood pressure was soaring.

"No." Reluctantly he leaned back, taking her with him. "Garner's a crook. There's no way around it. But if he was involved with this particular gang of hoodlums, he isn't now, at least, not that we can prove."

Anna was disappointed. In her best fantasies she had envisioned a shoo-in primary election for Grady. And if he won the primary, the election was only a formality. Now Rand Garner was still a threat, albeit not too serious a one. From what she read and heard on television, Grady was the favorite by far. "You'll still win," she said, leaning down to kiss him.

The kiss was much more than reassurance. By the time it had ended, Anna was suffused with pleasure.

"Is Ryan sleeping?" he whispered.

"Like a rock."

"I want to make love to you."

There was a pocket door between the living room where Anna slept and the kitchen. It could be locked for privacy. She didn't hesitate, rising quickly to her feet and holding out her hand.

Grady followed her inside. He grabbed and kissed her before she could turn out the one lamp that was burning. She made a helpless protest, aware on some fading level of consciousness that they could be seen from the street. "All I could think about tonight," he said, "was coming here to tell you about the bust."

"That was *all* you could think about?" she asked, pulling his tie from under his collar.

"That and this. Anna, I didn't know I was this person."

Anna realized Grady's thoughts were taking him where her own had earlier. "We're both possessed."

"No exorcisms, thanks."

She fell back on the sofa and reached for the lamp, plunging the room into darkness. The last thing she thought of as Grady fell down beside her was that *he* had exorcised the demons of her past. The woman emerging was the person who had been suppressed by fear and secrets. She had a moment of panic because this woman was someone she barely knew. Then the panic subsided, melting away under the passionate caresses of the man she was beginning to know very well.

Grady was gone the next morning when she awoke. She didn't know when he had left, only that it had been well after midnight. She stretched and realized that there were parts of her that felt as if they had been touched for the first time. She and Grady had stirred each other to fever pitch. For the brief hours they had been together they had forgotten his campaign and her secrets. They had reveled in each other, like children with the Christmas present they had wished for all their lives.

She ached this morning from their love play, but the pain she always carried inside her was soothed. Grady had soothed it with his kisses and caresses and his words of love. She didn't know what their future held, but she did know that Grady was slowly healing her. She had tried to heal herself; now she understood that only so much could be done alone. Grady saw things in her, drew things from her, that she hadn't even known were there.

Ryan was still sleeping, and it was early. Anna flicked on the television to watch the early morning news. She rarely had time for the papers, and she wanted to see if last night's drug raid had been announced.

She caught the weather first, then a short sports segment. With freshly brewed coffee in hand she came back from the kitchen in time for the local society reporter—which was a fancy way of saying gossip monger. Anna wondered how many stations paid someone to spout inanities about people only a very few residents were privileged to know and hardly anyone cared about. Hollywood and

New York might have excuses, but Ponte Reynaldo? It was pretentious, but that was a hallmark of certain communities of Florida's Gold Coasts. And Ponte Reynaldo was one of them.

She suffered through a who's who of Reynaldo Beach, where Grady's parents lived, and a description of a Palm Beach wedding so elaborate that it had obviously set the bride's parents back an easy quarter of a million.

She hadn't known what it meant to suffer, though, until the next item was aired. It was short and simple. It recapped the top news of weeks ago: the broken engagement between Grady and Susan. Then, it added the day's juicy tidbit in the form of an update.

"For those of us who wondered what could have interfered with the wedding of this perfectly suited couple, a glimmer of light has appeared on the horizon. Our young Mr. Clayton has taken up with another woman so quickly that the word 'rebound' need hardly apply.

"His new flame, Miss Anna Fitzgerald, is on the staff of First Day, a local shelter for runaways quartered in the former Garson mansion on Fort Carrol Boulevard. She is said to be an expert on that particular problem, as she is a former runaway herself. Miss Fitzgerald, the mother of a four-year-old son, admits to having supported herself on the streets from the age of sixteen, although the details of her life are, fortunately for all of us, discreetly hazy.

"Miss Fitzgerald and Mr. Clayton are said to have enjoyed a recent weekend together at his getaway cabin on Moss Run Creek. Do you suppose they were discussing the social implications of runaways in our society? And do you suppose that this discussion was the reason that, on tastelessly short notice, Mr. Clayton canceled his appearance at several charity benefits? Stay tuned for more details. Until then..."

The leather-skinned, bleached-blond matron gave a satisfied smile, then was replaced on the screen by a breakfast cereal commercial.

Anna was stunned. That blessed shock lasted only seconds, however. When the enormity of what she had just heard finally filtered through, she gasped in pain. Her life, her agonizing past, had just been trivialized for all of Sun County to see. And why? Who had done it? Who could have benefited from that kind of vicious exposure?

She had not been a politician's stepdaughter without learning something. She had the answer before the question was fully formed. Rand Garner had benefited, and would benefit immensely the more the story was publicized. Grady had just been involved in a huge drug sweep; the voters were going to be overwhelmingly in support of him. Garner had only one chance to win in the primary. He had to discredit Grady. Thoroughly. Absolutely. The only aspect of Grady's life that was anything other than picture perfect was his relationship with her. She was fair game for Garner.

And Garner had tapped a gold mine. He was a desperate man, a desperate man with connections. There were enough people who knew how she had survived on the streets that it would only be a matter of time before the horrors of those years surfaced. And how safe was the rest of the story? How long would it take for a desperate Garner to connect her with Hayden Barnard? What would Hayden, with all his clout, have to say about her if he were asked? What lies would he tell?

The telephone rang. She stared at it. She knew how reporters devoured each other's stories. She had watched them close in on Hayden often enough. This story was too good for anyone to pass up. Scandal was the bread and butter of too many newspapers today.

The phone continued to ring. She knew it was going to wake Ryan, and she had to have a few more minutes to try to pull herself back together. She lifted the receiver and heard Grady's voice.

"Anna!"

"Grady." She sank to a chair and squeezed her eyelids tightly shut.

"Have you seen the papers?"

She gripped the telephone harder. She knew what the papers would say. "I just heard a Channel 6 report. We were in the society news."

His cursing went straight to the point.

"Who did this to us?" she whispered.

"Garner, obviously. I don't know where he got his information."

She wanted to weep. "Someone at the house must have talked to him. No one else in town would know anything about my background."

There was silence for a moment. "Did anyone besides Tom known that you went to my cabin over the weekend?"

"I left Tom a message and told him where I was. One of the residents took it and apparently passed it around. At least one kid asked me if I'd had a good time." She could almost hear Grady thinking out loud. She had been stupidly indiscreet.

If that was what he was thinking there was no hint of it in his voice. "You were driving my car. You could have been followed."

She wanted to believe that was the answer, but she knew that even if it were true, it was only part of the explanation. "That might explain how they knew about the cabin, but it wouldn't explain how they knew about my being a runaway. I don't advertise that, Grady. I don't tell everybody I meet. Just the kids and staff know."

"Who would sell you out?"

She was too upset to think. Only one thing was absolutely clear to her. "You've got to stop seeing me. Give an interview and tell the reporters we're just friends." She pushed on when he tried to interrupt. "Tell them how you got to know me, that I was helping you identify possible drug pushers. That will link me to the sweep last night and put you in a better light. Tell them we have no future plans, that you're going to be much too busy serving as prosecutor to have a personal life now."

"Tell a bunch of lies, in other words."

"Not lies, Grady!" She was glad they weren't face-to-face. "This is the end. Even if you can't see it, I can. Your career is on the line. You can't be tied to me."

"I'm coming over."

She gripped the phone harder. "Don't be a fool! You can't be seen with me again. You've got to stay away. Look, it's been wonderful, but it's over now. I should never have let it go this far, and neither should you. I'm a hazard to you." She hesitated, but she interrupted as soon as he began to argue. "You're a hazard to me, too," she said over his arguments. "They could trace me to Hayden. Nothing that's happened so far is irrevocable, but it could be if we don't call this quits right now."

There was silence on the other end of the line.

Anna realized she was crying when tears splashed onto the receiver. "Grady," she pleaded, "tell me you understand."

"'Nothing that's happened is irrevocable.'" He repeated her words as if they were poison. "Is that so, Anna? What's this been for you, then? Some cheap little affair?"

"You know it hasn't."

"But it hasn't been important enough to fight for. *I'm* not important enough."

"You're too important."

If he heard her tears, his voice didn't soften. "Let's see if I've got *your* priorities straight. My career is more important than our relationship. And even if I could still have both, fighting for them sounds too difficult."

"Dangerous! Don't you see? I've got more than just you and me to worry about. I've got Ryan, too. I can't take the chance that Hayden would find us."

"Hayden Barnard wouldn't dare touch you, not if you told your story first. The media knows about us now. That's no reason to hide anymore. Tell your story and let the election be damned. You've never done anything wrong. If the voters can't see that, who cares if they elect me!"

She couldn't bear the exposure. Just the thought made her sick. "I can't!"

"Let me tell you why, then. You've lived behind your secrets for six years. You've hidden behind them! You've built up such a wall of secrets and fear and rage that you can't climb over it now. You can't climb it to forgive your sister, and you damn well can't climb it to forgive yourself. And, apparently, you can't climb it to love me, either. You'll hide for the rest of your days, and you'll never be the person you could be, because you're a prisoner!"

"It's so easy for you to say!"

"Sure. Easy, Anna. This is real easy for me."

"Give that interview. Tell them what I said. We can talk about this after the election." Anna wiped her eyes. "Promise me you will Grady."

"We won't talk after the election. We've just done our talking. And there won't be any interview unless you give it. I don't deal in scandal and half-truths. Never have, never will."

"You're not thinking clearly."

"Goodbye, Anna."

She listened to the click that meant he was gone from her life. She wanted to scream her anguish. She wanted to scream at him. But there was no one to hear her now. Grady was gone. She had sent him away because she loved him.

A wall of secrets and fear and rage. You'll never be the person you could be, because you're a prisoner.

She had sent him away because she loved him.

You couldn't climb it to forgive your sister, and you damn well can't climb it to forgive yourself.

She loved him. She had sent him away.

You're a prisoner.

She closed her eyes and sobbed. She had sent Grady away because their love would make a prisoner out of him, keeping him forever locked away from the life he wanted and needed. He couldn't be right.

But when she opened her eyes after all her tears were spent, she knew her house was no longer the haven she had believed it to be, her life no longer the story of a young woman who had prevailed against all odds. There were bars on her windows and, more important, bars on her spirit.

She was trapped behind them as surely as if she were serving a life sentence. And Grady, the Sun County State Attorney, had given her the key to freedom. If she could bring herself to use it.

Chapter 12

Wesley had sold her out.

Anna arrived at First Day to find that sometime during the night Wesley had packed his backpack—along with someone else's that he "borrowed"—and left for parts unknown. His cast had been successfully removed the previous afternoon. He was to have had two weeks of physical therapy to help overcome any lingering problems, but apparently that had seemed less important than getting out of town.

When the residents awoke the next morning both Wesley and any cash they hadn't hidden well were gone. He left nothing but a note for Anna. "I never liked pizza," it said. It was sitting on her desk; the desk had been ransacked.

She knew Wesley hadn't been looking for money in her office. He had been looking for more information that he could turn into money. Anna thought she understood why he had sold her out. She had gotten too close; he had gotten scared. She had expected things of him; he had been forced to show her that he couldn't live up to anyone's expectations. She had told him that she saw good in him; he had told himself that he had to show her how bad he was.

He had needed money, and he had already proved that there was nothing he wouldn't sell for it. Not human flesh, not secrets, not friendship and trust. In the most hurtful way he could find, Wesley had told her to get out of his life.

Tom was standing in the doorway when she looked up. The note was still in her hand. The hand was trembling.

"You told me once that I'd set the odds too high in favor of Wesley making it," she said.

"There was always a chance he would. That's why he was here."

"He's an enterprising young man. He sold my life story, or what he knew of it, to Rand Garner's people. I'm all over the papers this morning."

Tom didn't try to refute her theory. The fact that Wesley had disappeared the night before the story hit the papers made it that much more obvious. "What are you going to do?" he asked.

Anna had been asking herself the same thing ever since her phone call with Grady. She shrugged.

Tom crossed the room and took her into his arms. She let him hold her, but her tears were all cried out. "You've got a vacation coming," he said, giving her a final squeeze and releasing her. "Take it now."

"Won't it look like I'm running away?"

"What it looks like is less important than what it does for you."

"I just got back from some time off."

"Things are quiet here now that the conference is over. Take Ryan and get out of town for a while. I don't want you burning out. You're my secret weapon with these kids. If you don't take some more time to sort things out, you'll be shooting blanks."

She knew he was right. "What if Wesley comes back and I'm not here."

"You want the odds of *that* happening?" he asked gently. "Sometimes you've just got to give up on a kid, Anna. If you don't, there won't be room inside your heart for all the ones you *can* help."

"I'm furious at him anyway. If he was here I'd probably strangle him!" She took a deep breath. "But he always reminded me of Matt. You know?" She swallowed hard. "I was the only one who ever saw the good in Matt. I thought maybe it was the same with Wesley. Maybe there wasn't any good...."

"There was."

"I've already spent the whole damn morning in tears," she said fiercely.

"I've seen a lot of lives made out of nothing but."

"Why mine?" Anna shuffled the papers littering her desk. "What did I ever do wrong, Tom? When do I get to stop crying?"

"Do you want to know?" He put his hand on top of hers and forced her to look at him. "When you face all those ghosts in your past, Anna. Then they can't keep coming back to haunt you."

"Not you, too!"

"You don't want to hear it?"

"No, I don't."

"Stock up on tissues, then."

"Enough, Tom."

Tom lifted her calendar off the floor where Wesley had thrown it. "I'll see you in two weeks." He set the calendar in front of her. "Let me know where you are in case of emergency."

She stared at the calendar and wondered where she could go. Wherever she went, and whatever she did, though, she had one person she had to see first.

The man who showed Anna to a seat amid flowering orchids and nagging parrots looked as if he really wanted to show her out the back door. He left immediately after mumbling that Miss Powell would be with her in a few minutes.

Anna had lived in the midst of Washington, D.C. society and attended school with girls whose wealth rivaled Susan's. But never had she seen anything quite like the atrium in which she was seated. She felt distinctly uncomfortable, as if some mustachioed bandito with a machete might jump out from behind one of the tall rubber trees shading the closest doorway and insist she recite something in Spanish or Portuguese in exchange for her life.

"Anna?" Susan came through the doorway instead. "I hope you haven't been waiting long. I was on the telephone."

Anna had been there less than five minutes, but it had definitely been too long. She stood and held out her hand to Susan. "Thank you for seeing me."

"Would you like to talk out by the pool? I can have Pim bring us something to drink."

Anna would have preferred almost anything to remaining in the atrium. She was already suspicious she might have contracted malaria. She followed Susan through the house, noting no details but gaining the impression of luxury, exquisite taste and old money.

The pool was pure fifties nostalgia, kidney-shaped and Olympic-sized. The landscaping around it was reminiscent of the atrium, although it was slightly more subdued and the only birds in sight were wild and North American.

Susan led Anna to an ornate iron table with a floral-print umbrella shading it. Pim, the man who had deserted Anna in the atrium, appeared with two tall frosted glasses of lemonade and a plate of tiny cakes.

"Pim still likes to play tea party," Susan said, after he left. "When I was a little girl, my parents would leave me here while they traveled. I always had a nanny, but Pim considered it his job to be sure I played all the proper little girl games. I'm not sure he's noticed I've grown up."

Anna thought that if he hadn't, the man was blind. Susan Powell was as perfect an example of womanhood as existed. She lifted her lemonade off the tray at Susan's urging, but the last thing she could think about was hunger or thirst.

Susan fell silent, waiting for Anna to begin.

Anna could think of no way to ease into the subject of Grady. "Have you read the papers?" she asked.

"You mean the gossip about you and Grady? And me," she added as an afterthought. "I haven't been able to avoid it. And if I had, the reporters who've been calling all morning would have made sure I knew.''

"I should have realized they'd try to talk to you."

"I haven't given any interviews."

"I'm sorry they've tried to involve you."

"Why are you sorry? You certainly didn't put them up to it." Susan picked up her own lemonade, but she didn't take a drink. "Is that why you came? To tell me you were sorry for something you didn't have anything to do with?"

"One of the kids in the house told the story to Rand Garner. Apparently he made a nice profit off it, because he's gone now."

Susan touched Anna's arm. "I'm sorry. That must have been a blow."

Anna had expected almost anything except warmth. She didn't feel worthy of anybody's sympathy. Especially not this woman's. Unexpectedly, tears sprang to her eyes, and she thought of Tom's warning. *If you face the ghosts in your past, they can't keep coming back to haunt you.* With an effort she blinked back both the tears and the warning. She had cried enough tears, and the warning had already accomplished what Tom had intended. In the hours since she had talked to him she had made a decision about both her past and her future. She managed a smile to let Susan know she appreciated her words.

"You must feel so proud of what you do accomplish, though," Susan said, almost wistfully.

"I'm afraid that's the last thing I'm feeling right now." Anna sipped her drink, swallowing more than lemonade as she did. "Look, I didn't come here to tell you my troubles. I know I have no right to ask you for anything, but I need your help."

Susan didn't even hesitate. "What can I do?"

"You can talk to Grady for me."

"Why don't you talk to him yourself?"

"Grady and I aren't going to be seeing or talking to each other again." Anna thought what a contrast she and Susan were. She could hardly sit still, but despite the things she had already told Susan, Susan was completely composed. If she felt anything, she didn't seem to think she had the right to show it.

"Was that Grady's idea or yours?" Susan asked when Anna didn't continue.

"Mine." Anna couldn't stand to sit another moment. "Would you mind if we walked?" Without waiting for an answer, she rose and began to pace the perimeter of the pool. Susan joined her, and Anna tried to explain. "Look, we both know Grady. You better than me, because you've known him longer. But the one thing I'm sure of is that even if he wanted to forget he'd ever known me, he would be too considerate and too conscious of doing what was right to tell me. Susan, he wants this job, even if he says it's not that important to him. And Sun County needs him. He's not going to get the job unless I step out of the picture."

"So you told him goodbye." It was not a question.

"I had no choice."

"I imagine Grady doesn't see it that way."

Anna didn't want to think about the way Grady saw things. She couldn't bear to think of him feeling anything at all. She cared about him too much to imagine him immersed in the same torment she was. "Grady thinks he's a white knight. He believes he can battle off this publicity and still come out a winner. I know he can't. You know it, too, don't you?"

"My opinion doesn't matter."

Anna stopped and faced Susan. "It matters to me. And it will matter to Grady. He needs to hear the truth from you. He values your opinion."

"And he loves you."

Anna was surprised Susan could say those words, much less with no apparent pain. "I don't know if he does or not. But even if he thinks he does now, how would he feel in a year or two when he realized he was chained to a woman who was going to keep him from a career he desperately wanted?"

"And why would you?"

"Because all the things the papers are intimating about me are true," Anna said, looking Susan straight in the eye.

Susan shrugged.

"Can't you see what that could do to Grady?" Anna asked.

"I think you've underestimated everybody involved. Yourself, Grady...the voters. You're not nearly as important as you've let yourself believe," Susan said with no malice. "You've got a story worth telling, Anna. Your life could be the kind of example that people need. And the American public is a forgiving public. There will be people who hold your background against you, but there will be more who cheer you on because of it." She paused, and then, as if she'd made a decision, she went on. "I won't go to Grady for you. If you want to ruin his life, do your own dirty work. But maybe you ought to be clear about your reasons."

"I've told you my reasons."

"I guess I don't believe them."

"I want to protect him!"

"Funny, but I get the feeling it's *you* you want to protect."

The blow had come out of nowhere. Anna wondered how Susan could deliver a punch to the gut and still look as calm as she had moments before. She began to walk again. Susan stayed beside her.

"I'm going away for a while," Anna said when they reached the table. She picked up her purse to leave.

"It had better be far away if you're trying to get away from Grady and the press." Susan hesitated, then added, "And even farther if it's *you* you're trying to get away from."

"I'm not getting away from me. I'm going to find me."

Susan put her hand on Anna's arm. "Do you have a place to go?"

"I've had a place waiting for me almost seven years." Anna tried to smile. "And you know, I'm so scared I can hardly put one foot in front of the other to get there."

Susan had no way of knowing what Anna meant, but her eyes registered understanding. "Have a safe journey."

Anna knew no journey into her past could be safe. But whether it was safe or not, Grady and Tom were right. It had to be made. On an impulse she extended her hand to Susan. The other woman clasped it, and they stood that way for a moment. "You, too," Anna said at last.

"I'm not sure I want my journey to be safe," Susan said. "I think I'm ready to take chances."

"Good traveling, then."

Susan smiled. "I like that better. Good traveling."

Anna's journey into the past began with two plane tickets. Ryan was so excited that he was going to fly in an airplane that he stayed awake most of the night. To avoid reporters and the telephone, Anna had taken a room at an airport motel, and Enrique and Isabella had delivered Ryan to her there, along with a suitcase of clothing for both of them. Enrique had made sure he wasn't followed, and after his experiences smuggling his family from his homeland, he was both competent and thorough.

Anna hadn't found the courage to call Krista to let her know she was coming. She knew she was taking a chance that Krista might not be there, but the alternative was worse. She had no idea what she would say to her sister when she saw her again, but at least, when they were face-to-face, she would be forced to say something.

Early the next morning she and Ryan boarded their flight to Virginia. Ryan bounced and chattered the entire way. Anna fought the apprehension and, worse, the hope, welling inside her. The past felt like a human presence with its hands wrapped around her throat. She knew the time had come for its stranglehold to be broken; she just didn't know if she had the strength or the courage.

They landed in Roanoke and rented a car. The Blue Ridge Mountains were green and lush. Picturesque farms and towns dotted the land bordering the interstate. Once they stopped for a gallon of cider to drink along the way, then once more for country ham biscuits.

Just past lunchtime they turned off the interstate and onto a winding country road leading up the side of a mountain.

Half an hour later Anna pulled into a long narrow driveway, bordered from the road by a neatly kept apple orchard. At the drive's end stood a large, white frame house. There was a split-rail fence surrounding it, with summer's red roses splayed luxuriously over each post. Just behind the house was a long, low structure that looked like a stable with a riding ring beside it. There was an historical marker by the roadside explaining that the house had once been a stop on a regular stagecoach route.

"We're here." Anna pulled into a parking place in front of the house.

"We're gonna see those people now?"

"Krista is your aunt, and Jess is your uncle. You say Aunt Krista and Uncle Jess," she instructed yet again.

Two teenage girls came out the front door, shoving each other playfully. They started toward the apple orchard.

"Are we gonna go in?" Ryan asked.

Anna had been asking herself the same question. But she had come too far to turn back now. She reached over and finger combed Ryan's curls. Then she opened her door.

Stagecoach Inn had a large, tarnished brass knocker instead of a bell. Anna let it fall once, then again. She stepped back and waited. From inside there were footsteps and an "I'll get it" before the door was flung open. A big-eyed waif with Orphan Annie red hair and no shoes stood in the doorway.

Anna introduced herself and Ryan, then stepped inside at the girl's invitation. "Is Krista here?" Anna asked.

"She was a moment ago. She expecting you?"

"No."

"You been here before?" At Anna's reply, the girl, who said her name was Vivian, pointed toward the stairs. "Straight up. Down the hall to the right. She's in the office."

Holding Ryan's hand, Anna climbed the winding staircase leading to the second floor. The inside of the house was clean, with fresh paint and wallpaper, but there was nothing ornate about it or any of the furnishings. It reminded her of First Day. Runaway shelters had the habit of reducing even the most historic or elegant structures to the lowest common denominator. The house was cozy and thoroughly livable. It was not what Anna would have expected from her sister, who had once had champagne and caviar tastes.

She paused outside the door marked Office. It was closed, and she nearly turned back.

Ryan spied a moth-eaten black tomcat at the end of the hall and took off after it. The cat, who was obviously used to that sort of attention, suffered his caresses. Anna knocked on the door and opened it when Krista called, "Come in."

Anna stood in the doorway. Krista was on the telephone, and her back was turned. Anna was glad for the few seconds to adjust to seeing her sister again. For the first time since she had made the plane reservations, she knew she had done the right thing.

Krista hung up and turned. Her eyes widened, and she stood slowly. "Anna."

Anna knew it was significant that Krista hadn't called her Rosie. They were starting over. It was the only hope for their relationship. "I can come back if this is a bad time."

Krista stared at her; then the corners of her mouth turned up. Her eyes grew suspiciously moist. "You've got to be kidding."

Anna edged her way around the desk until they were in touching range. "I should have called."

"I'll take you any way I can get you." Krista took a step forward, then stopped.

Anna took a step forward; then she stopped, too. "I've brought Ryan, too."

"I'm so glad." Krista lifted her hand and touched Anna's shoulder, almost as if she wanted to be sure she was real. In a minute they were sobbing in each other's arms.

Much later, with Ryan napping on Krista's lap and Anna curled up on the sofa less than an arm's length away, they were still greedily catching up on years of stories. Jess found them that way. He stood in the doorway until Anna looked up and saw him.

She rose and went to him, and he held her as if she had never been away.

"I knew you'd come," he reassured her when she tried to apologize. "Seeing us was a shock. You had to have time."

"The only thing that got me through all those years was anger. And Ryan," she added, trying to explain.

"Don't you think we know that?" He hugged her hard before he released her.

"I'm just so sorry." Anna wiped her eyes.

"There's nothing to be sorry about." Jess put his fingers under her chin and lifted her face to his. "How long can you stay?"

"Do you have room for us?"

"She keeps asking questions like that." Krista came to stand beside them, a just-waking Ryan still in her arms. "Can you imagine?"

Jess smiled tenderly at his wife. "We have room for you," he assured Anna. "Always. Tate's at school, so you can have her room."

Jess piggybacked Ryan as he and Krista took Anna around the house for a tour. She was duly impressed. Stagecoach Inn was set up to deal with runaway girls other agencies had given up on. It was a long-term residential program. The girls stayed until they were ready to make a success of life on their own or until they ran away again. Three of Stagecoach Inn's former residents, including Tate, had gone on to college. Four had run away back to the streets; two had graduated from high school and founds jobs in the local community. One had married, and one was serving a sentence for burglary in a juvenile detention center.

There were six girls in residence now and two more expected in the next few weeks. Stagecoach Inn could take no more than eight at a time because of space and the expensive, intensive program of therapy and support that was offered. There were four full-time staff other than Jess and Krista, and several part-timers. Anna saw the quiet pride and competence with which Jess and Krista described what they were doing and what they planned for the future.

The tour ended in the kitchen, where one long-faced resident was tearing lettuce and chopping tomatoes as she muttered under her breath.

"You were a librarian, not a social worker," Anna told Krista as they took iced tea out to a small sun porch in the back of the house. Jess had taken Ryan to see the three horses they kept for the residents' enjoyment.

"And you were once a pigtailed kid who wanted to be an astronaut," Krista reminded her.

"You were talking about marrying Scott Newton."

"I almost did." Krista patted the cushion beside her on the wicker loveseat, and Anna joined her. "He told me that if I didn't stop looking for you, the wedding was off."

Anna realized they were getting uncomfortably close to talking about their stepfather, a subject they hadn't yet broached. She didn't retreat, however. It was too important. "Did he just want you to himself?"

Krista considered softening the truth, but she realized that she and Anna had to be absolutely honest with each other if they were going to reestablish their relationship. "Scott knew why you ran away. He was trying to protect Hayden. I didn't know that, of course, but when he threatened to cancel the wedding if I didn't stop looking for you, I canceled the wedding instead. Later I found out what kind of man he really was."

Anna realized, yet again, how much Krista had given up, too. "Have you seen Hayden?"

"Not since the day I left to search for you."

"I know Mother died."

"It was very sudden."

"Did she know the truth, Krista?"

Krista couldn't mistake what Anna meant. "I think Hayden told her I'd gone off the deep end and was trying to destroy his career with lies, just like you had. She called me once, just after Jess and I married and came here. I told her that if she wanted to hear the truth about her husband, I'd be glad to see her again. It was the last time we spoke. There was no funeral or memorial service after she died. Hayden claimed publicly that she had made that request, but I'm sure he dispensed with ceremony to halt any questions about why his stepdaughters were so noticeably absent.''

Anna hadn't really expected to hear anything different, but it still hurt. ''What did they tell the world about me? One day I was there in D.C. with them, the next I was gone. They used to trot me out like a show dog at their parties. Didn't anyone notice I wasn't there?''

''Supposedly you were sent to boarding school overseas. I'm sure Mother's death put an end to the need for any other explanation. You were only Hayden's stepdaughter, and so was I. No one would necessarily have expected us to continue to be a happy family after Mother died.''

''Boarding school.'' Anna wasn't sure whether to laugh or cry. ''Switzerland, no doubt.''

Krista heard the ragged emotion in her sister's voice. She draped her arm around Anna's shoulders. ''Don't. It's all over now.''

''Not until I tell the world.''

Krista stroked Anna's hair. ''Is that what brought you here?''

''I came because I needed to be with you.'' Anna told her about Grady and the story that had circulated. ''Grady says I've been hiding behind walls of fear and rage for so long I'm a prisoner. He said that's why I couldn't forgive you. He was right about that much.''

''And all those years ago *I* was so afraid to hear the truth about Hayden and so angry when I did that I wouldn't believe it. I was hiding, too.''

Anna hadn't realized how similar their reactions had been. It was another reason to forgive her sister. ''I've gotten all kinds of free advice in the last day or so. In one way or another, everybody's told me I have to face my past.''

''You did that by coming here.''

''You're the good part of my past, Krista. There's still Hayden.''

''You said you were going to tell the world.''

''I'm going to let Jess do it, if he will.''

''What will that do to Grady?''

Anna was surprised at the question. Making a public statement about her past would affect Krista and Jess almost as much as it would affect her. But Krista was worried about Grady. "I've told him goodbye."

"Did he want you to?"

"No."

"Do you love him?"

Anna couldn't face the answer. "I don't know. It doesn't matter now."

"Doesn't it?"

"No."

"What doesn't matter?" Jess, minus his nephew sidekick, came out to join them.

"Anna wants you to publish her story."

Jess dropped into a chair across from them. He was silent for a few moments. Then, "You're ready for the publicity? The lies Barnard will tell about you? The scandal?"

"I'm ready."

"There are people who love to blame the victim. You'll be destroying a well-loved public figure."

"Will I be believed?"

Jess considered again before he spoke. "Eventually, I think. Kris and I will add our own part of the story, the threats we received, the photographs with an *X* over your heart. There were other girls, too. He's frightened them into silence, but maybe someone else will come forward after you do."

"Am I putting us in danger?"

"It will be harder for him to get to you when the story's public. But I think we'd better make it soon."

"Do you think he knows I'm here?"

"I think we should assume it's possible."

Anna shuddered. "I'm ready when you are."

Krista felt the shudder. She wanted to protect Anna as she once had, but those days were past. Her sister was an adult now. And she had made an adult's decision. "I'll take Ryan for the evening, so you can begin." She looked at Jess and saw concern; she also saw excitement. Jess wanted to expose Hayden Barnard before his party's convention as much as he wanted to breathe.

"Where is Ryan?" Anna stood. She needed some time to herself.

"Helping Vivian make cider out in the orchard. She loves kids. He'll be fine."

"I think I'm going to lie down for a while."

"That's a good idea. Dinner won't be for another hour." Krista stood, too. "We'll keep Ryan occupied."

Anna sent her a grateful smile and escaped.

Upstairs, she lay on Tate's double bed and stared at the ceiling. She didn't dare think of all the years she had spent alone while all the time Krista had been there for her. She couldn't analyze the peace she felt knowing that now her sister would never be more than a phone call away. And right now she couldn't face the fact that in a short time everything she had suffered would be laid bare in newsprint, and Hayden would know where she was.

Right now she could only think of Grady.

She wrestled with herself. She had no right to call him, and perhaps even the reasons she was manufacturing were poor. The simple truth was that she needed to hear his voice. She needed him, even though she had sent him away.

In the end she convinced herself that she had to tell him where she was and what she was about to do. He had to be prepared, because when her story hit the papers, he would be questioned and questioned again. She contacted the operator and asked to have the call charged to her home phone. Then she waited to be connected to his secretary.

In what seemed like moments he was on the line. She cleared her throat. The sound of his voice was like thunder echoing inside her. "Grady, it's Anna."

"Hold on a minute," he said. She could hear some noise in the background, then, finally, quiet. She guessed he had gotten rid of whomever had been in his office. He came back on the line. "Where are you?"

She told him. "Jess is going to print the truth about Hayden," she said. "I've asked him to. I wanted you to know so you'd be prepared."

He was silent.

"Grady?" She hadn't meant to sound so needy.

"When are you coming back?"

"I don't know. I don't know anything right now." She realized she was going to cry.

"Anna." His voice softened.

His gentle tone was her undoing. Furiously, she sniffed back tears. "Do you hate me?"

"Anna."

"I meant everything I said, Grady. I'm not changing my mind. I just don't want you to hate me."

"We can safely say I don't."

She sniffed again. "Good."

"When are you coming back?"

"I told you. I'm not sure."

"You've got a week."

"What do you mean, I've got a week?"

"Before I come up and get you."

There was nothing she could say to that. She gripped the telephone receiver and waited for him to say something more. Then she heard an unmistakable click and the line went dead.

"Grady!" Her answer was a dial tone.

"Grady!"

She was still staring at the telephone when Krista came to tell her it was time for dinner.

Chapter 13

The night before the story about Hayden was to run in the Washington paper, Jess and Krista unplugged every telephone at Stagecoach Inn. All the residents were instructed not to talk to anyone who appeared the next morning, whether they were reporters or just friendly strangers asking questions about the program. Jess hired two off-duty policemen to patrol the grounds in shifts, one at a time, and another to stay close to the house. Jess felt fairly certain that Hayden wouldn't be foolish enough to retaliate, but he wasn't about to take chances.

It was past midnight when Anna went up to the room she shared with Ryan. He had been asleep for hours; luckily, the mounting tension hadn't affected him. There was a full moon shining, and she knew she would be able to see the valley below from her window. She parted the lace curtains and stared out at the countryside.

She had never seen anything more beautiful than the Blue Ridge Mountains in the moonlight. In a month or two the vast stands of poplar and oak would be red and gold with autumn's arrival; then the mountains would be traced with snow. Spring would come next, with its bevy of delicate wildflowers, its lilacs and orchards of fragrant apple blossoms. Krista had described the change of seasons almost as if the mountains were alive. She had told Anna that she was welcome to stay and see all the seasons. Welcome to stay forever.

Anna knew she could be satisfied here. Stagecoach Inn would soon be losing a staff member who was getting married. With Anna's experience and training, she would be an asset to the program. She could stay, find a house in the nearest town and raise Ryan in this peaceful, unpolluted place, with its small-town values and Southern mountain charm. Ryan would grow up with relatives who loved him, and she would have the help she needed raising him.

It was too soon to make a decision, but even as she considered it, her heart was somewhere else. She looked out over apple orchards and poplar forests and saw palm trees and the dancing surf melting into white sand. Crickets and katydids chirped their nighttime lullabies, yet she heard the rhythms of the city, the cries of babies, the laughter of families sitting on their porches to catch the night breeze. She was alone, yet Grady was beside her somehow. She hadn't heard from him since their one, brief telephone call, but each minute she had felt his presence, his reassurance, as certainly as if his arms were around her.

Tomorrow morning her story, her life, would be reduced to black ink on newsprint. There would be people who didn't believe it, and others who believed it but didn't care. There would be sympathy, too, but nothing could ever make up for the agony of having to reveal the truth. Hayden's reaction was an unknown. He was a powerful, devious man. But powerful men had been brought to their knees before. With Watergate in the not-so-distant past, the nation was making new demands on its leaders. No longer could they preach a morality they didn't live.

Anna wondered if any of Hayden's other victims would step forward now that she had. If they did, it would strengthen her story's credibility and guarantee he would lose his party's nomination. If the evidence was overwhelming, no one could accuse her of lying. And if her story was absolutely validated, it would establish her credibility as a person, too.

She had told her whole story to Jess, and they had cried together. He had told her it wasn't necessary to include any of the horrors of her life after running away, but she had asked him to. The American public was going to get an education tomorrow. No thoughtful person would go to bed tomorrow night with the misconception that running away today had any of the romance of thirties' youths hopping freight trains, or sixties' flower children living in communes and grooving at love-ins. Anyone whose mind was open would understand more clearly the horrors of child abuse and of children alone and defenseless on city streets. It had happened to a senator's stepdaughter. It could happen to anyone.

"Grady." She whispered his name to bring him closer. What would tomorrow bring for him? She would be exposed for all the world to judge. And he would have a choice to make. He could tell the press that he and Anna had only worked together on identifying suspects for the drug raid, or he could tell the truth. She no longer knew which she wanted. Emptying herself, exposing herself, had made her so vulnerable that she could no longer think of Grady and what was best for him.

"Mommy?" Ryan sat up, rubbing his eyes sleepily. "Are we back in Florida?"

Anna crossed the room and sat on the edge of Ryan's bed. "No. We're still at Aunt Krista and Uncle Jess's." She brushed his curls back from his forehead. "Did you have a bad dream?"

"I dreamed I was playing with Teresa."

"Then it was a good dream."

"When can we go home?"

Anna slid under the covers and put her arms around him. "I don't know, bunny-nose. Right now you just need to go back to sleep."

"I miss my room."

"I know you do."

"And my fish."

"Go to sleep."

Ryan sighed and turned so that his back was to her. Anna kept her arms around him and felt him relax. She wondered where Grady was and what he was thinking about. She fell asleep wondering.

The next afternoon Grady stood on the steps of the courthouse and faced the reporters that the power of his office had helped him avoid for most of the day. From the moment the first bit of gossip about his relationship with Anna had appeared, he had refused to answer any questions about her. Now her life was no longer grist for the gossip mill; it was hard news. The local papers hadn't yet printed the story of her abuse by Hayden Barnard because it had only appeared in the Washington paper that morning. But all through the day, television, with a news deadline of only minutes' duration, had been full of it.

"I'll make a short statement," Grady told the reporters standing just steps below him. The local television channel was videotaping every word he said, and one of their newscasters was standing to the side, ready to make a comment on camera when he finished. There were two radio stations broadcasting live, and reporters he recognized from the local paper and from a Miami daily that had a wide audience in Ponte Reynaldo. The other reporters were unfamiliar to him. He wondered idly if he was going to get national coverage.

"This is all that I'm going to say now," Grady continued. "So questions will be useless. I came to know Anna Fitzgerald when I was involved in trying to establish the identities of the drug ring that our police force exposed last week. She is a fine young woman, a credit to this community.

"In the course of our relationship she shared her personal story with me. I have also spoken to Jess Cantrell. I have every reason to believe what has been said in the Washington paper today and no reason to doubt it. Our nation has trusted Hayden Barnard to lead us, and his personal destruction is no one's pleasure. I believe, however, that we must look at the truth, not what we want the truth to be.

"It would be convenient and more pleasant for citizens everywhere if Anna Fitzgerald and Jess Cantrell were lying about her stepfather. I can only say that I believe with everything inside me that they are telling the truth."

Grady started down the stairs, making his way slowly because every step was blocked. Two policemen moved in beside him and helped him push through. He heard the questions being shouted at him but made no attempt to answer.

What was the true nature of his relationship with Anna Fitzgerald? He would have liked an answer to that one himself. What did he think about her life on the streets after she ran away? What did he think about Hayden Barnard's response to the article? Did he think Barnard was protecting himself when he said that his stepdaughter had always been a liar and a troublemaker and was sadly in need of psychiatric help? Was he impressed that some of the most powerful people in the Senate seemed to be rallying to Barnard's defense?

Grady pushed his way into the passenger side of the car waiting for him at the curb. He slammed his door shut, and the car tires screeched like a teenager's hot rod as the car pulled away. "Good job, Dad," he said, leaning back and closing his eyes.

"I thought I finished getting you out of scrapes when you were eighteen."

"I was never *in* any scrapes. I was the perfect son."

"Well, you're in one now." Stan Clayton made a quick left, then a right. In a moment they were immersed in rush-hour traffic. "I was listening to you live on the radio. You may just have lost yourself the election."

"If telling the truth loses an election, it wasn't worth winning."

"What *does* this girl mean to you?"

Grady might have laughed at the tone of his father's question if he'd had the energy or the concentration. Instead his thoughts were with Anna, as they had been all day. "Everything," he said.

Stan Clayton was silent until they were almost to Reynaldo Beach. "You may not believe this, son, but I understand," he said gruffly.

"Who?" Grady asked, and they both knew he meant what woman had taught his father about that kind of love.

"Your mother, of course," Stan said, gruffer still. "Who in hell did you think I meant?"

This time Grady did laugh. "She drives you crazy. Always has."

"She'd drive any reasonable man crazy."

Grady was left to ponder the idiosyncracies of the human heart and the sweet taste of his father's understanding.

"All three of the major networks want you on their morning shows," Jess told Anna that night as they sat in the kitchen and tried to eat dinner. The residents had eaten earlier and gone with two counselors to spend the evening at a shopping mall. For the kids' sake, Jess and Krista believed it was best to act as if things were normal, even though policemen patrolling the house and grounds seemed anything but. Anna had fed Ryan at his usual time and put him to bed, and she, Krista and Jess were just now getting around to eating.

Anna had little appetite, but she pushed food around her plate in an effort not to worry anyone. "Did your editor tell you about the shows when you called him?"

"He's acting as a clearinghouse for requests."

"Do you think I should go on TV?"

"It's not necessary."

"Hayden's not going to resign or even pull out of the presidential race, is he?"

"It's too early to tell."

"I heard him on the news, remember?"

"How many times have you heard a politician say he was going to fight to the end, only to resign the next day?" Krista asked.

"Whether he resigns or not, he's lost his bid for the presidency," Jess assured Anna.

"Unless the convention delegates are so outraged at my 'lies' that they nominate him out of spite." Anna gave up the pretense of eating and sipped the wine Krista had poured, instead.

Jess sat back with his wine, too, and so did Krista. No one had much appetite, but then, no one had expected to. "You knew there were going to be people who didn't believe you."

"I didn't expect to hear myself denounced by the same men who used to show me pictures of their grandchildren at cocktail parties." Anna thought of one senator in particular, a man who had never ceased chucking her under the chin, even when she had grown taller than his five feet four. According to the news he had been one of the first to speak out against her. "It's just tough to spill your guts and have people accuse you of lying for publicity."

"The story's out there now. Every reporter in America will be trying to dig up something about Hayden. He's a condemned man." Jess drained his wineglass and set it on the table. "I'm supposed to call Carl and see if anything else has come up." He stood. "I'd better do it now before the girls get back and I have to watch them model whatever clothes they bought."

Krista stood, too, and started taking dishes to the sink. Anna joined her. "Are you going to call Grady?" Krista asked.

"No."

"This could have had a pretty large impact on him."

Anna couldn't call, because she was afraid that if she did, she would break down and admit to Grady how much she needed him. She was also afraid to find out what the Sun County media were saying about her. She wasn't ready to face the fact that she might never be able to go back to Florida again, even if she wanted to.

"Old habits are hard to break. I can't seem to stop giving you advice," Krista said when Anna remained silent. "I'm just worried about you. And I know how much Grady cares."

"If you thought you were going to hurt Jess, wouldn't you back away from him?"

"Hurt Jess or hurt his career? The two aren't the same. I don't think there's anything I could do that would hurt Jess more than backing away."

Anna felt a rush of frustration. "How could Grady be happy with me if I was the cause of his failure in politics?"

"Can he succeed if he's not happy to start with?"

Anna had asked herself the same questions over and over, but she had no answers. She helped Krista with the dishes in silence.

When Jess came back into the kitchen, Krista was making coffee and Anna was slicing an apple pie she had no appetite to eat. Morose, and still contemplating Krista's advice, she didn't even look at him. She was forced to, finally, when he stood directly in her path as she started to the table.

Jess's smile was remarkable for its contrast to the rest of the atmosphere. "Did you expect to hear yourself defended by the vice president's wife?"

"You're kidding."

"No. A reporter asked her about you today, and she said that she remembered you well and fondly. She had always wondered about your abrupt disappearance and suspected the truth wasn't being told when she never saw you again."

"She wasn't the vice president's wife when I knew her. But she always liked me." Anna tried to smile. "And even then I could tell she thought Hayden was a creep. Maybe he chased her around the Capitol rotunda a time or two."

"One of Barnard's former aides has admitted he resigned from your stepfather's staff because he'd heard rumors about him and didn't want to be any part of a scandal."

"Did he say what kind of rumors? Did he have proof?"

Jess shook his head.

"Damn."

"The point is that some very influential people are coming out in support of you and strengthening the case against Barnard. And this is just the beginning."

"Do you think he'll resign if more evidence comes in?"

"Whether he does or doesn't, every time someone supports you, Hayden's credibility will be damaged even more than it is now."

Krista came over and put her arms around them both. "When it gets really hot, he'll resign *and* drop out of the presidential race. He doesn't have the courage or the strength of character to face the music. If he resigns there will always be some gullible souls who believe he was framed by the media. He'll find them and live out the rest of his life among them as a quasi hero."

"There are going to be very few people who think of him as any kind of hero when this is finished." Jess hugged them both.

Anna felt numb. She wanted the whole thing over with.

Jess kept his arm around Anna. He didn't like her pallor. "In the meantime, we'll keep the security guards here until we're sure Barnard's not going to strike out. But I don't think he'll touch us. His freedom's about the only thing he'll have left when this is done. And he'll be lucky to have that."

Anna needed time to put everything together. "I think I'm going to go check on Ryan." She gave Jess and Krista another hug, then moved away.

Jess looked concerned, but Krista held him back when he started to go after Anna. "Anna," she called. "We'll be up for a while if you need us."

Anna turned and managed a smile. "I'll *always* need you."

She checked on Ryan, who was sleeping peacefully, but she was in no mood to try to sleep herself. Too much had happened too quickly. She wasn't sure she would ever sleep again until, somehow, she was able to put her life back in perspective. She went back downstairs to tell Krista she was going outside for some fresh air. Neither Krista nor Jess were there, however. Anna imagined they were up in their own suite, resting and taking advantage of the few minutes of peace and quiet before the house was filled with teenage girls again.

The policeman at the back door wasn't happy about her leaving for a moonlight walk and offered to accompany her, but she refused, promising she would stay near the house. She stopped at the edge of the apple orchard and waved, then ventured in a few rows, where she would still be in sight.

Moonlight filtered through the thick canopy of trees and illuminated the heavy clusters of fruit. The Stagecoach Inn girls had picked many of the early ripening varieties and marketed them in town for pocket money. They were just beginning to make cider and would make it through the fall until the first frost.

Anna picked one particularly enticing apple and bit into it. It was at its peak, juicy and firm, with just the hint of tartness that she liked. She remembered, for the first time in years, a summer at a Minnesota uncle's farm and the fresh, sweet taste of apples right from the apple tree outside his window. Uncle Neal had been a funny man who carved her puppets out of firewood and danced the sailors' hornpipe whenever anything was going well.

She hadn't thought of him in years. His wife, her Aunt Hildy, had been a notorious scold, but she had baked cinnamon apple dumplings that made up for her complaining. And late at night, when Krista and Anna were supposed to be sleeping, she would sneak into their room and check to see that they were comfortably covered. Then she would sit in the corner in an old hickory rocker and rock and watch over them. Now Anna could almost hear the comforting, monotonous creak.

There was going to be other memories, too. She knew they were going to flood through her, because the dam had been blown to pieces with the morning paper. There had been so many good things she had been forced to repress along with the bad. Now she knew she was ready to face them all.

It was the future she couldn't yet face. It was Grady.

She walked a little farther into the orchard. There was one old tree, gnarled and bent, that was made for climbing. She swung herself up to recline on the bottom branch. There had been a maple tree in the backyard of her childhood. She and

Krista had tried to build a treehouse. Anna had stepped into it one day and fallen straight to the ground—followed closely by the treehouse. Screaming, Krista had come running to pull her out of the rubble. They had both been convinced she was dead, but except for scrapes and one impressive bruise, she had survived intact. Later the treehouse had been chopped into kindling by a local handyman and used for starting winter fires.

Anna climbed higher. The apple tree held her like an old, dear friend. Perched in its top, she could see over most of the other trees to the road and the valley beyond. The moment was one she would remember all her life. The air was sweet, cool and crystal clear, and the night flooded by golden moonlight. She was perched somewhere between past and future, completely aware of the present.

An owl hooted nearby, and at the next farm over, dogs began to howl, as if disturbed in the midst of sleep. Anna looked toward the house and saw the silhouette of the man standing guard. She felt no need for protection. The reality of her new freedom was just beginning to wash over her. She *was* free. Hayden *couldn't* touch her now. Her life was her own.

She wasn't sure how long she sat that way, but when she turned back toward the road she saw a moving shadow beyond the trees bordering it. For a moment she thought she was mistaken. The shadow blended into those thrown by trees at the road's edge. Then, as she watched, it crept along the ground again. There was no identifiable form, but it was too elongated to be an animal's.

Anna knew there was a man patrolling the grounds. The shadow could belong to him. Yet wouldn't he be trying to stay out of sight? Why would he patrol the roadside where he could easily be seen?

She dropped down one limb, where she could be screened by denser branches. She wasn't afraid for herself; she was well hidden, but she was becoming afraid for those inside. She could still see nothing but a shadow, but it took on frightening proportions in her mind. It seemed to slide along the ground with sinister intent, stopping, moving slowly, stopping again. It grew and diminished with ghostlike undulations.

She was considering climbing down to warn the man guarding the house when the shadow stopped moving, then slowly faded into the shadows cast by the trees in the orchard. Whoever the shadow belonged to was walking through the apple trees now.

Anna wrapped her arms around the trunk of her tree and sat very still. She waited, hardly breathing, for the man—she was sure it had to be a man—to appear. Just as she was beginning to wonder if she had imagined the entire thing, she heard the sound of leaves and twigs crackling under the intruder's feet.

The sound was coming from her left. She strained her eyes but saw nothing. The noise grew louder as she listened. The man didn't seem to be trying to hide his approach, but why should he? Who would expect the orchard to be occupied?

She sifted frantically through explanations for his presence. He could be the policeman on patrol; he could be a reporter trying to find a way to get an interview; he could be someone Hayden had hired. She tried not to panic. Whoever it was, he would be intercepted near the house. He wouldn't know that guards had been hired and that the residents of Stagecoach Inn weren't the sitting ducks they seemed to be.

Just as she thought she couldn't stand the suspense any longer, the man appeared. He was tall, but she could tell little else because he was still too far away. He picked his way through the trees with an easy, confident stride. He was two rows away when she recognized him.

"Grady!"

He stopped, suddenly tense, and looked around as if he was hearing the voice of a ghost.

Anna felt such a rush of elation she could hardly breathe. She plucked an apple off a nearby branch and lobbed it in his direction. Then she chose another and did the same.

The second apple landed at his feet. The third hit him on the shoulder. "Anna?"

"Grady!" She slithered down at top speed and ran to him.

He grabbed her and swung her around; then she was in his arms. She kissed him as if time were running out and every second was an ending. Grady couldn't hold her tight enough or feel enough of her against him.

Somewhere behind them, someone else was not as elated as they were. "Hold it right there!"

Anna swung around and saw the policeman who had been at the back door. He was pointing a gun.

"It's all right," Anna reassured him. "He's my...my..."

"Lover," Grady supplied. "And I'll take care of her now."

"It's really all right," Anna said. "We'll be going inside in just a moment." She turned back to Grady. "Where's your car?"

"Parked up the road. It's a rental with a broken gas gauge and an empty tank."

"How far did you have to walk?"

"A mile, two maybe."

Behind them the policeman holstered his pistol and slipped away.

"You must be exhausted," Anna said, framing his face in her hands to take a better look at him. He did look tired, but, more important, he looked wonderful. Perfect.

"I'm not exhausted now. But I was getting there. That's why I took the shortcut through the orchard." He kissed her again, then pushed her away. "What did you mean throwing apples at me?"

She laughed. "My aim was great, wasn't it?"

"Anna." He clasped her close and wrapped his arms around her. "I'm so proud of you."

As much as she'd missed him, she hadn't realized how she had needed to hear him say those words. She felt vindicated again. "It was so hard," she admitted, slipping her arms around his waist. She knew she could stay this way forever.

"What made you decide to tell the whole story?"

"The things you said to me, the things others said, including Susan."

"Susan?"

"I went to her. I thought she would back me up, Grady. I wanted her to talk to you and make you see reason. She helped *me* see reason instead." She rushed on before he could misunderstand. "I realize how destructive it was to keep running away. I saw that I had to face up to the past, not just for myself, but for everybody."

"What does that mean for us?"

She lifted her face to his. "I don't know. Grady, please, let's not tackle that tonight."

"I gave a statement to the press today. I told them I believed everything you'd said in your interview with Jess. The next time I speak to them, I'm going to tell them how I feel about you."

"It's still just my word against Hayden's, and right now at least half the country thinks I'm lying." She put her fingers against his lips to silence him. "But even if that changes, I was still out on the streets for most of two years, Grady. I told the truth about the things that happened to me out there. Some people will never forgive me for that. I'll never be clean enough or pure enough for them. I'll never be the woman they want to see with their State's Attorney, or their governor or their senator."

He kissed her fingers until she rested them against his shoulders. "Marry me."

"How can you ask that now?"

"I'm asking because I need you. You wouldn't be marrying the Sun County voters. You'd be marrying me. *I* love you."

There was nothing she could say to that. He loved her. He had all the reasons in the world not to say it, and yet the words had come forth as naturally, as fluently, as the clear spring flowing at the base of the orchard. "I love you, too," she whispered. "Don't ever think I don't."

"Then tell me you'll marry me."

"I can't. Not now. Don't you see?"

"No."

"We've got time. Everything's happened so fast. Can't we just take it slowly?"

Grady heard the plea in her voice. She had been through a nightmare, and he wanted to protect her and keep her safe for the rest of her life. But by pushing her, he was making things worse. He wanted her, needed her, but he had no right to rush her because of what he felt. He let his kiss be his answer. It was slow and thorough, with his demands held in firm check. He could wait for her, would wait for her, until she saw that they had to be together. But he wouldn't give her up.

Headlights swept the road in front of the orchard, followed by the appearance of the Stagecoach Inn van. The shouts of teenage girls enlivened the quiet night as the van pulled into the driveway.

"Is there a place for me to stay?" Grady asked. He put his arm around Anna's waist, and they started toward the house.

"I'm sure we can find one." Anna thought of something that hadn't occurred to her before. "Does anyone know you're here?"

"I imagine the whole county suspects. I disappeared into thin air two weeks before the primary and just after all the publicity about you."

"Grady, no!"

"Am I here?"

"Of course you're—"

"Then I did."

"When do you have to leave?"

"Tomorrow afternoon. When are you coming home?"

She knew that the later she went back, the better Grady's chances of being elected. "I'm not sure. I've still got another week of vacation time, and Jess and Krista want me to stay."

"I want you beside me the last week of the campaign, Anna. I don't want you hiding. You have no reason to."

She still had all the reasons she had already mentioned. And one more. "There's still Hayden."

Grady frowned. "What about him?"

"We don't know what he'll do, or even if he'll do anything. But I'm going to have to be careful for a while. I don't want to drag you into that."

"I'm already in it." He stopped and turned her to him. "I *am* in your life," he said, enunciating each word. "The bad, the good. I'm here. That's what being together is about. You've been alone too long, so you don't know. But you're not alone now."

He kissed her hard, and there, at the edge of the apple orchard, she began to believe that maybe he was right.

Chapter 14

Anna and Ryan went home to Florida with a bodyguard. Every day there were more stories about Hayden making the rounds, rumors that couldn't be substantiated, second and thirdhand accounts that led back to sudden silence or disavowals. Hayden's network of support was shaken, but as yet hadn't crumbled. He was still a powerful man, and his grip on those he had mistreated was still firm enough to keep them from following Anna's example and telling their stories.

Now that Hayden could no longer use Anna's safety as a weapon to keep Jess in line, Jess was working through every waking hour to follow leads to bring Hayden to a final reckoning. He assured Anna that justice was inevitable. Hayden hadn't been particularly careful; he had relied on his wealth and power to cover the mistakes he made. Even a mistake buried six feet under could be resurrected with careful, skilled digging.

Anna had resigned herself to the fact that Hayden's final downfall might take months. She couldn't wait in Virginia. The kids at First Day needed her, and she needed Grady,

even though she had tried to convince herself that the latter
wasn't true.

Grady had flown back to Florida the afternoon after their
apple orchard encounter, but he had warned her that he
would be back to get her if she didn't come home on her
own. Anna had no doubt that he meant it. He seemed willing to throw away his career for her. What was almost more
frightening was what she was willing to throw away for him.
In Virginia she could stay out of the public eye. At Grady's
side, she would be forced to face accusations that she had
lied and questions about her past. Her safety would be
threatened in Florida, too. She would be more exposed,
more vulnerable. No one knew if Hayden would retaliate for
the things she had made public. He had everything to lose
if he was linked to an attempt on her life, but the more his
credibility was questioned, the more chances he might be
willing to take.

Jess and Krista had insisted Anna allow them to hire a
bodyguard to stay with her once she went home. Zeke was
a silent man, a retired Secret Service agent with the gray hair
of a grandfather and the sharp eyes of a teenager. He missed
nothing that went on around him. He could survey a scene
in seconds and report details that no one else would have
noticed after an hour's investigation. Zeke didn't crowd,
and he didn't lecture. He simply kept watch and casually, if
it was necessary, steered Anna out of potentially troubling
situations. Ryan loved him, and when they were alone,
Zeke's stern face often softened into a smile.

When Anna and Ryan stepped off the plane into the
Florida sunshine, Zeke had been with them for two days. He
had wanted time to get used to Anna and Ryan, to observe
how she did things and how Ryan behaved, before they
ventured into public. Since he made a point of dropping into
the background, Anna was comfortable with him now, if
not happy that he had to be there.

Anna followed Zeke down the steps onto the airport runway, and Ryan followed closely behind her. She hadn't given
anyone the time or even the date of her arrival. The last
thing she wanted was to be welcomed by flashbulbs and

screamed interrogations. She wanted to go home, pure and simple. She wanted to see Isabella and her family, and experience the pleasure of being in her own house once more before the press discovered she was back.

Zeke stopped on the bottom step and scanned the runway before allowing Anna and Ryan off the stairs. They crossed the hot asphalt and opened the door. Inside, their arrival gate was bedlam.

Anna had taken the precaution of not giving anyone her flight number and time, but she hadn't reckoned with the devious tactics of the press. Now all she could think about was how she was going to get past the microphones being shoved in her face. Even with Zeke's help, the crowd was too dense for her to push right through. She held Ryan's hand tightly in hers and allowed Zeke to take her arm.

Repeating a firm "no comment" into each microphone, she put her head down and slowly began to make her way through the crowd. Ryan stayed close behind her, goggle-eyed at the unexpected attention. She had explained what she could to him when they were still in Virginia. Now she hoped he remembered what she had said about always staying close and doing what he was told.

An overweight man wearing plaid Bermuda shorts and a tie-dyed T-shirt stepped solidly in her path. He took the next in what must have been a long series of photographs and began to wind his film. Zeke tried to steer around him, but he stepped in their way yet again. Zeke signaled to two uniformed airport security guards who were coming toward them.

"Out of the way," Zeke told the photographer. "Or I'll have to move you."

"You and who else, pops?" the man quipped, snapping gum in emphasis.

Zeke moved so swiftly that Anna hardly knew what had happened. His arm shot out, and he shoved the photographer's shoulder hard enough to make him stagger. Then, before the man could recover, Zeke tugged Anna around him. The maneuver would have been perfect except that just as Anna was passing the photographer, someone else moved in at her side and suddenly she was no longer holding Ryan's hand.

"Ryan!" Anna spun around, frantically trying to find her son. She caught a glimpse of him behind two reporters who had shoved their way to her side. Then one of the security guards circled the crowd and headed straight toward Ryan. He lifted the little boy in his arms.

Anna breathed easier and allowed Zeke to continue guiding her through the crowd. She saw that he was aware of Ryan's situation and apparently thought it best that for now the guard continue to carry the little boy.

The reporters began to trail them at a greater distance, convinced at last that they weren't going to have their questions answered. They had as much of a story as they were going to get. Anna Fitzgerald was back.

Zeke had already told Anna that if there was any trouble in the airport he would arrange to have her luggage delivered after she was safely home. Now he steered her toward the cabstand at the nearest exit. The guard carrying Ryan trailed behind them.

Zeke signaled a cab and almost pushed Anna inside, blocking the doorway with his own body as several die-hard reporters came out to the curb. His eyes scanned the sidewalk for Ryan, and he nodded with satisfaction as the guard brought him to the cab and deposited him inside with Anna. Then Zeke locked and shut their door and got into the front with the driver. In a moment, after a nod to the guard, they pulled away.

Anna tugged Ryan into her arms. The entire scene had been unpleasant, but the only truly frightening moment had been when she had lost hold of Ryan's hand. "Are you all right?" she asked as she buried her face in his curls.

"That man who carried me was nice."

"I was holding your hand so tight, but somebody bumped me and knocked you away."

"I got to ride instead," Ryan said with youthful resilience. "And I got a present."

Anna barely paid attention to what he was saying. She was more shaken than she had thought. Now that the onslaught was over, she was beginning to feel its effects. "Well, I'm glad you're all right," she murmured, hugging him a little tighter.

"Do you want to see it?"

"See what?"

"The present."

Anna wondered if the guard had slipped Ryan a quarter or a pack of gum as a reward for making it through the trying situation. "Sure."

Ryan wiggled off Anna's lap on to the seat. He reached deeply into the pocket of his cargo shorts and pulled out a small package wrapped in bright red paper and tied with a gold bow. Anna looked up just in time to see Zeke reach for it and take it from the little boy's hands.

"That's mine!" Ryan insisted.

"I know, son," Zeke told him. "But remember what we said about checking everything? That's my job, remember?"

Ryan pouted.

Zeke carefully held the package to his ear. Anna's stomach dove to her toes. "Zeke?"

"Now who exactly gave this to you?" Zeke asked calmly.

"The man did." Ryan stretched out his hand, but Zeke shook his head.

"Which man?"

"The one who carried me."

"The guard?"

"He was a policeman!"

Zeke nodded calmly. "Did he say anything when he gave it to you?"

Ryan screwed up his face. Anna wasn't sure if he was thinking or ready to cry. "Think, bunny-nose," she said, pulling him against her. "It could be important."

"He said it was from my grandfather," Ryan said with a trembling lip. "He said I should tell my mom. I told him I don't have a grandfather, but he said to tell you anyway. I don't have a grandfather, do I?" he asked.

Anna was staring at Zeke. She was cold all over. Zeke was examining the package. He didn't look at all surprised. "I'm going to have to keep this," he told Ryan. "I'm afraid he gave it to the wrong little boy."

Ryan whimpered his distress, and Anna pulled him onto her lap once more. Only she and Zeke knew that the guard hadn't given the present to the wrong little boy at all. Hayden Barnard had instructed him well.

Grady took the long way to Anna's house, zigzagging through suburban subdivisions and city neighborhoods with children playing dodgeball in the middle of the street and teenagers lounging on the corners. He drove a plain white Dodge from his office, since his Audi was too easy to identify, but he suspected that as soon as he arrived at Anna's he would be seen anyway. Her house would be under observation, just as his condo and his parents' home were. Cynically, he wished for a hurricane building in the Atlantic or a nice bloodless bank robbery to take the minds of the press off Anna's revelations and the upcoming primary.

He knew Anna was home. He had asked Isabella to phone as soon as she arrived, and the call had come two hours before. Anna hadn't called herself, but that was just what he had expected. She was convinced that she had to stay out of his life until the election was over, no matter how much she needed him. She didn't understand that she was in his thoughts every minute, that he dreamed of her, fantasized her presence, remembered every detail of their moments together. She was as much a part of him as if she were by his side. She couldn't stay out of his life because she *was* his life.

He parked one block over and cut through an alley running beside a neighboring house. With summer's waning, twilight came sooner now, and he used the lengthening shadows to shroud his arrival at her back door. The hard-faced man who intercepted him didn't seem impressed by his maneuvers.

Grady was pulling out his wallet to prove his identity to Zeke when Anna came to the door. In a moment she was in his arms.

Later she told him what had happened at the airport. "It was just a dime-store toy pistol." Anna let Grady hold her tight. With Grady there to watch over Anna, Zeke had taken Ryan to the store to pick out a present to replace the one he hadn't been allowed to keep.

"Did Zeke have it checked out thoroughly?" Grady stroked her back with a lover's thorough caresses.

"Yes." Anna thought how good it was to be in Grady's arms again. "The gun hadn't been tampered with, and the airport insists that they have no security guards that meet Zeke's description of the two men."

"So Barnard's made his first move."

Anna shuddered. All the safety precautions Jess had insisted on had proven to be necessary. Her stepfather had declared his intentions. Unfortunately, there was nothing they could do about it. There was no way to prove that the "present" had come from Hayden. And even if had been possible, who else would see it as the threat it was? Hayden had proved his cunning. He had shown that Anna's movements were known to him, that he could get close to her anytime he wanted, even if she had an experienced bodyguard. He had also shown that he understood the most effective way to get to her: through her son.

"I'll have police protection begun immediately," Grady reassured her.

"Can you do that? Won't that look like you're using your office for your own benefit?"

"If you're being threatened, that's the only excuse I need. After the hornet's nest you've stirred up, I doubt anyone would question the need for protection." Grady ran his hands through Anna's hair and turned her face to his. "Do you know how much I've missed you?"

She wanted to tell him to get used to it. Now that Hayden had made his intentions clear, she had to get out of Grady's life for good. She was nothing but trouble; there was nowhere their relationship could take him except down. "Grady." Her voice was as tormented as her thoughts. He understood immediately what she was about to say and silenced her with a kiss.

"I'm prepared to lose this election," he said after he'd reluctantly pulled away. "I know that may happen, Anna.

I know firsthand all the things you're going to tell me, so
don't bother saying any of them. I know something else,
too. Eventually Hayden Barnard will be exposed and your
reputation will be cleared. Then, if I ever have the desire to
run for office again, I'll be free to.''

"Can't you see that's not true? Maybe someday people
will know I didn't lie about Hayden, but they'll also know I
lived on the streets for two years. Do you think I'll ever be
forgiven for that?''

"You were a kid with no place to go. They'll forgive you
if you'll forgive yourself!''

She was stunned by the force of his words.

He pushed her away, frustrated and angry and sick of the
roadblocks she kept putting up. "Let's just get right to the
truth, shall we? You're using my damn career as an excuse
not to commit yourself to me. You keep talking about the
way the public will look at you. Hell, it's the way you look
at yourself that's all screwed up. Deep down inside you still
feel like the kid who Hayden Barnard wanted to use as his
plaything. Somehow you think that was your fault. And
later, when a fast-talking New York pimp tricked you, well,
that was your fault, too! Ryan's birth, Matt's death, all of
that was your fault, wasn't it? You do penance every day of
your life because of all the mistakes you made. That's why
you've made Ryan and First Day your whole life. You can't
take anything for yourself. You won't let yourself think
about a future with me because you know you don't deserve to be happy!''

Anna felt all the blood drain from her face. "I *am* thinking of you," she said in a near-whisper.

"I don't think so."

"I'm in danger. If you don't get out of my life, you could
be in danger, too."

"The only danger I'm in is of making a fool of myself
over you." Grady ran his hand through his hair. The last
weeks had taken their toll on him, just as they had on her.
He and Anna were caught up in circumstances they couldn't
completely control, but they had to stand together. Instead, she was standing a hundred miles away.

Anna's head was spinning with the things Grady had just said to her. "After the election—"

"Now or never, Anna." He didn't touch her, but he might as well have shaken her, his gaze was so intense. "I'm calling a press conference tomorrow afternoon to answer questions. We both know what's going to be asked. I want you there beside me."

"You ask too much!"

"I don't ask enough! I want you to marry me, but I know what your answer will be. So instead I'm asking you to come to the press conference with me tomorrow. Stand beside me. You don't have to say a word. Just be there. Do it for us."

For us. By going to the press conference to be with Grady, she would be advertising their relationship to the world. Now the question of whether they were still seeing each other was conjecture, but if she went to the press conference, every rumor, every theory, would be confirmed. Grady's chance to win the primary would be ended, and Hayden would have a new target.

"I can't." She shook her head.

"You put on a good show, but underneath all the bravado you're a coward about the things that really matter. I guess it's good I found out."

"You found out nothing. I have to protect you!"

"You have to protect yourself," Grady said. "You're afraid you'll find out that you could be happy, and you know you don't deserve it." He stared at her for a moment, as though he were trying to understand more about her than he already did. Then he started for the front door. He didn't care who saw him leave, since he wouldn't be back.

"You don't know what I feel!"

He didn't answer.

"You don't know what it's like living every day with the things I've had to live with."

He turned in the doorway. "No, I don't know exactly. But I do know this. You have nothing to be ashamed of. Nothing! And you have no reason to protect me, because I can protect myself. Get rid of the guilt and the fear, Anna, and what have you got? Love? I honestly don't know if there's been any room inside you to let it grow. And I won't know unless you show up at that press conference tomorrow."

He didn't slam the door, but its closing echoed through the tiny house. Anna was still staring at it a few minutes later when Zeke and Ryan walked in. And it was only when Zeke happened to mention he'd seen Grady parked outside her house that she discovered Grady had driven to her street and waited for Zeke to return before he left for good.

Isabella's house was still brimming over with relatives, although they now rented two nearby houses so that Isabella and Enrique could have some privacy at night. Isabella was in the final days of her pregnancy. She had already been to the hospital once with false labor, and she was due to go any day for the real thing.

Although her own life was full of turmoil, Isabella still appeared at Anna's door an hour after Grady left with a plate of freshly baked cookies and a shoulder to cry on. Anna didn't even know how Isabella had guessed she was needed. "My family, they are all at the beach. Me, I look like a . . ." Words failed her for a moment, then she said, ". . . bloop in my bathing suit."

"Blimp." Anna took the cookies and stepped aside so Isabella could come in. Ryan and Zeke were in Ryan's room playing cards, and Anna had called out Isabella's identity to Zeke before opening the door. Now Zeke came out to be introduced before he disappeared back into Ryan's room.

"Grady was here, too, no?" Isabelle asked.

Anna swallowed hard, refusing to cry. It was a vow she'd had to make to herself every minute since his departure. "I'll get us some tea to go with the cookies." She went to the refrigerator to get the pitcher.

"This Zeke, he's here to take care of you?"

"My life and Ryan's could be in danger."

Isabella knew enough of Anna's story not to have to ask why. "Grady's mad because you have a man here?"

Anna wished it were that simple. As briefly and unemotionally as she could, she repeated what Grady had said to her.

Isabella accepted the iced tea Anna poured, but she waited to speak until Anna was sitting across from her at the table. "These things Grady said, they are right. I have read your story in the paper, Anna, and I am not so..." She searched for the right word. "Dense?" She watched Anna nod. "...dense that I have not understood some of it before from the things you have said. You hide from Grady now because you are ashamed."

"What do *any* of you know about shame?" Anna exploded. "Did you ever lie and steal from strangers? Did you ever stand on a street corner and offer your body because, if you didn't, the pimp who put you there would beat you until you had nothing left to offer?"

Isabella looked down at the table. "I have offered my body, too," she said.

Anna knew Isabella couldn't be lying. "I'm sorry. I didn't—"

"Enrique and I, we couldn't find a way to get out of our country. Enrique had a small newspaper. The politics of it were not like those of the soldiers who ran our town. Enrique said some things in the paper that marked him for death. We were in hiding, but one night the soldiers came. They took Enrique away, but they let me go because of Teresa. I knew where they had taken him. I knew he would be killed."

Isabella toyed with a cookie on the plate between them. She still hadn't looked at Anna. "I followed them. When I got there, they wouldn't let me inside. I could hear a man screaming...." She swallowed convulsively. "The soldiers asked me what I would give them to let me go inside. So I told them I would give them whatever they wanted."

Anna put her hand over Isabella's. The tears she had denied herself all afternoon were spilling down her cheeks.

"They would have taken me there, on the ground outside, but a man who had gone to school with my brother came by. He was a soldier, too, high up, I think. He pushed them away from me. He told me to go home, that there was nothing I could do for Enrique. I told him they must shoot me there, then, because I would stay until I died with my husband."

Anna could only imagine the horrors that Isabella had described. She wanted to stop her, but there were no words to do it.

"The soldier had been a good friend of my brother's. My brother was dead by then. Maybe he was sorry that my brother had died and that I would die, too. He made the soldiers promise not to...to touch me, then he went inside. I waited all night. I could still hear screaming...."

Isabelle lifted her eyes to Anna's. "At dawn, the gates were opened. Enrique's body was thrown at my feet. At first I thought he was dead, but then I saw he was breathing. They had left him alive for me. Much later, when Enrique was well enough to travel, we left our town. Before we left, someone told Enrique that I had offered myself to the soldiers. He only spoke of it once to me, but when he left me here, Anna, I knew it was because of what I had done. I knew, because I was still dirty, inside." She touched her chest, just over her heart.

Anna couldn't bear Isabella's suffering. "But he didn't leave you! He went to help your families escape."

Isabella nodded. "That is what he did and why he did it. But I believed it was because of what I had told the soldiers. I said this to Enrique after he came back. He told me that he felt dirty inside, too, because I had been put in such great danger and suffered such shame. He went back to get our families to make up to me for what I had been through." Tears escaped down Isabella's cheeks. "I was ashamed, and he was ashamed. And if he had died trying to bring our families across the border, I would never have known."

Anna thought of all the things that could have happened to Isabella and Enrique. Isabella could have been raped, Enrique killed. Instead, they had lost much, but gained much, too. And through the humiliation and shame, their love had remained. Despite the things they had suffered. "Then Enrique has forgiven you?" she asked at last.

"There was nothing to forgive. I see that now. And you have nothing to forgive yourself for. Can we control what other people will do? Must we suffer always for what they do to us?''

Anna thought of all the times she had suffered because of Hayden and because she had run away to escape him. He was still making her suffer, because she was afraid of what he might do to her, to her son, and to her lover. But, worse, she was still suffering because, in some way, she *had* blamed herself for the things that had happened to her. Just like Isabella, she had felt dirty inside.

And none of if was my fault.

She must have spoken the last words out loud, because when she looked up, Isabella was nodding. "No, it was not your fault," she said, her eyes glistening. "Just as it was not my fault that the soldiers stood between me and my husband. The fault was theirs.''

"You protected your man," Anna said. "Don't I have to protect mine?''

"Perhaps you must protect his heart and trust him to protect his own safety." Isabella stood. "My family will be home soon. I want to be there when they come.''

Anna understood. After everything Isabella had just revealed, she needed the comfort of having Enrique close beside her. Anna leaned over and hugged her as best she could. She felt Isabella's baby kick against her own abdomen. For some reason, it seemed the ultimate symbolism. After everything that Isabella and Enrique had endured, they still had enough faith in the world to bring another child into it.

And where was *her* faith? Why hadn't she seen how her own guilt and shame had destroyed it?

Isabella hugged her back, then moved away. "Enrique and my mother will take Ryan for you tomorrow if I am at the hospital. Enrique will not let him out of his sight. He will be his body—body—''

"Guard," Anna supplied. "If I never have the chance to tell you again, please know I love you, Isabella.''

Isabella blinked back tears. "And I love you. That is why I spoke. Don't make a mistake, Anna. This world, it's already filled with them. Live for something better.''

Chapter 15

Grady planned to hold his press conference at his campaign headquarters, a large, airy suite in Ponte Reynaldo's business district, not far from his office. One narrow room had been cleared of desks and tables and set up with folding chairs for the reporters. Someone had set up a lectern similar to the one used by the president of the Unites States for news conferences from the White House. All it lacked was the presidential seal and a microphone that didn't screech.

Grady got to his headquarters well before the press would begin to arrive. He did not want to make a late entrance, pushing his way through the crowd like a man who thought his time was more precious than anyone else's. He was dreading the conference, anyway. He didn't want to get off to a poor start.

He hadn't heard from Anna since their fight. He hadn't expected to, but her silence hadn't hurt any less because he'd expected it. Somewhere inside him, in some foolish, childish part of his heart, he had hoped she would see the truth in the things he'd been forced to say. Instead, he thought, he had driven her away.

Phil Stuart, Grady's campaign manager, intercepted him as soon as he walked through the door. Phil, a tall, wiry cowboy of a man, was holding a sheaf of papers in front of him and pointing them right at Grady. Grady felt a twinge of regret that he had been so absent during the campaign. His job and his personal life had combined to make the election a lower priority than it should have been. Phil had been given a difficult job. Now, with all the rumors about Grady's relationship with Anna and Anna's connection with Hayden Barnard, it was almost an impossible one.

Phil didn't waste any time on pleasantries. "You know the latest poll I told you about?"

Grady nodded, prepared.

"You and Garner are running neck and neck."

Grady thought that was pretty good, considering. "How many points have I fallen?"

"Fourteen."

"That's not a fall, that's a suicide leap."

Phil consulted his notes. "You're seen as too young for the job, too emotional..." He flipped the page, saying, "...too impulsive. Garner's seen as too secretive, too indecisive and too tied to people with poor reputations."

"How wise our voters are." Grady started across the room with Phil at his side.

"You've got to counter your image today, Grady. You've got to be mature, thoughtful and poker-faced. No heart-to-heart chats with the media, please. Just give them the facts, nice and straight and calm."

"They don't want facts—they want blood."

"Then show them you don't bleed. That's what the voters want."

Grady had done all the bleeding he ever wanted to. He thought of Susan and the serene progression of their relationship. His election had been almost assured at that point in his life. Now he didn't have a snowball's chance in Sun County.

And the damnedest thing was that he wouldn't change anything that had happened. He still wanted to be elected State's Attorney, but, more than that, he wanted to be a man who did what was right. And no matter how his relationship with Anna turned out, he had been that man when he pursued her.

"Why don't you spend the time until the conference at my desk looking over the week's worth of papers you're behind on?" Phil asked when Grady didn't answer him.

"Let me know when everybody's here."

"What *are* you going to say, Grady?" Phil asked. "Don't you think you ought to tell me, so I'll be prepared?"

"I don't know what I'm going to say," Grady admitted. "Whatever it is, though, it'll be the truth."

"God help us, then."

"If He's inclined to want to, He'll be pleased I'm telling the truth, even if you're not."

Anna entered Grady's campaign headquarters alone. She had insisted that Zeke let her go to the press conference without him. He had compromised, driving her there and stationing himself just out front after first making a tour of the building to learn its layout. She had been nervous before, but after Zeke's heavy-handed detective work, her heart was in her throat. She wasn't nervous about Hayden, however. She didn't expect her stepfather to strike in a roomful of reporters. She was nervous about seeing Grady, nervous about what he would say about their relationship.

Perhaps most of all, she was nervous that he would still be angry and say nothing at all.

The large suite of offices was bustling by the time she walked through the door. She didn't ask for directions to the press conference; the location was obvious. She followed the buzz of voices like someone who knew where she was going, and nobody in the reception area stopped or even noticed her.

She had planned her arrival for the beginning of the session because she hadn't wanted to field questions before it began. She hadn't called Grady, because until the moment she walked through the door she hadn't been sure she would have the courage to see this through. Now, as she entered the room where the press conference was being held, she lifted her chin and started toward the front.

The small room was so crowded that at first no one paid her any attention. Then, as she stepped around some photographic equipment, someone recognized her.

Grady, dressed in a dark blue suit, was just standing to begin when he heard someone speak Anna's name. He was prepared for the better part of the questions today to be about her, so at first he didn't understand the significance. Then he glanced toward the side of the room where heads were turning, and he saw Anna coming toward him.

She had never looked lovelier; she had never been more welcome. She was wearing a bright gold dress and a tentative smile. He caught her eye, and for just that second no one else in the room mattered. He held out his hand, and she didn't hesitate. She picked her way around reporters and photographers, microphones and cameras, until she was standing beside him. Grady clasped her hand and spoke so that only she could hear. "I love you." Then he leaned down and kissed her.

"And today at his press conference, Grady Clayton, Sun County's acting State's Attorney and candidate for that office in the upcoming primary, addressed his relationship with the controversial Anna Fitzgerald, stepdaughter of Senator Hayden Barnard of Minnesota. Clayton informed reporters that he and Miss Fitzgerald are in love and that he has asked her to marry him.

"He spoke of the courage it took for her to reveal Senator Barnard's abuse and said that he is going to try to be as courageous and caring an individual as she is. Clayton asked the public to be careful about making judgments, to look over their own lives and count their own acts of courage before they decide how to mark their ballots.

"Miss Fitzgerald spoke briefly, making a plea for the public to show compassion for the thousands of runaway teenagers living on this country's streets. Miss Fitzgerald pointed out that Sun County has a significant population of runaways, and that the only shelter serving them depends largely on private donations to continue its work. Miss Fitzgerald is herself an employee of that program, First Day, and a former resident.

"When asked about her accusations against her stepfather, Miss Fitzgerald replied that she feels certain that it will just be matter of time before she is completely vindicated. She pointed out that child abuse comes in many forms and in all segments of society. She asked the public to be sensitive to the needs of children and teenagers, and to do their part to help the young who are incapable of helping themselves."

The Channel 8 newscaster blinked, as if reading that lengthy a statement from the TelePrompTer screen had tired his eyes. "A fire on the West Side today—"

Anna flicked off the television. Then she turned, arms folded across her chest, to wait for Grady's comments.

He was smiling. "I think *you'll* be elected."

She relaxed and crossed the room to fall into his arms. "They were so much more positive than I thought they'd be."

"They fell in love with you." Grady buried his face in her hair and thought how lucky he was. That morning he had been afraid he had lost her forever. Now she was in his arms; they were alone in his condo, and they still had an hour together before he had to take her back home. Even her bodyguard was nowhere in sight. At Grady's insistence, Zeke had taken a few hours off. Ryan was at Isabella's under the watchful eye of Enrique and family. Even Zeke was satisfied with Enrique's skills.

"You don't really think it was that easy, do you?" Anna asked. She felt herself becoming lost in Grady's arms. They had things they had to settle first.

"No." He nuzzled her neck and felt her shiver. He smiled against the silky softness of her skin.

"There will be people who *won't* vote for you now who might have if you hadn't aligned yourself with me."

"And there will be people who will." Grady's lips trailed to her earlobe, and he gave an experimental tug. Anna shivered again. "Right now, I don't care."

Anna pushed herself off the sofa, aware that one more minute in his arms would make it impossible to finish the conversation. She walked on curiously weakened legs to the window. The lights of Ponte Reynaldo sparkled below them. Grady's ultramodern beachfront building was ten stories high, and his condo was on the top floor. From this window, much of Ponte Reynaldo was visible, and from the windows of his bedroom, white sand and deep blue water provided the view.

"I've thought about what you said to me yesterday, Grady. You were right. I have been ashamed about the things that happened to me and the things I've done. I never really understood that before. I'd counsel the kids at First Day to be proud of themselves and to stand tall, but all the time I couldn't be proud of myself. Maybe they sensed it, too. I hope not."

He came up behind her and rested his hands on her arms. "Another thing to be ashamed of?"

She laughed a little. "Hayden's legacy, I guess. It's going to take me some time to learn to be proud, really proud, of myself."

"I'm proud enough of you to help you over the hump." He turned her gently. "I love you, Anna. I meant what I said today. I love you, and I want you in my life. I don't care about the things you've done, or your stepfather's threats, or whether the election is going to be affected. I love you, and I want to marry you. Are you going to let me?"

She wanted to say yes. She could no longer imagine a life without Grady. The election loomed in their immediate future, though. Until it was over, until she was sure that Grady still wanted her, even if he lost, she couldn't say yes. And as long as Hayden still prowled the shadows of her life, she couldn't go into a marriage with a clear conscience. She had to protect everyone involved.

"I'm not saying no. But I can't say yes. Please don't make me say either."

Frustration warred with love and lost the battle. Grady knew her fears; she didn't have to express them. He also knew he had no right to force her to make a decision. Her life had been anything but easy. He wanted their years together to make up for all the pain of her past. He could not begin those years by insisting she overcome her doubts. She needed time, patience and love. And right now he had the perfect opportunity to show her the third.

"Then just say maybe," he told her.

She smiled. "Maybe."

"And tell me you love me."

Her turquoise eyes were lit with a thousand stars. "I love you."

This time, when he kissed her, there were no more words that needed to be said. He found and undid the zipper snaking down her spine. Gradually he savored the softness of her skin, the gentle slope of her hips. He felt Anna's hands under his shirt, and he longed for the luxury of no clothes at all.

With an effortless lift she was in his arms, and then they were moving toward the bedroom. She laughed exuberantly, and the sound filled his apartment with the shimmer of quicksilver.

"Caveman," she said, nuzzling his neck.

"My woman." The words sounded right. He said them again, capturing her mouth and murmuring them against her lips. She drank the words, drank the taste of him, the warmth of him. She murmured love words in return against his lips, the faint rasp of his cheeks, the strong line of his jaw.

In his room she caressed him with her whole body as he lowered her to her feet. They undressed quickly, without helping each other, as if even that intimacy would delay fulfillment of a greater need. Naked, Anna stood in front of Grady and stroked the broad width of his shoulders with her palms. Touching him, looking at him, brought her more pleasure than she had ever known she could feel. And there was more pleasure ahead, much more.

He cupped her breasts gently, possessively. "My woman."

"Always." She moved against him again, smoothing her hips against his, feeling him grow harder against her. She knew how well they would fit, how perfect their union could be. She knew in that moment how weak her defenses were, how impossible it would ever be to deny herself Grady's love.

He kissed her again. She tasted him, felt him, sensed the very essence of him, as if they were no longer bound by the restrictions of flesh but had somehow merged their spirits. They moved to the bed as one, striving to prolong this almost unearthly communion.

Grady touched Anna, and she felt the brush of his fingers send heat to places he couldn't touch. She touched him, and he knew a mindless joy he'd thought himself incapable of. Touch was pure, undefiled connection, the words they wanted to say to each other but couldn't, the feelings there were no words for.

Love was a rising tide inside them, and they were buoyed by it, riding its crest together, unafraid. Anna opened herself to Grady as she hadn't before. There was no part of her, nothing inside her, that she wouldn't give him if he asked. And he asked with every kiss and caress, with the exploration of every curve and hollow of her body.

He opened himself to her, too. In their first encounters, he had given, she had taken. Now the ebb and flow of their lovemaking left no room for those roles. Each of them gave, each took, until there was no giving or taking, only being together, sharing, floating, soaring.

When they finally became one flesh, there was nothing between them. Nothing except the love that flowed boundlessly and the joy that made thought impossible.

* * *

"Your watchdog will be barking at my door if I don't get you home in the next half hour." Grady stretched lazily, keeping his arm around Anna as he did. He was loathe to let her go, because he knew that until the primary was over, they wouldn't have any more time alone.

Anna draped herself over him. Her soft breasts pressed against his chest, and her hip nestled perfectly in the cradle of his. She didn't want to leave.

"Are you trying to make this difficult?" Grady asked.

"Impossible."

He groaned and wrapped his arms around her. Desire, which had been wrung from him by their mutual passion, filled him again. He thought of the lifetime to come with Anna, the hours of passion, the fulfillment of nights and the joyful sharing of days.

"I'm going to take a shower." Anna swung her leg over him and sat on the edge of the bed before his prediction came to pass and Zeke came to fetch her.

"Hours alone together. Days. Years. Imagine it."

Anna smiled. "Alone? Don't forget, I come with a small child. We're a package deal."

"I'd like to adopt Ryan, Anna."

Her smile faded. She turned to him. "Do you mean it?"

He sat up and pulled her to rest against him. "I'd like to be his father. He already feels like he's mine. Would you mind?"

There was little need to consider. "Matt would want that. His own life was so sad. He'd want the best for Ryan."

"Go take your shower."

She searched his eyes and saw compassion and desire and the full flame of love. She knew she could never deny them both what they wanted, could never deny Ryan a father's love.

He leaned forward. "I'll count to five, and if you're not off this bed, Zeke's going to get a surprise if he comes looking for you."

She blew him a kiss on the way to the bathroom, and in the end, the shower ran cold before its two occupants came out together.

Anna phoned Zeke while Grady finished dressing. She had agreed to meet him at her house, but she knew that Grady's joke about the other man coming to get her if she wasn't on time wasn't far from the truth. She let the phone ring once and hung up. Then she dialed her number again and let it ring until Zeke picked it up, recognizing the prearranged signal.

Before he had a chance to do more than say "hello," Anna explained that she would be late. Then she listened to his response. She was at the window staring at the lights of Ponte Reynaldo when Grady joined her.

"We turned off the news too soon," she said without turning around.

Grady felt a chill prick of foreboding. He wanted nothing to spoil the good feelings of their afternoon together. "Anna, whatever it was, it doesn't matter."

"But it does." She faced him, and he saw that her eyes were shining. "It matters, Grady. Two women have gone to the press with their own stories about Hayden. Jess called my house to tell me, and Zeke got the message. It happened late this afternoon. The story ran at the end of the national news. He made terrible threats to one and apparently paid the other one off. Now they've both come forward to try and put their lives back together again. Hayden almost destroyed them. Now they've destroyed him."

Grady knew what this meant to her. "Anna..." He gathered her in his arms.

"Jess told Zeke that there's substantial evidence to prove their claims. One of the women even has a tape of a threatening phone call made by one of Haydens' aides. Jess says it's the end of Hayden's career. No one will doubt me now, Grady. No one!"

"No one who matters ever doubted you."

"I know. But, Grady, don't you see? After all these years
Hayden's finally been shown up for the man he is. He
thought he was so powerful he could live any way he
wanted, step on anyone he pleased. But I showed him that
he couldn't. Those two women showed him that he couldn't.
He'll never be able to bring anyone else the misery he
brought us!"

Grady saw her slowly blooming pride. Both of them could
talk forever about shame and fear and self-esteem. But
nothing, nothing, would ever heal Anna as this would. He
could almost see the years of Hayden's oppression vanish-
ing as he watched her. She had shown great courage through
all those years, but the greatest display had been her decision to go public with her story. And her courage had
brought the giant to his knees.

"I have always been proud of you," he told her. "And
now I'm humbled."

She grinned, cocky and sure of herself in a way he had
never seen. "Fat chance of that." She rose on her toes and
gave him a long, exuberant kiss. Then she spun around the
room, a frantic, ecstatic ballerina. "And now your voters
will know I wasn't lying, Grady!"

"Anyone who saw the press conference will know that
anyway."

"I've got to call Krista."

"Call her now."

Anna stopped dancing and ran back to him for a kiss.
"From my house. Can you stay while I do? Just for a little
while?"

"For a little while."

"Then let's go."

Grady followed her to the door. Her energy suffused him
too. For that moment he believed that nothing could go
wrong again. He and Anna would marry and live happily
together as they raised their son. Perhaps there would be
other children, some with Anna's exuberance and some with
his thoughtful caution. There would be laughter and love,
and whatever tears there were would be shared.

Anna flung open the door, then stopped as suddenly as if she had run into a wall. For a moment Grady didn't know why; then he saw.

Sitting on the dark wooden bannister outside his door was a doll. Its face was porcelain—a perfect replica of Anna's.

Chapter 16

Grady's election day party, victory or defeat, was to take place at the Ponte Reynaldo Plaza. The elegant presidential suite had been reserved as a place for him to join his family and campaign officials to wait for the results. It was widely known that he would secrete himself there in the late afternoon in order to get firsthand information. Later in the evening, when the election was called and the winner declared, he would go downstairs and accept congratulations or regrets.

By midafternoon the atmosphere in the State's Attorney's office had moved beyond its usual repressed panic to all-out chaos. Grady had disappeared from view by late morning, refusing to subject himself to questions or election theories. For once Polly's army sergeant discipline had served an important purpose, and she had protected him from phone calls and unwelcome visitors. But at three in the afternoon one phone call made it through.

Grady was in the middle of a meeting with some of his staff when his buzzer sounded. He listened to Polly's explanation, then punched the flashing button on his telephone. His responses were terse; he listened more than he spoke. When the call ended he stood to end the meeting, but his staff was already on their collective feet, heading for the door. He admired their savvy as he nodded his goodbyes.

When the door closed behind him, he sat down again and dialed the First Day number. He drummed his fingers on his desk as he waited to be connected to Anna's office.

"Hello."

Grady felt relief spiral through him. "Hello yourself."

"Now how did you find the time to call me?" Her voice was warm with feeling. He could almost see the look on her face. He knew her that well now. He had known her forever.

"I'll never be too busy to call you," he said.

"Are you about to head over to the hotel?"

Grady paused. "Anna," he said at last, "something's come up."

There was a long silence; then she sighed. It carried across the line. She didn't ask any questions; she knew better. "I wish you were here," she said. "Right here."

"So do I."

"I'll be heading home in a few hours."

"I know."

"And then, as soon as I've spent some time with Ryan, I'll be at the Plaza to congratulate you."

"I'm counting on seeing you there."

There was a short silence. "I've told you, haven't I, that I love you?"

Grady shut his eyes. "I don't plan to get tired of hearing it. Not ever."

"I'll see you tonight."

"Tonight." Grady replaced the receiver. Silenty he blessed his predecessor, Harry Traltor, who in the process of renovating this office had thought to construct a well-concealed exit that only a few people knew existed.

In seconds the office was empty.

* * *

By the time the polls were emptying Anna was finishing up at First Day. Two staff members had taken vacations following her return, and everyone was working longer hours to compensate. She was preparing to go home when Tom knocked on her open door. He didn't wait to be invited in.

"What's up?" Anna asked.

"I just got a call from the Dade County police. Want to guess who they picked up?"

She didn't have to think for long. "Wesley."

"Our favorite son."

"What was he doing?"

"Loitering."

"You're kidding." Anna leaned against her desk. "Do they know how lucky they are that's all he was doing?"

"The man I talked to said that Wesley practically begged to be taken in. Apparently he volunteered all kinds of information about his stay here, the money he stole from the others kids, his vandalism of your office."

Anna frowned. Wesley's actions were just one more puzzle to solve in a week filled with them. "What did you tell the cop?"

"What would you have told him?"

"Is this a test?"

"You might say so."

Anna considered. There came a time in every person's life when he had to take the rap for the things he had done. Wesley had been given every chance at First Day, and he had turned on them. He had turned on her most viciously. If he came back, he could turn on them again—most likely *would* turn on them again.

Once upon a time there had been two other street kids. Their trust and most of their humanity had been bled out of them by a life not meant for the young. They had tried to survive any way that they could, but the boy had died on the streets. The girl hadn't. She had come back to the world she had left, one step at a time. She had trusted slowly, incompletely. And if it hadn't been for her son...

Her son. Everybody's sons and daughters. Some at Harvard, some in jail, some out on the streets, some trying... trying to find their way back home.

"I guess I would have told them to send him back here." Anna looked up at Tom. "Did I pass the test?"

"With flying colors." He crossed the room and kissed her cheek. "He's coming back tomorrow."

"He's a real little bastard. You know that, don't you? I don't know why he wants to come back."

"There's a spark of good in him."

"I get tired of fanning that spark. But someday..."

Tom put his arm around her. "Someday, if that spark ignites, you'll be glad you kept right on waving your hand."

Anna's drive home was through the last remnants of rush-hour traffic. Somewhere in the cars surrounding her was a plainclothes cop, assigned to follow her home. Zeke was no longer at her side. He'd been replaced by Sun County police who came and went, drifting in and out of her life, shadows at twilight, silhouettes at dawn.

She missed the physical reality of Zeke's protection. He had been a solid reminder that someone stood between her and Hayden Barnard. Now she was never sure exactly where her protectors were.

Supposedly, no one knew exactly where Hayden was, either. He had resigned from the Senate, a step that surprised everyone. His shot at the presidency was a thing of the past, his reputation tarnished beyond redemption. But no one had expected him to give up his bid for the presidency or his office with such grace. He had resigned with a poignant speech about the stress of politics and the fallibility of human beings. He had said it was time to step down, to reflect on mistakes made and honors won. He had gone immediately into seclusion, for all practical purposes disappearing from the public eye, perhaps forever.

In Anna's possession were two children's toys to prove that Hayden's grace, his humility, his talk of honor, were as fraudulent as his long-ago pretense of being her loving stepfather. The doll sitting on Grady's bannister had been hers as a child, a gift from a great-aunt who had been a doll collector. Anna had last seen it before she fled Hayden's Washington home. Hayden's message had been clear. He knew her every step; he was watching her closely.

Anna parked in front of her house. No car pulled onto the street behind her, and she noticed immediately. Tonight she didn't feel the invisible aura of protection she always did on her block, even though there were people sitting on their porches, luxuriating in the warm summer breeze. She waved to several and stepped off the sidewalk as a skateboarder in neon green shorts came whizzing past her.

At Isabella's, relatives were cooing over the new baby. Esteban was five days old, chubby, big-eyed and thoroughly adorable. Ryan was holding him on his lap when Anna walked in. She had never seen Ryan so still.

She exchanged greetings with all the relatives, every one of whom, including the children, already spoke better English than she spoke Spanish. Onions and garlic scented the air, and Isabella was in the kitchen cooking supper. She didn't look like a woman who had just had a baby. She had taken the experience in stride, and nothing, nothing, was going to make her relinquish her kitchen to any of the other women in the house.

"You will stay for supper?" Isabella asked.

"No. I'm going to take Ryan home and feed him before I bring him back for the evening. Are you sure you want him here? You must be worn out. Grady insists I can bring him to the party."

"He will be better here. And soon I won't see him every day."

Anna tried to imagine what her life would be like when Isabella left for Canada. But it was just one more closed curtain between her and the future. Right now she could only live from moment to moment. She thought of Grady's phone call. From moment to moment . . .

"Anna?"

Anna shook off her thoughts. "You'll be able to come back to visit."

"Toronto, it's not so far that you won't be able to come, too."

"You know I will." She hugged Isabella and went back to play with Esteban for a few minutes before she and Ryan went next door.

Outside, the evening seemed strangely quiet. The sounds that usually wrapped her in security were stilled, perhaps because it was dinnertime and everyone was indoors. She listened hard, but except for someone's barking dog, the neighborhood was silent. She hurried Ryan along.

The house seemed cold, and she turned off the air conditioners, which had been running all day, and opened a window. She started the water for Ryan's bath and put clean clothes for him by the bathroom sink. When she went back into the kitchen he was pouting, because he liked Isabella's cooking better than hers, but he brightened when she pulled out a frozen pizza shell from the local deli and covered it with sauce and cheese.

"Take your bath while it cooks, bunny-nose," she ordered. "Put on the shorts and T-shirt by the sink. You can sleep in them tonight."

Ryan grumbled, but since bath time wasn't really so bad, he did as he was told.

Anna waited until she could hear him splashing contentedly before she turned on the television. She had already missed the news, but she knew there would be primary updates throughout the evening. She knew from her conversation with Grady that the first results from the exit polls had shown the race between Grady and Rand Garner to be close. She had attended campaign functions with Grady in the last week, and she had developed a real appreciation of the grueling length of his days and the tension he had lived under since announcing his candidacy. She knew what he would be feeling now.

There had been an interesting, subtle shift in his support. Since his unrelenting and public defense of Anna, he was no longer seen as the rich man's candidate. Among those who were registered but hadn't voted recently, Grady had a decided edge. If they went to the polls today, they would turn the tide of the election.

The last week had been a tumultuous seesaw ride. Anna wanted the election over with, but there was a part of her that wondered if everything else would ever end.

She watched a repeat of a popular sitcom as she set the table and made a small salad. Then she went to the closet she shared with Ryan to take out the dress she had bought for the party tonight. It was black and slinky, with a sunburst of rhinestones on a sheer chiffon overskirt. She had never felt more beautiful or desirable than she had the day she tried it on and paid a good chunk of a week's salary for it.

Now she hung it in the bathroom as Ryan finished so that it would steam when she showered later.

She was in Ryan's bedroom, helping him select a few toys to take to Isabella's, when she heard the voice of a local news reporter on television. By the time she got to the living room the update had ended. Since this was only the primary, Anna knew the updates would be few until the outcome was definite.

She served the pizza and watched Ryan eat as if he hadn't eaten all day. "Too bad you don't like it," she said wryly.

"Isabella puts peppers on hers. Hot peppers."

"Sounds scrumptious."

"Huh?" Ryan looked, his mouth full of pizza.

There was something about the way he was cocking his head that reminded Anna of Grady. She had noticed it before. Her son was copying her lover. In the years to come others would undoubtedly notice it, too, and those who didn't know would believe Ryan was Grady's child. And he would be, in all the important ways. If she told Grady yes...

"I love you, bunny-nose." Anna reached across the table and wiped his mouth. "Finish up now, okay? I've got to get going."

Ryan jumped up from his chair. "I can go to Teresa's by myself."

"No!" Anna took a deep breath. "I mean, I want to see Esteban again, so I'll come with you."

Ryan's blue eyes saw more than a four-year-old should see. "You're scared."

"Maybe a little. It's getting dark." She forced a laugh. "You could get lost."

"If Zeke was here he'd take me."

"But Zeke's not here. Remember? He had to go home."

Ryan slurped up the last of a glass of milk. "Let's go." He made it one word.

Anna came around the table. She couldn't stop herself from giving him a fierce hug. "Now, do whatever Isabella and Enrique tell you to. Promise? And I'll be there to get you tomorrow morning."

"*They* let me stay up late."

She smiled. "Good. Have fun doing it."

"C'mon."

Anna went the back way to deliver him next door. She left him eating cookies and finishing another glass of milk at the kitchen table with Isabella and her family.

The cheerful kitchen scene haunted her on her short, still-silent journey home. Isabella and Enrique had faced hell, but they had come through it together. She knew enough about hell to realize that not every trip through it ended so happily. Where would she and Ryan and Grady come out? And when?

At home, she stacked some dishes in the sink and ran water over them to soak. Then she prepared for her shower. She stayed in longer than she had planned, letting the warm water sluice over her until she felt a small portion of her energy return. When she was dressed in her new dress, her makeup applied, she fluffed her hair and fastened dangling crystal teardrops on her earlobes, then stood away from the mirror on the back of the door to view the whole effect. Satisfied, she opened the door and stepped into the kitchen.

Hayden Barnard sat at the table. A small pistol lay across the placemat before him. The lights were off, except for the low-wattage fluorescent bulb over the sink. All the blinds were lowered. He examined her. "My, how you've grown."

Anna considered backing into the bathroom and locking the door, but, as if he had read her mind, Hayden shook his head slowly. He casually rested his hand on the butt of the pistol. "It's too bad I just missed your son. I've been anxious to meet my grandchild."

She took a deep breath. "Then why don't I just pop next door and get him? We can have a family party."

"You know, I'm surprised, really surprised, that you didn't thank me for my little gifts."

"And I'm surprised you've had the guts to do more than make threats. You threaten so well, why branch out?"

Hayden laughed. He was a large man, but most of his bulk had gone soft in the last years. He looked older in person than he had on television the day he resigned, and much older than the man she had run from so many years before. His hair was thin and almost white now, and his face showed evidence of years of dissipation.

"You always had a sense of humor, Roseanna. That was one of the first things I loved about you. I'm glad you didn't lose it out on the streets of our noble country."

"I lost something else."

He lifted his brows in question.

"My fear of you."

"Now that's too bad. A little fear is a healthy thing. It can make the difference between safety and death. And death . . . is so final."

"You're doing what you do best again. You truly shine."

"I hate to admit it, but I underestimated you and that sweet big sister of yours. I didn't know Krista had the courage to stand against me and her mother, but she did. Sonya went to her death wondering if I had told her the truth. You girls drove a wedge between us."

"How inconsiderate."

Hayden shrugged. "And now you're all grown up. You even have a lover. A politician. You must have thought of the irony."

"It's crossed my mind."

"Come sit with me and let's have a little heart-to-heart chat." He picked up the gun and motioned to a seat across from him.

She didn't move. "Are you going to kill me, Hayden? Surely you've thought of the suspicion that would raise. I can't think of a single soul who would want me dead, other than you."

"But I'm not here. I'm in Minnesota, at our getaway cabin on the lake. You remember it, don't you? I went into town for the mail just this morning. The neighbors were noticeably cool. Some people will believe anything. Nobody would believe I was here, though. Not when I was seen there..." He paused for effect. "And not when my aides insist they were with me this afternoon and evening. The same aides, by the way, who got me the key to this house."

She forced more bravado. "Where *would* you be without those men to do your dirty work? Is Scott Newton one of them?"

"Newton abandoned ship. That boy always had good instincts. Course, he'll never be elected dogcatcher. His instincts weren't good enough to keep him from getting his nose dirty a time or two, and I've got records...or, I should say, the press has records now."

Anna thought briefly of Krista and the fate she had escaped when she gave Scott Newton back his ring. Something good had come of all of this. Something good...

"I'm surprised you don't look scared," Hayden said, as if he were making an observation about her dress or her earrings.

"This is a small house, and there are people next door who will hear the shot if you kill me."

"People will hear the shot." He shook his head from side to side. "The shot heard round the world. Some shots are always heard, Roseanna. Some things rise to the surface, no matter how hard you try to keep them submerged. Some *people* rise, and some people fall. And sometimes... sometimes they die."

Anna felt a surge of fear as he lifted the pistol from the table. "Hayden, your life will be over, too, if you pull that trigger. Grady won't rest until he's pinned this shooting on you."

Hayden waved her to silence with the gun barrel. "Grady Clayton is a fine young man. I've been watching him closely ever since I learned you were associating with him."

"Since I gave my story to the press—"

Hayden shook his head. "No. Since I learned you were associating with him. I've known where you were for most of the last four years. Ever since you wrote the state of Minnesota for a copy of your birth certificate so you could get a social security card. You've been watched. Everything you've done has been recorded."

"You would have killed me if you'd known!"

"If I was smarter, crueler...sicker, perhaps. Yes, I might have. Would have, I suppose." Just for a moment, his eyes wavered from hers. "But, you see, I had feelings for you, and, whether you believe it or not, feelings for your mother."

She wanted to believe he was lying, but somewhere deep inside her, she sensed he was telling the truth. Somehow this revelation was more chilling than reassuring. *Sicker.* Did Hayden know he was a man with a warped sense of what he was due? "But you would kill me now?"

He toyed with the gun. "I was at the top, Roseanna. I don't suppose you know what that means, do you? You've been at the bottom so long. I was at the top, and you were at the bottom...." He let the gun dangle toward the floor, and feature by feature his face seemed to dissolve. "I told myself you were no threat. I *believed* you were no threat. I was at the top."

Anna's stomach had cramped into a hard knot. She didn't know if she could stand to face him this way any longer.

"It's been a long, long trip down." But he didn't point it at Anna. He turned his wrist, and suddenly the gun was pointed at his own temple.

Anna realized what everything he had said added up to. He had not come to kill her. Or perhaps he had, but once there, he had changed his mind. He was going to escape the torment of the last weeks, perhaps the torment of his life.

"No!" Before she thought about what she was doing, Anna flung herself across the small room. She didn't have a chance to reach him. Suddenly the kitchen door had been kicked off its hinges and Grady was there, followed closely by two uniformed policemen.

In a moment Hayden's gun was on the floor, and his head was pillowed on his arms on the table. He began to sob.

Anna felt Grady lift her to her feet. She stared at Hayden. For the last six years he had controlled every waking moment of her life. He had taken her adolescence and molded it into something agonizing and shameful. She had hated him as few people learned to hate. Yet now she felt pity eat away at hatred's roots. He no longer had any power over her, and he never would again. He was broken and bleeding; and she could not rejoice.

She heaved a deep, shaken sigh. Then her eyes met Grady's. And she exploded.

"What the hell took you so long!"

The Ponte Reynaldo Plaza was lit up like fairyland. Men in tuxedos and women in evening dress, as well as men and women in blue jeans, streamed into the ballroom to celebrate Grady's victory. Anna entered the hotel on Grady's arm as camera flashes lit the night. She was smiling, although it had taken an hour after Hayden had been led from her kitchen before anyone could coax a smile out of her.

"Are you surprised at the strength of your victory, Mr. Clayton?" a reporter asked, worming his way to the front of the pack by sheer elbow power.

Grady held Anna closer. "I'm learning not to be surprised at anything."

Anna's snort was only for Grady's ears. His victory had not been as narrow as her escape. Surprisingly, the Sun County voters had rallied to support him, and a strong lead had been established early.

"Imagine the voters' surprise tomorrow when they find out you were playing cops and robbers tonight while the votes were being tallied," she said under her breath.

He squeezed her arm. For a few minutes that was the best he could do.

"Are you really all right?" he asked later, during a momentary lull before they started into the ballroom where he would make his victory speech.

"I still want to know what took you so long!"

He grinned and kissed her quickly before he answered. "You knew I was there, didn't you? You knew we were waiting for the right minute to come in. You were never in any danger."

"Next time, make it a little earlier, okay? I'd prefer an early wrong moment over a late right one!"

Grady was engulfed by well-wishers and suddenly too busy shaking hands to answer her. Anna watched him being carried away by a tide of exuberant supporters. She was surrounded, too, accepting congratulations for him.

"There are a couple of people here to see you."

Anna felt a hand at her elbow and turned to see Zeke, stern as always, in a dark suit. "Zeke! You're back from Minnesota already?"

His face was more than stern; it was furious. "If I'd been back earlier, the police wouldn't have screwed up, I'll tell you."

She thought for a moment, then shook her head. "No one screwed up. It was best this way. Hayden won't be a threat to me again. Too much was said in front of too many witnesses. Maybe he'll even get some help. God knows he needs it." She paused and then added the rest from her heart. "Grady wouldn't have let me get hurt, Zeke. I was in good hands."

He mumbled something that sounded like a maybe and began to guide her toward a distant corner. She was stopped every few feet along the way, and it wasn't until she was almost there that she saw who was waiting for her.

"Krista! Jess!" She flung herself toward them, and in a moment they were indulging in a three-way hug.

When they parted, Anna saw that Krista was blinking back tears. "Nobody will tell us what happened! Zeke said you'd want to be the one to do it."

"It's over now." Anna said the words, and for the first time she knew they were true. "Hayden can never bother either of us again."

"But what happened?"

"Hayden made it known that he could get to me, no matter what I did, no matter who we hired to protect me." She explained about the toy gun and the doll. "Grady and Zeke and the police decided the only way to be sure he didn't harm me was to catch him or one of his aides in the act of threatening me."

Krista looked horrified. "Put your life in danger, you mean?"

"No one thought it would come to that. I know I didn't."

"You were in on it?" Jess asked.

"Right from the beginning." Anna shook her head at his frown. "I couldn't go on the way I had been any longer. I was afraid I'd spend the rest of my life looking over my shoulder. I *made* them go ahead with it. I just wanted this over with so that all of us could live a normal life."

"So they set you up?" Jess asked, obviously still angry.

"Not really. My protectors just vanished into the shadows. I was still watched constantly. And Zeke went to Minnesota to keep his eye on Hayden and his henchmen. We thought if Hayden believed I no longer had a bodyguard, he might threaten me again, only this time we'd be watching and waiting."

"Is that what happened?" Krista asked.

"I got a call from Grady this afternoon. He told me something had come up. It was our signal that Hayden

could be making a move." She told them the details of what
had happened in her kitchen."

"So they knew Hayden was coming after you, but they
still didn't keep him from getting into your house?" Jess
demanded.

"Zeke telephoned Grady from Minnesota and told him
that he hadn't seen Hayden since early that morning. He'd
taken long afternoon walks around the lake every day, so
today Zeke got suspicious. By then, it seems that Hayden
was already here, watching for a chance to slip into my
house. He got inside before anyone could stop him."

"How could they have let that happen?"

Anna put her hand on Jess's shoulder. "No one understood Hayden and what he was capable of, Jess. Not even
me. Until today we never thought he'd come after me himself. And even though he did, I was never in any danger. Not
really. Grady and the police were right there. I knew it." She
paused. "I just had a moment or two of wondering if they
were going to get inside in time," she said wryly.

Krista wrapped her arms around her sister, and for a moment the two embraced as if they never wanted to part
again. "Then it's really over," Krista said at last.

Anna blinked back tears. "Life just plods on from here.
I don't know about you, but I can use a little plodding."

"What are you going to do now?" Jess asked, slipping his
arm around her waist. His other arm slid around Krista.

"I'm going to stay here and continue at First Day. This is
my home and the place I need to be."

"I thought you'd stay." Krista gave a tremulous smile,
but the tears behind it were good ones. At last. "And
Grady?"

"I've got to talk to him tonight."

Jess turned her toward the speakers' platform. "You're
going to wait until he gives his speech, I hope. He'll need
some concentration for that."

"I think he's just about to give it."

The lights flashed on and off in the ballroom, and the exuberant crowd quieted. Then there was a roar of applause

as Grady stepped onto the platform. His parents stood just
behind him, along with his campaign staff. Anna had refused to join him. There were things she and Grady had to
settle before she stood beside him for victory speeches. As
she listened to him accept this honor and heard the roar of
the crowd each time he paused, she knew there would be
other chances to stand by his side.

The lights of Ponte Reynaldo were disappearing into the
color-rich haze of dawn before Anna stood at Grady's window, looking out over the city. "Ponte Reynaldo is yours,"
she said, turning to smile at Grady, who was coming toward her bearing two cups of coffee. The party had lasted
all night. The coffee was to stave off the exhaustion that
both knew would claim them soon. "The election in November will be just a formality. You're the State's Attorney
for the next four years, Grady."

"My mother says that her tarot-card reader sees big things
in my future."

"I like your mother. And your father. But how have they
stayed married this long?"

"They love each other." Grady handed her a cup. "Big
things," he went on, as if she hadn't sidetracked him. "I
think I know what she meant."

"You're going to be governor? President?" Anna toasted
him with her coffee cup before she took a sip.

"No, I think she meant something else. Big mortgage
payments. Big family. Big happiness with the woman I
love."

Suddenly the coffee didn't seem important. Anna set it
down on the windowsill. "Grady—"

"Why wouldn't you stand beside me tonight?"

"It was your night. And there wasn't time to talk...."

"There's nothing left to say." He put his coffee cup down,
too.

"You know I'm all wrong for you. I'm going to keep
working at First Day. I won't have time to campaign or en-
tertain. I'll say whatever comes into my mind. And there will

be people, lots of them, who'll think I'm not good enough for you.''

"Finished?" he asked.

She wasn't sure she liked his tone of voice. She hurried on. "On the other hand, I'm smart and not too bad to look at. I photograph well." She backed toward the window. "I can cook, as long as it doesn't have to be fancy. I can even cook Cuban, which is a plus here. I speak a little Spanish. Well, actually, very little." She backed up another pace. "And I have had experience in the political world. I'm on a first name basis with the vice president's wife."

"Are you or are you not going to marry me?"

For a moment Anna let all her vulnerability show. "Do you still want me? After everything I've put you through?"

Grady groaned and clasped her to him. "Idiot. I almost got my head shot off for you tonight."

She had just one more question. "If you had lost the primary, would you still have wanted me?"

He shook her, but he didn't let her go. "There was a big part of me that *wanted* to lose the damn election, Anna! Didn't you see that? I don't even know if I want a career in politics. I want you first, and Ryan. I want a real marriage and more kids. That's what I really want. I'll take the other a step at a time."

He had been telling her that in a thousand ways since she had met him, but now, for the first time, she could believe him. Her past—that haunted, terrifying void—had been exposed and, somehow, returned to her, cleansed and new. She was whole at last. Past, present and future could flow together. She could be happy now. She *deserved* happiness. And so did the man holding her.

"I don't want a big wedding," she said. "Not after everything. Can we run away?"

"When?"

"Oh, I don't know. Right now, maybe?"

He lifted her in his arms and kissed her. "How about in an hour or two?"

"That will do nicely." She draped her arms around his neck.

"Do you want Krista and Jess to be there?"

"And Ryan and Isabella's family. And Zeke."

"My parents?"

"Sure."

He started toward his bedroom. "That's not exactly running."

She smiled and reached up to kiss him. "Close enough," she said. "As close to running as I ever want to get. I've found my way back home, Grady. I won't ever be leaving again."

* * * * *

Silhouette Sensation

COMING NEXT MONTH

CHANGE OF LIFE
Judith Arnold

On Lila Chapin's birthday, something snapped.
She packed her bags, wrote a note and left — just
like that. Lila decided to give herself the present she
wanted most: a month's holiday. Ken and the boys
had been taking her for granted.

How was Ken going to react to Lila's domestic
rebellion?

DUNCAN'S BRIDE
Linda Howard

Reese Duncan needed a wife who would be willing
to work on the ranch, bear his children and settle for
lovemaking instead of loving. So he advertised for a
bride.

Madelyn Patterson was all wrong for the job; she
was New York and bright lights, but after one look
he had to have her. Madelyn knew marrying Reese
was a risk, but it was a risk she had to take!